A Song Without a Melody

A novel of the '90s by Ace Boggess

ISBN: 1-988292-05-2
ISBN-13: 978-1-988292-05-2

For Grace

CONTENTS

ACKNOWLEDGMENTS

The author wishes to thank the following publications in which excerpts from *A Song Without a Melody* first appeared, often in slightly different forms:

The Circle: "The Scene"

Erosha: "Naked and Bleeding," "The Morning After," and "The Chuang Tzu Routine"

Lily Literary Review: "First Day at the *Domestic-Chronicle*"

Megaera: "Second Encounter with Billy Ray Rose"

SN Review: "The Country Singer Wants to Die, and That's What I Like About Him"

Subterranean Quarterly: "The Sound Room"

Part One

Riffs, Rifts, and Ripples

CANTO ONE

The Scene

I didn't get drawn into the scene, the culture, the counter-culture, the movie-of-the-week kind of chaos that emanates from small clubs with numbers for names, built around black lights and darkness. I didn't wake up one hazy morning with a blue-black misery from one too many hangovers and whisper, "What happened to me? What have I become?" as if the walls, the air, or my own superficial spirits offered up a care. No, that's not the way it went. Nobody shanghaied me or dragged me kicking and screaming into that a.m. asylum, that sunset commune lifestyle. I walked in with dignity and ease, head high, eyes forward, notebook in hand. I wanted it, hungered to be a part of it. It spoke to me in my own words.

The case with December Leigh was something else—a story I never expected to tell, and one perhaps that should never be told. What the hell. Everyone has at least one story that shouldn't be told, and it's the most entertaining. Even now, alone, I can see her dyed black hair dangling down over pale skin, dry lips, yellowish cat's eyes. I can smell aftersweat from a good show or a heavy, emotional trip. I can feel calloused fingertips from her fretting hand brushing across my cheek or down my back like claws, grabbing for my buttocks and that extra bit of pull. She's a vision and a shadow, as much now as then. Times, lives, and personalities have changed, but December's a constant, the same no matter how much she evolves.

I certainly didn't expect to spill out all my emotions or flick them away like dying cigarette embers left to flitter to the concrete in some back room after hours. I never planned to fall in love with my work. But why not? That's what it all comes down to. My work took me up. Why shouldn't I have given myself to it entirely, let it maneuver me, instruct me, plot my strategies and see them carried out? I existed for a headline on the *Life* page, so why not write a few new pages for my life?

December's band Cancer Moon had a gig at Club Zero, Pittsburgh's newest alternative hangout, though of course the owner preferred the term 'eclectic.' Zero was your classic Smoke and Toke: booze for those with identification, and smoke-filled black-light bathrooms filled with peddlers of other less acceptable indulgences for those too young to imbibe. Its newness and rich early business kept the eyes of the city temporarily deflected or enticed city officials to defer enforcing penalties for ordinance violations and other *mala prohibita* crimes, so long as they occurred inside and their perpetrators never staggered half-naked out onto the public streets.

I'd been to a hundred of these during my tenure at the *Domestic-Chronicle*, and when I walked through the front door of this particular cultural niche, nothing surprised me. I took careful note of an energetic crowd expressed as a collage of bohemian believers ranging from the lost and forlorn to the naive and therefore fascinated. Straightening my tie, I smiled. "Welcome home," I mumbled, playing the Hannibal of this foreign land. "You've returned at last."

"I need to see some I.D.," said the serf behind the bar.

The request didn't offend me, but I became indignant just the same. "Yeah," I said with more cockalorum than a battle-weary Green Beret. "Surely you recognize *this* face."

"Sorry, man," he said, leaning on the bar. Sweat-soaked sandy brown curls draped down around his cheeks, sticking to his skin. "Never seen you before in my life. Now show me some identification."

I drew my wallet like a pistol and aimed it, shooting from the hip. With calm, practiced leisure, I opened it one-handed to the spot where my driver's license slept in its plastic slot. I held it there for several seconds, making sure that sap saw the sleeve above with my carefully placed press card glowing neon purple under the haze from vast rows of black lights over the bar.

"Twenty-three." He mouthed the word, almost inaudible under blaring techno-pop pouring from manmade mountains of speakers arrayed along each wall.

"Have a good look, and don't forget. I'm a professional. I *will* be back."

He nodded, raising his hand in a mock salute as if to say, *Yes, your majesty. As you wish.*

I grinned, showing purple teeth.

After a brief pause, he smiled back. "What can I get you?"

"Give me something I've never had before, something I've never heard of." It was an old trick I used to earn free drinks. Good bartenders love guinea pigs. They experiment, playing the mad scientist with different brands of booze. If they find somebody willing to taste their concoctions, nine times out of ten they'll respond by making a gift of each.

He rubbed his chin with his thumb and forefinger. "That's a tough order," he said. "How about something I came up with?"

"Ideal, man. It's casual. Go with it."

He returned a couple minutes later, holding a Styrofoam cup filled with sinister-looking liquid: thick, brown sludge with foam like steamed milk. "Drink up. You asked for it."

"How much?"

"It's on the house. I don't get too many lab rats in here."

I grinned like the devil after a good deal. "That's cool," I said. "What is it?"

"I call it a Sausage Link."

"Why? What's in it?"

He laughed. "You don't want to know."

Staring at the cup of brown bile, I considered backing out. I couldn't. It'd blow my con. Besides, I'd done worse things. "Praise the Lord," I said, and swallowed it all in one gulp. Going down, it tasted like oatmeal flavored with turkey gravy, but the aftertaste was sharp and crisp, almost sweet like a custard pie. "Ideal. Now for something more conventional. Give me an Absolut Screw, and make it a stiff one."

He appeared content. Nodding emphatically, he said, "Sure enough. Coming right up."

As he went to work, I belched silently and turned to study the crowd. I saw a lot of familiar faces, a lot of clumsy legs dancing, a lot of sullen eyes—like mine—searching the room, staring with unfulfilled longing. My kind of people, all of them. They just didn't know it yet.

When the bartender returned, I faced him, still flashing what I imagined to be a truly maniacal glare. Accepting my drink, I again asked how much.

He waved me off with both hands. "This one's on the house, too. You're a professional."

"That's unethical," I replied, and took a hefty sip. "Thanks."

"No problem." He turned and went to serve someone else.

No discotheque, this place. The Zero enticed a darker, more somber clientele, covered in a hundred different shades of black. They came for the madness, the abyss in which to lose themselves. On the wall behind the bar hung a pseudo-Picasso more than six feet wide: a colorful canvas displaying the twisted, tortured form of a green-skinned Aphrodite with triangular breasts, spiraling thighs, and bloody teardrops mushrooming out from square eyes— one pink, one orange. This macabre masterpiece could've been a self-portrait of Club Zero, with every element untuned, untamed, and way out of proportion.

As if confirming this, a dye-blond doll, maybe nineteen, strolled by me with her face blurred by grease paint and clown make-up. In contrast, she'd dressed her near-perfect figure in a red lace brassiere and matching pair of crotchless panties worn on top of a black spandex body suit. She turned to look at me as she ambled by, offering up a comical smile. "Nice outfit," she said, as if I were the clown. I understood. She fit right in, whereas I was out of place.

Then again, even my conservative attire didn't blacklist me from any part of the Zero. My persona bought the ticket.

My eyes were unrelenting as I watched the clown goddess strut out the front door. They followed her all the way, even as she stopped to flirt with a heavyset bouncer leaning up against a wall under the neon *Exit* sign. Laughing to myself, I figured he probably was checking to see if she wanted him to stuff her in the back of a crowded Volkswagen with a group of his friends.

Crazy world. Cool world. An unconventional world. Crazy, cool, unconventional people, hanging out in this crazy, cool, unconventional world. I could circle the globe blindfolded and still find my way back here, or somewhere similar in New Jersey, Maryland, or West Virginia. Oblivious to the oblivion of these indulgent excessives, I've strived for that abyss, to stare into it longingly, tranquilly, valiantly, regardless should it stare back into me. I accept the humanity of these black shadows, wandering the wastelands of the Earth, unconcerned with precedents and politics, dancing in avoidance of the light. A Cheshire grin leads us homeward, wayward, skyward, every which way but the most direct: into the self, where we confront our thoughts alone. Far better to make the day on National Public Radio, or in clubs and newspaper columns, than to face that same day, exposed.

Even an individual can lose himself in the masses.

I lost myself, offering no complaints.

Slamming my drink, I crumpled up the Styrofoam and dropped it onto the counter to drip out whatever residue remained. Feeling the call, I crept through the quilted crowd toward the restroom, taking note of all eyes I came into visual contact with. These friendly eyes, these lustful eyes, these hopeless, sad, dispirited eyes, these energetic amber eyes needing no escape, these serpent's eyes, cat's eyes, sorcerer's eyes, the eyes of future family men, funeral directors, and unsuspecting officers of the law already building themselves the criminal pasts that will make them the best of cops, the mischievous eyes of plotters and planners, soon-to-be soldiers, or underworld attorneys on retainer, the gentle but critical eyes of potential youth league football coaches watching the first sprouts of a budding beer gut, the eyes of maniacs and fanatics, hipsters and wallflowers, dreamers and the objects of dreams, I gazed into them all and knew that they were human eyes, each pair offering insight toward a new tomorrow. I took careful note of them, as always, and continued on my way.

The restroom published volumes of libelous gossip about the Zero's clientele, including but not limited to names and numbers, call signs, tags, encyclopedias of graffiti from the sexually obscure to the soft, subtle philosophy of semi-famous porcelain poets. Each pen stroke glistened from freshness. Even before I entered, I knew what to expect by a quick glance at the door, where someone had scratched out 'MEN' and replaced it with a stick-figure prick and balls, poorly drawn but never faltering in its message: *You ain't got one of these, stay the hell out!*

Meeting the strict admission requirements, I pushed through the doorway into this blacklit dingy den of iniquities. By my calculations, Club Zero opened less than two weeks prior, but already these plastered walls were home to a hundred hieroglyphs, or a hundred thousand. I chose not to read them all, preferring to stick to my purpose. I headed for a free urinal on the far wall. Twin scents of pot and opium all but hid the typical reek. I took a deep breath, remembering.

As I relieved myself of a burden, I got that tingling at the back of my neck, that special sense that comes from being watched. Swiveling my head to the right, I saw two scrawny, roughhouse types in thick, khaki army coats. They were sitting up against a wall, staring at me with their faces bathed in blank expressions that made them look like prisoners of war just back from psychological torture.

Perverts? I wondered. *No, not likely. They're more covert. Dopers, more like it, probably scared of a shirt and tie.* I considered blowing their minds by asking for a hit of whatever parcel they were passing. But, not that. Not yet. Not until I made my name and face a fixture at the Zero. Then my tie, or even a red power tie, wouldn't stand out any more than clown make-up did.

Looking at them with the intensity of one who knows, I flashed a smile and mocked them by sucking imaginary smoke through pinched fingers holding nothing.

They flinched, but neither took their eyes off me.

"Enough fun," I said, barely audible amidst the heavy, rhythmic bass from a rap song blasting over the speakers outside in the club proper. Zipping up, I flushed and fled the scene with a practiced dégagé strut. "Time for work," I said to no one in particular.

As I approached the bar, I motioned with my left hand, summoning the barkeep. "Hey, man," he shouted, almost in sync with the beat of artificial drums, "ready for another shot?"

"Not now. I'm looking for Knox."

"What?" he said, cupping a hand to his ear.

"Knox! I'm looking for Nick Knox."

"What the hell for?"

"Business. He owns the place, right?"

"That he does."

"So, where can I find him?"

He glanced down at the bar, reached for a soapy rag, and began to wipe up a small pool of spilled beer. He was buying time, allowing himself a moment to consider the consequences of betraying the boss's whereabouts, and of the opposite action, denial. When he finished wiping the bar, he deposited the rag on a shelf down below, and then looked up, studying the intent in my eyes. Seeing no mischief in me, or just enough, he nodded. "Well, you're not a cop."

"No, man. I'm a reporter."

"That's just as bad."

"Only if I'm not on your side."

He grinned, sly but serious, the way a serial killer might grin at a potential victim. "Through that door," he said. He pointed to a short wooden portal into a closed-off room jutting out halfway between the bar and stage. Large square mirrors circled the room, showing off the club like surreal, living art. Two-way, I guessed. "Knock first," the bartender added.

"Thanks." I headed toward the door, stopping for a moment in the midst of the crowd as another colorful character caught my eye. Tattoos covered his entire body, or at least every inch of visible flesh, highlighting him in rainbow colors standing out against a backdrop of deep black. It was a mural of the cosmos, a map of constell-ations and solar systems, suns, stars, and all the other somewhere else of space, carefully etched onto his skin. Even his bald head housed a portrait of a planet on a black background. Jupiter, I later found out. The same name by which this sublime spaceman chose to be known. I watched him as he danced with a relatively normal-looking girl in a tight black mini-dress and high heels. I found it an intriguing combination of companions: the common sex-queen type ruling her personal universe, dancing with the heavens, occasionally reaching down to caress secret stars. I could've spent the night composing sonnets to such a scene, but I had more important images to portray, with more specific topics about which the paper kept paying me to write. By comparison, the universe was a trivial thing.

I reached the door and knocked.

No answer.

I knocked again, louder, harder, longer.

No answer.

No rush, I thought. *Take your time.* I knew the deal. They were sizing me up, checking out the threads from the other side of the two-way mirrors. Also, it's likely they were hiding their drugs. *Cool*, I thought. *It's cool.* I understood the rules.

After a lengthy pause, I knocked again.

This time, the door shot inward. "What?" this aging burnout on the other side screamed at me. He was an absurd display of ambivalence to social custom, dressed in a faded tie-dye with clashing striped suspenders holding up his bright white jeans. "What's your problem?"

I didn't know whether to recoil in fear or laugh in his dirt-crusted face. I chose neither, instead breaking into my Respectable Journalist routine. "Are you Nick Knox?"

"No!" he spat back with a shower of saliva. "Who are you?"

"Collin Hearst," I said, offering a hand to shake, "reporter for the *Domestic-Chronicle*."

He ignored the hand. Without looking over his shoulder, he groaned, "Knox, there's a catfish here to see you!" The cords in his neck were bulging, ready to explode from his scarlet skin. My impulse was to say, "Whatever drugs you're doing, they're the wrong ones." Instead, I waited for him to take a breath, at which point he said, "What do you want, bottom fish?"

"Answers to a few questions."

"Questions? What kind of questions?"

I shook my head and then tried to stare him down. "I'm not looking for a Pulitzer Prize. I have questions. Everyday, run-of-the-mill, who, what, when, where, why, and how kind of questions. I'm not here to steal your thoughts. I'm after stories. Chaos stories, vibe stories, stereotypical sex, drugs, and rock'n'roll kind of stories. I cover the scene, man. Now, unless you have more questions of your own, I'd like to get some answers to mine."

This tirade numbed him faster than *Novocain*, with all his rage not so much dying as simply fading for a while with a false feeling of death, skin tingling, thoughts strained, emotions grayed or in hibernation. It left him speechless. He hesitated. Voice calmer, he said, "Wait here. Nick's got to play the next disc. He'll be out in a minute."

"It's casual," I said, and watched as he staggered around me, out onto the dance floor, disappearing in the masses. While I waited, I turned momentarily and caught a glimpse of myself in one of the mirrors, gazing at the round, cadaverous face staring back at me from underneath prescription sunglasses—a solemn portrait painted under waves of bourbon brown hair filled with more hot air than a zeppelin. The face said Journeyman Beatnik, but the body, less than fit, said Never Been Far From Home. I wasn't sure how to take this character, dressed all in black save for a red and gray tie. *What's your deal?* I thought. *What crazy god spliced your patchwork parts together?*

Before the face in the mirror could respond, I sensed new movement at my periphery and turned in time to see this carrot-top, anorexic type head my way. His eyes, only partly shielded by John Lennon spectacles, were glazed, sterile, but far from sad. His jaw hung open about twenty degrees, closing every few breaths to push out straying strands from his lengthy orange curls. He was dressed in maroon Bermuda shorts and a gray tee on which someone had handwritten the word 'Mugwump.' I couldn't tell from this guy's demeanor if the word referred to the long-dead political party or the slimy creature from a Burroughs novel that ejaculated intoxicating fluids. At a guess, I presumed the latter, it likely being some sort of pseudonym, or perhaps a coded invitation to young girls.

"Nick Knox?" I said.

"True enough." He flashed me a peace sign with his fingers. "And you are?"

"Collin Hearst. I believe we spoke on the phone." I offered my hand.

He didn't speak right off, but after a brief pause his face lit up with far too much excitement. Taking my hand in both of his, he shook it vigorously, violently, coating my fingers with thick sweat. "Cool, man," he said. "Cool. I forgot you were coming. No, I didn't. That's not it. I didn't forget, but I didn't really expect you to show. It's cool you did, though. I'm glad you made it." His words came so fast and frantic with anxious energy that they made me feel like some stunning doll he'd just asked out, never expecting an affirmative answer.

"You're going to love this band," he continued. "Without a doubt. Hey, you did come to check out the band, right? Well, this chick, she's explosive fucking gorgeous. She's got a voice to make you cry and come back to back in perfect synchronicity, and a face to make you beg for more of both. It cost me a couple grand to bring her here but, man, she's worth every penny. The band sparkles, too. It'll be a great show."

"That's casual. I know they're good."

"You've seen them?"

"No, but I've heard about them."

"Cool," he said. "That's so cool. So you're here for a review?"

I shook my head. "Sorry, Nick. The paper's full tomorrow. I'm just here to kick back, have a few drinks, and catch the show. If it works for me, I'll do a preview next time they're in."

He looked at me quizzically, but his mood brightened fast. "That'll work. We got 'em booked again next month." He paused. "Listen, we're setting up the sound board now. Why don't you come inside? We can talk about it while I work."

"Good, Nick. You can tell me what you've got lined up, so I can plan my schedule."

"Cool."

"*I* think so."

"Cool. You have many bands lined up?"

"You could say that. A lot of bars, a lot of gigs. Punks, hicks, metalheads, rappers, alternative angsters, even the occasional gospel Godsquadder. You better believe I'm busy."

He grinned from ear to ear with comic-book glee. "Cool," he said. "Cool." His redundancies drew my attention to a fact I'd thus far overlooked: Knox was my age, though maybe a couple years older. What made this kid so special, unique, enterprising? Owning his own cult-classic club, plopping down a couple thousand dollars in one night for a trendy but not yet superstar music group, giving orders rather than taking them—these were signs of someone who'd lived the life and learned how to succeed. I wondered if he'd gone to college and gotten a degree in business, economics, or maybe juvenile psychology. Or had he taken a trust fund from Dear Old Mom and Dad and spit it straight into the wild wind of contemporary culture? Would he make his mark on the scene for months before burning out with an ounce-a-day heroin habit, two broken legs from unpaid debts, and a six-inch stack of subpoenas from the IRS? Would he steal a quick glimpse of the good life, only to reminisce from a vantage well below? Or would he succeed, perhaps transforming the

Zero into a landmark for the city and the scene? I didn't know the answers, but I looked forward to finding out.

The Sound Room

"Step inside," he said, "and close the door behind you. Have to keep the patrons out, you dig. First rule of business: never let the revelers near your expensive equipment."

"Logical," I said, and did as instructed. When the door clicked into place, the air went silent, save for a low vibrating hum barely heard through walls and windows. *How odd*, I thought: the sound room had been soundproofed. The inside looked like a voyeur's paradise, with backs of two-way mirrors facing three directions—one toward the bar, one down the hallway leading to the restrooms, and one facing the stage, peering out at an angle slightly above the dance floor in between. Except in the bathrooms themselves, Knox could tell exactly what went on at all times inside his club. Below the mirror facing the stage, a P.A. mixer that could've doubled for a battleship extended from wall to wall, exposing its exoskeleton: a thousand knobs in reds, yellows, greens, and blacks. A hundred cords sprouted from the sound board like roots or colorful rubber hair, reaching in all directions through holes in the walls and floor. At the other end of the room, some musical Dr. Frankenstein built a patchwork stereo system with dozens of components. Like the mixer, each part stretched tentacles through walls and floor. The rest of the place, except for a short walkway, looked like a teenage boy's Christmas wish-list, stacked end to end with compact discs, cassettes, digitals, albums, and even a handful of eight tracks.

"Quite a setup."

"That it is," he said. "The bank has no idea how much quality stuff it owns."

So that was his story: a borrower. Those types are the hardest workers, the dreamers, the romantics. Someone owning a club like this with help from Daddy's bankroll likely wouldn't have the heart it takes to entice eager college kids or keep a crowd that's constant. Debt riders, on the other hand, tend to struggle to keep whatever it is they've got, no matter how big the bills, how slow the business, how fast the profits seem to disappear.

"Your first time here?" Knox asked, twisting knobs and checking connections.

I thought he meant the sound room, which was spectacular, but as the cobwebs cleared from my head, I caught his intent. "It is," I said.

"Opinion?"

I shrugged. "As a reporter or patron?"

"Take your pick."

"As a reporter, I'd have to say it's madness left to run its course, a cross between a sex farm, an amusement park and a disco with anxiety. It's a place for the weird and weird at heart to shed their calm and come be entertained."

"Some trip. Can't tell if that's a compliment or a moral decree. What about as a patron?"

"Refreshing change of pace."

He shook his head vigorously. "Damn, that's cool of you. I hope you come back."

"I'll be around. I cover the scene. I can't get too far away or I might lose touch. When you write about food, you're never far from the kitchen. When you write about crime, you hang around with cops. When you write about the twisted and insane, you have to stay within the walls of the asylum. This is my nuthouse. I have to stay with the nuts."

Knox didn't respond, so I used the pause to examine a couple compact discs I saw resting in a prominent place away from the others. The first was an album called "Greasy Gray Go-Go Juice" from a band named Lunar

Landscape. It had a picture on the cover of three pampered preppies sipping martinis while laying on beach towels on the moon's surface. "Odd," I said.

Knox turned to see, then groaned as if his bowels were tightening. "Last night's band."

"No good?"

"The worst. I've heard better music at funerals."

"That's bad."

He scowled at me. "Man, those cats drew a huge crowd. Biggest we've seen. But by the time they finished their set, this place could've passed for Monday night at church. Not a soul around except me, Carl, and Cliff the bartender, and we would've split if we could've. Dig the other one, though—the one beside it. Much better."

I looked at the second disc: "Touched" by Cancer Moon. The glossy displayed a flushed foursome—two males, two females—stripped bare except for black bars over breasts and genitalia. Each person had an arm outstretched with hand disappearing behind the black box of a neighbor. "Suggestive," I said.

"No doubt. They're hot, too." He turned away and resumed his preparations. Talking over his shoulder, he said, "I caught'em a couple months ago in Philly. That's where they're from, I think. No, maybe not. Well, they knocked me cold. This chick comes out on stage with a classical guitar, playing Mozart or Beethoven, I don't know what, and she just starts improvising these hick-ass country lyrics over top. Blows my mind. After about thirty or forty seconds, I hear the conception of feedback gestating in Marshall stacks, getting louder, louder, higher, higher, biting my ears, sending shivers down my spine. The next thing I know, the rest of the band's on stage, and these four demons are wailing away with some of the most drastic noise pollution I've ever heard. Distortion and discord roaring in the background, classical guitar up front, and at the mic the girl's singing rock'n'roll Hosannas, alternating between melodies, extended rants, and bloodcurdling, cacophonous screams. It was like listening to a sound-track for a movie about my life—sometimes passionate, sometimes frustrating, often incomprehensible, and always out of control."

"So, you're saying it's a good show."

He took my padded sarcasm and ran with it. Turning to face me, he said, "I've seen Picassos in my time, and I've seen posers. This band's at least a Van Gogh."

Overlooking the obvious pun about earsplitting noise, I said, "So, Nick, what's with the moon theme? Last night Lunar Landscape, Cancer Moon tonight. You on some astro vibe?"

He squinted. "I didn't even catch that. Must be some sort of sick irony. I guess you could say last night there was a '*bad moon rising.*'"

I feigned laughter. "Let's hope there's a better moon tonight."

He walked toward me and slapped me on the back as if we were old friends, before moving past me toward the stereo system. Sorting through his discs, he planned and programmed the next few tracks. "Fits, though," he said.

"What's that?"

"Two moons," he said. "Look at the crowd, man. These kids ain't exactly normal. All a bunch of space cadets."

"Sounds as if you don't care for them much."

"Care for them?" he said in a calm, serious tone. "I love them. All of them. Hell, if I could, I *would* love them all. But I'm a whore." He turned and went back to work.

As I considered the possibility, seeing this orgy of the damned played out in my head, I missed his subsequent comments. "What's that?" I asked.

"I said you're pretty cool for a catfish, man. None of the scavengers I've ever met would've come into a place like this just to hang out and talk trash."

"Is that a compliment?"

"That's straight up."

"All right," I said. "Thanks. I appreciate it."

"What makes you different?"

I had to consider that before answering. "I just enjoy my work, I guess."

"That's cool," he said. "Do you smoke pot?"

"I beg your pardon?" I said, caught by surprise.

Turning to face me, he said, "Collin, man, do you smoke pot?" Then, when he saw the hesitation in my eyes or the lines on my face, he added, "Don't be offended. It's a simple question, one I would've asked of any book that reads like you. If it bothers you, don't answer."

"I'm not offended, Nick, just a little stunned. I've seen patrons and club owners alike entertaining every habit known to man from drugs to self-mutilation. Sometimes I've joined in and sometimes I've deferred, but Nick, I've always had to figure out the game. I've had to pick it up with a careful eye, a little luck, and a hunger to learn more. Not once, no matter how crazy things have gotten, has anyone ever come right out at the first meeting and said, *'Collin, do you smoke pot?'* You just gave me blunt trauma to the brain."

"Cool," he said, with enthusiasm. "Guess that makes us both unique."

"That it does, Nick. That it does."

I swear I thought I saw him start to glow. After a few seconds spent with eyes locked to eyes, he broke the trance. "You didn't answer the question."

Repeating my earlier qualification, I replied, "As a patron or reporter?"

"Patron," he said.

Voice sly, gaze averted, I said, "I've been known to play along."

"Cool," he said. "What about as a reporter?"

"None of your damn business."

This time, we both laughed.

"That's cool, too," he said. "So listen, Collin, you want to do a hit?"

"Right now?"

"Best time."

I nodded. "Yeah, you're right. That might be agreeable."

Knox whipped his arm into a back pocket and pulled out what appeared to be a pack of Kent cigarettes. He pointed it in my direction, going in for the kill. As if reading my thoughts, he explained, "It's a wooden dugout hidden inside an empty pack. It's for privacy. You know how it goes. Cops stop me all the time, but they're too stupid to strip search a pack of Kents." He pressed the top and a small brass pinch hitter popped up. "Go ahead, man. It's cool."

No hesitation. When you're laying down the Journalist routine, you have to ask the right questions. When you're playing the Ego Trip Hipster, you have to flash balls of steel. When you're exhibiting the Worldly Sinner lie, you have no choice but stick to the story, through all its twists and turns, highs and lows, all the way to the end of the exposition. I was masking myself beneath a carefully woven cloak made of all three. "*Gracias, amigo*," I mumbled in mock Spanish, pulling the brass bat from its resting place.

"Need a light?"

"No, thanks." I removed a red disposable lighter from my shirt pocket.

"You don't look like a smoker."

"I'm not."

"Then why the lighter?"

"Club chicks that smoke. Never get caught short. Girl comes up. She says, '*Hey, man, you got a light?*' You better be prepared to say yes, or she'll go ask somebody else."

"Never get caught short, eh? What else you got in there?"

"A Trojan and a Vicodin, for before and after." Pause. "Oh, and my unspent nine-millimeter slug that was given to me by a friend who said it was good luck because it was in the chamber the night he tried to blow his head off but couldn't. Those three things get me through."

"No doubt," he said, and started to laugh.

I lifted the pseudo-cigarette to my lips, lit it, and inhaled heavily until my lungs were so full that the smoke escaped through my nostrils. My throat burned, my eyes dripped sorrowless tears, and my chest screamed. I fought the pain, holding the smoke in for fifteen, twenty, twenty-five seconds, before that uncontrollable marijuana cough forced it back into my mouth. I exhaled and sucked in a fresh breath. "Lively," I gasped.

"It's seeded from Amsterdam, man. Some of the best."

I handed him the pinch hitter. He refilled it from his stash inside the Kent pack. Lighting up, he sucked down a treasure trove in plant matter. Ticking off the seconds in my head, I counted nearly a minute before the door opened and, surprised, Knox spit out his cloud. "Je-ee-sus," Knox snapped. "You know better than that, Carl. Knock first."

"Sorry, Mugwump," said the angry, old burnout, his carrot-top head turning away as if he'd seen us naked. "Band's ready for a quick sound check, and the chick wants to see you."

"Which chick?"

"December."

"Perfect," he said. "I want to see her, too. Preferably in the buff."

Carrot-top Carl offered no appreciation for the boss's humor. "What's the deal with the catfish? You not afraid he'll expose you for showing off your wares like that?"

Knox cut loose with mean guffaws. He filled the pinch hitter and passed it back to me, watching me hit it without a word. "You were saying?"

The burnout shook his head. He backed out of the room and closed the door behind him.

When the door slammed, I exhaled and allowed a little laughter of my own. Fighting it back, I said, "What's his problem?"

"Too many drugs twenty years ago," Knox explained, "too much tolerance now. He has the damnedest time getting high these days and it really pisses him off. Besides, the chicks don't dig him. Carl's past his prime and past his time, and if it weren't for me giving him a job, he'd be out on the street, maybe up at the stadium after Steelers games with a sign saying 'Kick butt' on one side and 'Will work for food' on the other. He's miserable, melancholy, and as paranoid as a field mouse on coke. But you get past all that and he's a nice guy deep down inside."

"So, why's he call you *Mugwump*?" I said, reading the suddenly blurry word on his chest.

"Haven't the foggiest."

"It's on your shirt."

He shook his head. "People been calling me that since I was twelve. I don't know why and I don't really care. I answer to it, the same as Nick or Dickhead or damn near anything else. I'll tell you, it gives me endless opportunities to lie to ladies that never know the difference between a story and a fact. So, I wear it on my shirt and use it every chance I get."

"I can see where it might come in handy." And I could. "I'll have to remember that." And I would. "That's a game I know how to play." And I did. The next words staggered out unintended, more an anathema for a high head than the poetry of actual insight. With a spine turned something akin to jelly, I leaned back against a CD rack, got my balance, and said, "Everyone has a sacred name, an unintended epithet for the being inside, the *Dasein*. It's a secret name, incomprehensible to others, hidden to ourselves. We spend our lives trying to learn that name, and then to define it, to give it meaning, or to understand its nature, its essence that may not yet exist. To others, we tend to exaggerate the passion of the name. To ourselves, we play it down and suffer grief from self-pity and self-doubt. Regardless, we're labeled by this name, defined by it even as we seek to define it. So, when I introduce myself and ask, 'What is your name?' you should answer, 'It's my *destiny*.'"

This soliloquy seemed to shock Nick. "What does it mean?" he asked, eyes glazed over, muscles lax, lips twitching awkwardly. "Don't leave me hanging. Tell me what it means."

"That's what we strive to figure out."

"Man, you're a true obstacle for a sane mind."

I couldn't figure him for serious or sarcastic, so I brushed his statement aside. "So Nick," I said, "what bands you got lined up? Anybody I might want to write about?"

It took him a few seconds to regain his composure. He stood still, his expression just as calm. I knew in his head he heard the question played at snail speed. "Cancer Moon," he said. "They'll be back next month."

"You already told me. Others?"

"Uh…" He hesitated. "Smashed Love Bug. Ever heard of 'em?"

"I think so," I lied. "Not really sure. What do they play?"

"Alternative. What else?"

I laughed and felt my glasses slip, so I took them off and dropped them in the black pocket of my dress shirt, my red tie shifting to hide them there.

"They're here next Friday. Saturday, we've got the Hemlocks, a punk band from Seattle."

"I've heard of them." I hadn't.

"What about Puritanical Sex Queen?"

"Oh, yeah." No. Would've remembered a name like that.

"Got them booked in a couple weeks for the Tired Bones Festival. It's a charity thing with all the profits going to give some little girl in Jersey a bone marrow transplant.

PSQ's the headliner, with Jock Itch and Smells Like Burning Hair. It's a good cause, I'm supposed to say. Anyway, it's sponsored by the local Hells Angels chapter and their biker brethren. It's not bad. Killer bands, hard-drinking bikers, you know the deal. Of course, it means the place will be packed with those smelly bastards. Still, it's for a good cause, like I said."

"Sounds respectable."

"Well, after that we've got Clam Safari, one of my favorites. Ska band out of Florida. You can't miss that one. You'll crack up all through the show."

"I'll keep that in mind."

"Do," he said. "Then there's a solo show with the lead singer from Rusted…"

A loud knock cut him off.

Without pausing to consider his actions, he slapped the pinch hitter back inside the Kent pack which, in turn, he forced into a back pocket. "Yeah," he screamed at the closed door, his fire-stained throat crackling under the strain. "What is it?"

The door opened, and I got my first glimpse of December Leigh. She was so beautiful she could've been a drug-induced daydream. Strobe lights released behind my eyes, while whole galaxies were born and destroyed within the infinite smallness of my emotions. Shapely as any comic book villainess, but ragged as lost love or worn carpets, she reminded me of a morning shadow—tortured, ailing, eager to pass on with the approaching sun, and then no longer as perfect under the moonlight, still breathtaking in its weariness. Short black hair reinforced the image, drawing fresh shadows on her face, under her eyes, all around her gaunt, tight neck.

I wanted to kiss that spectral neck. I wanted to bury my lips under her chin, to taste the salty sweet flavor of her sweat-stained skin. Instead, I acted more like some meek geek, or like myself before I started covering the scene. I stood there leaning against a shelf, silent and immobile with a fear she might look me in the eyes.

She did, in passing, thankfully and regrettably taking little notice. Turning to the medicine man, she said, "Smells like ceebee smoke in here. You two been elevating?"

Knox flashed that pseudo-sly grin. "You caught us, babe. Burning sagebrush stogies straight from the fruited plain. Call the cops. We'll go quietly."

"I don't think so," she said. "Just give me a hit. Then start a stick of incense or something, Mugwump. Your place smells like the creeping crotch rot. Toxic. Got to get rid of the stench."

Knox shrugged his shoulders. "Anything for the lady. Just close the damned door. Can't have people lining up to beg for helpings."

She came all the way in, easing the door shut behind her. Seconds after the latch clicked, Knox proffered the Kent pack with a prestidigitator's sleight of hand. Before I could gasp or blink, this girl took two quick drags, holding in the second. Next thing I knew, she had her hands wrapped around the back of my head, lips pressed tight to mine, exhaling smoke and forcing it into my lungs.

"Whoa," Knox blurted. "Surprise shotgun!"

The act stole my resistance and my breath. My first reaction was to gag and struggle, but her steady grip caught me and kept me still. Soon, my numb lips adjusted to the warm, coarse feel of hers. I relaxed, taking all she gave me and wanting more.

Backing away, she watched as I coughed. "You taste good," she said.

I nodded in reply, fighting suffocation. Head rolled, heart rocked, and my wonderful wish-granting genie drifted away in a cloud of heavy, gray smoke.

Turning to Knox, she asked about the mindless mark she'd played. "Doesn't speak much," she said. "What's his story?"

Laughing wildly, Knox managed only a single word: "Reporter."

"Oh, *fuck*," she said, returning her glazed gaze to me. "Man, I'm sorry. I figured you for one of those club flakes. You know what I mean? I thought you were one of the hang-arounds."

I tried to smile.

"Are you okay? If I'd known…"

Knox interrupted her. "Don't worry, doll. He's cool."

"What?"

"He's cool."

She didn't believe or didn't understand. "A reporter?"

"He's on a trip as we speak. You probably stunned him like a hooked fish, or I should say a hooked bottom fish." He waved his arms at me, trying to get my attention. "Scavenger! Yo, Scavenger! Stop reminiscing and introduce yourself before you give the lady nightmares."

My senses took their sweet time translating. Biting my lip to break the trance, I coughed, "Forgive me." I straightened, continuing to smile like some naive virgin. "I must have been in a coma, just now. Dreaming. This goddess in black, I saw her right here, kissing me, caressing me, breathing new life into these tired lungs."

"That was her," said Knox.

I played along. "I can see the resemblance," I said, making it clear with slow eye-motion I was studying her from head to foot. I offered a hand. "Collin Hearst, your servant for life."

"Dee Leigh," she replied, shaking with a soft touch that sent fresh shivers up and down my spine. "I'm sorry, Mister Hearst. God, I'm embarrassed. I didn't mean to attack you like that."

"She did, too," said Knox. "Don't listen to her."

"I didn't. I thought you were…"

I shook my head. "No big deal," I said, slipping into my Hopeless Romantic routine. "I enjoyed it." I pulled my hand away, but my eyes locked on. "And by the way, it's Collin."

She returned my gaze for a long pause before breaking the connection. "What's a reporter doing hanging out in the sound room of a second-rate club?"

"Hey," said Knox. "It's a third-rate club. But I appreciate the compliment."

"Why are you in here, of all places, smoking dope and maybe ogling alternative kids through the boss's two-way mirrors?"

"Enjoying myself," I said, as casually as I could. "I cover the scene."

"The scene?"

"The bands, the people, the business. I live for it."

"He called last week," Knox added. "Asked what bands I had booked. I told him…"

"He told me a troupe of wizards and witches would pass through tonight, singing rites to the moon god, practicing enchantments on a helpless, unsuspecting crowd. He said you were magical, the hippest band in the world. His exact words were 'like nothing you've ever seen.'"

"I said the *solar system*. Just like a reporter to go and misquote me."

"My fault," I said. "He said you were the hippest band in the solar system."

"I also told him the sexiest singer in the business would be center stage."

"I see he was right." I thought I owned her. The look in her eyes, the hint of a smile, they told me stories—fantastic stories, erotic stories, stories to be made into blue movies, or at least heavily edited movies barely maintaining an 'R' rating. I wanted to watch those movies, to write their scripts, to live each scene with her as my costar.

"All right, lovers," Knox intervened, "that's enough."

"What?" the lady and I said in unison.

"Don't give me that. I can see the static stagger back and forth between your eyes."

"No," I said.

"You're tripping," said December.

"You've flipped," I said. "You've gone mad."

"Oh, I get it. Execute the messenger. I only told you what I saw, so save it for later and let's get back to work. This *is* a real business, you know."

"Right," I said. "Sorry."

"No problem." He turned to December. "So Dee, baby, did you come in here just to abuse my stash or was there something you wanted?"

She staggered a bit in her head. After a long hesitation and a puzzled look, she replied, "We've got two problems."

"Big or small?" said Knox.

"Hopefully small. Guess that depends on you."

"Spill it. What's the deal?"

"Number one. One of Justin's mics crapped out. The rest are working, but his drums are shallow. If you've got an extra, we'll use it. Otherwise, we'll play short."

"No problem. I'll have Carl hook you up as soon as possible. What else?"

"Number two. This is the important one. I want you to kill the front lights."

"Front lights? *For fuck's sake*, why?"

"Can't handle front lights, Mugwump. They hurt my eyes, make me nervous, make me dizzy, give me this sort of creepy, claustrophobic feeling like the walls are collapsing around me. I can't take it. Besides, I like to see the crowd."

Knox shook his head. "That'll leave an awful lot of shadows on your face."

"The Jim Morrison look," I offered.

"Beg your pardon?" said Knox.

"She's going for the Jim Morrison look. You know what I mean? It's the sullen look, the spectral look, the deranged demigod look. You should go with it, Nick. Could be sexy."

He took all this in, renewing his grin. "You need a job, man?"

"Got one."

"Too bad." He waved his hands and sighed. "Okay, Dee. You got it. One extra mic. No stage lights. What else?"

"That's it," she said. "We'll start whenever you give the word."

"Good. I'll find that microphone and get it to you. After that, I'll let you know. Got to play a few more tunes, try to get the crowd jumping."

She nodded.

"While you're waiting, why don't you take the carp here and introduce him to the rest of the band. Try to get in cozy with him."

"That's cool," she said.

"Be sure you put on a good show, too. If he digs the gig, he might write you up when you come through town next month."

"*Real* cool," she said. She turned to me, smiling seductively. "In that case, come on. Let's go party with the others."

"Sounds good."

"I'll bet they'll love you."

"Bet they won't know how to take him," put in Knox.

December disagreed. "No, they'll know. They'll treat him with the *utmost* respect."

I laughed. "Dealt with reporters before?"

"Many."

"All stuffy?"

"What else would you expect? They all know about the press. They've been burned with bad quotes and lousy reviews a hundred times."

"Ain't that the way shit works?" said Knox. "Well, you go broaden their horizons."

"We're on our way. Just one more hit first." Turning to me, she was careful to add, "Don't worry. I won't attack you again."

"Too bad," I whispered under a halfhearted laugh.

Next thing I knew, I was outside the sound room, again part of the Club Zero mayhem. I tried to keep my balance amidst a dizzying barrage of high-decibel sounds and flailing bodies twisting and turning in their pagan rituals. I don't recall if it was rap or rock or weird folk they were dancing to, but whatever it was, it felt almost erotic on nerves subdued by smoke. I lost all desire except simply to feel and be. Before long, I'd followed December across the dance floor and down a shaded corridor trailing off behind the stage, leading to a hidden room. I'd seen dozens of these rooms, decorated in different ways—some featureless like this one with nondescript sofas and chairs scattered under nondescript walls. Within a breath, I was pressing the flesh like some politician—shaking hands, smiling, trying to act smooth despite the buzz.

December pointed to each of her friends in turn. "Collin," she said, "this is Justin, our drummer. Our bassist, Heather. And over there in the corner, that's B.J., the lead guitarist."

"How do you do? How do you do? How the hell are you?"

"Collin's a reporter for…what was it?"

"The *Domestic-Chronicle*."

"He's a hack?" said the haggard, balding guitarist.

"He's a hack," December replied.

"Yeah," I countered, "but I'm a damned good one."

CANTO TWO

First Day at the Domestic-Chronicle

Ragged in dress, anxious in mannerism, I entered the newsroom in a mixed-up strut, proud but timid. I twit-ched—a scared college sophomore stepping into a news pro's world.

"Can I help you?" asked a receptionist sitting behind what could've been a papier-mâché desk, stacked high with facsimiles, fliers, newspapers, forms, and other pulp.

"Collin Hearst," I said. "I'm supposed to start work today."

She told me where to go, and from there it was a jumble of introductions and instructions. I met a cranky middle-aged woman in a gray jogging suit. The *boss*. "I'm Kathryn Carter," she said, "the editor. Nice to meet you. Don't say the same. You'll learn soon enough it's not true."

With effortless grace, Kathy gave me the full-bore tour, presenting me to my colleagues, only stopping long enough for a handshake and a quick hello. "This is Gray, our obit clerk. He'll teach you how to use our computers. That's Michelle, our late cops reporter. She'll teach you everything you'll be doing on the weekends. Say hello to Arnold Baker. He's our city editor. If you have questions or problems and don't want to be yelled at, ask him. Arnie'll take care of you. Rick Dunlap, managing editor. Important enough for a little yelling, go to him."

She was distracted by the receptionist who wanted to check the importance of a fax. I used the opportunity to engage Rick. "Is she serious? Or is it all a show to scare the new guy?"

Rick's lip eased into a tired smirk. "Watch and learn," he said. "That's all I can tell you, Hearst. You'll have to watch and learn."

"Where were we?" Kathy asked. "Oh, yeah. This is Agatha, one of our copyeditors. Pay close attention to her. She'll show you all the trivial or superficial things that'll get you fired." Then, after pointing me toward my desk, she introduced me to a face I recalled from years of newspaper columns. "This is Hunter Delaware. Ignore him. Nothing *he* says has any value. If you follow his advice, you'll wind up doing something unacceptable. Then you'll get yelled at by everybody. The things he does, *you* won't get away with. He's allowed because, aside from me and the publisher, he makes more money than anybody here. Get the picture?"

I nodded.

"Good. Now this is…" Blah, blah, blah.

My first story, by assignment, I wrote about pumpkins, those balls of sloppy orange pulp and seeds, sliced into faces with crooked candlelight grins. Symbols of the season, these jack-o-lanterns soon to be are meant to be displayed on porches rather than newspaper pages. Reporters know that. I got the job that no one else wanted: the annual ritual of deifying dealers of overpriced holiday melons. I was supposed to make those people look golden, as if they served a Samaritan purpose by making their profits in the true take-the-booty-and-run spirit of Halloween.

This story never changes. It's the same as writing about Christmas trees or county fairs. Nothing unique, nothing original, but it has to be done at least once every year.

I had never done it. I expected it to establish me. It'd place my name in newsprint, and from there, it'd be all front-page features with banner headlines stripped across the top.

My contact's name was Jim Dunkin, owner of Dunkin's Punkins. He had a patch several acres across just outside of the city limits off I-279. The stink of rot and droning hum of a thousand flies assaulted my senses as I got out of the car. That scent repulsed me, but I contained my disgust as Dunkin greeted me from a distance, waving one gritty hand while using the other to continue stacking fresh produce in the back of a beat-up black Chevrolet truck. He was a portrait of man as an animal, an evolution-ary link. Hair oily, beard clotted with muck, skin eternally stained from sweat and soil—he'd given himself to the land, and the land, in turn, devoured him. The left side of his red flannel shirt was tucked neatly into his faded denim jeans, while the right side hung down parallel with his fly. Dunkin straightened up, revealing more than six feet. He stretched, cracked his knuckles, and extended a grubby paw, expecting me to shake.

I did, feeling dried pumpkin guts against my skin.

"How you doing?" he said. "You from the news-paper?"

"Yes, sir. Collin Hearst. Nice to meet you."

"Same to you. Jim Dunkin. Welcome to Dunkin's Punkins."

"Nice place," I said.

"Thanks. You like pumpkins?"

"Everybody likes pumpkins," I said, as evasively as possible. "So tell me, Mister Dunkin, how long have you been in the business?" I pulled out a pen and notebook, ready to capture every detail.

"Twenty-three years."

I wrote it down.

"My daddy ran the place for thirty years before that."

I wrote it down.

He put an arm up to his forehead, wiping away the product of his labors. "You'll have to forgive me," he said. "I've been loading pumpkins all day, and I'm sweating like a stuck pig."

I wrote it down. Hell, I wrote everything down: every word, every phrase, every colorful colloquialism. I wanted to get the story right, without a hint of a breakdown or misquote. The questions I asked weren't much help. I went in to my first interview well prepared with plenty of perfect preformed interrogatories intended to get a grasp on the story. But they were far from open-ended, and most earned a one-word response. "Do you like selling pumpkins?"

"Yeah."

"Have you sold pumpkins all your life?"

"Oh, yeah."

"Ever do anything else?"

"No."

"What do you do in the off season, when pumpkins aren't in great demand?"

"Play the lottery, watch the tube, hang out down at the Scratching Post. That's about it, really."

"Ever get tired of your work?"

"Nah."

"Do you make a good living?"

"Oh, yeah."

"Do you sell very many pumpkins?"

"Yes."

"Business pretty good this year?"

"Yeah."

"Do you intend to do this all your life?"

"Yes."

"Ever plan to retire?"

"No."

That's how it went: an hour of yeses and noes, yeahs and nahs, occasionally a usable line or two. I only stole one gem: "What is it about selling pumpkins that makes you enjoy it?"

He rubbed his chin before replying. "I'm filling a need," he said. "I'm not feeding the poor or finding a cure for cancer. This ain't brain surgery. All the same, I supply something essential to our culture, our tradition, our American way. I can get in my truck and drive around town, seeing my contribution grinning mischievous greetings from every porch or every other window. Sure, I know they're not all mine. But they could be. I'm doing something that, for a while at least, makes parents smile and kids glow. That helps me feel good. People only rely on me once a year, and I won't let them down." He turned away for a moment, perhaps reminiscing. When he resumed his oration, it was with passion, or perhaps conviction. "You know, I'm not the most educated man, not the sharpest, not the hardest worker. I'm not any of that, but I do what's expected of me. You won't see Jim Dunkin asking for handouts. You won't see Jim Dunkin down at the welfare office. I work for a living. I do my job. When the harvest's over, ten thousand freshly-cut faces tell me I'm a success. That's why I enjoy this. That's why I keep doing it. It's something even a dumb old farmer like me can do well at, and when I do well at it, I add to the tradition. Continuing the tradition's special. It gives me a tingling feeling, a fire deep down inside, just like one of those jack-o-lanterns."

My article made the *Local* page along with a head shot of Jim Dunkin, a photo of some little girl's truly evil-looking carved masterpiece, and a bold headline that read, *"Pumpkin man sells the fruit of tradition."* Not a brilliant story. Not much different than any before or after. Not the kind of article that adds insight to a reader's life. Still, I clipped it and added it to my portfolio.

"Nice story, kid," said Hunter Delaware. He was sitting at his terminal, just opposite mine, sandaled feet propped one on top of the other to the right of his keyboard. His faded blue jeans were rolled up, exposing bare ankles covered with thick, black hair the same tint as his bristly beard. "You did a hell of a job for your first effort. That's no shit. A hell of a fine job."

"Thanks," I said. "Nothing special, though."

"Holiday stories rarely are. Thanksgiving you do your turkey stories and your classic soup kitchen stories. Christmas, you got Christmas trees, toys, the mandatory weather story, and usually another take on the soup kitchen angle. On Valentine's Day it's paper hearts and love stories. Of course, Flag Day you got flags and old veterans. So, on Halloween, what else is there but to write about pumpkins and ghosts? They're staples in the fold. You write these once a year to fill a page, and in a day or a week, they're long forgotten."

"Yes, sir," I said. "I'll do what I'm told, but I'm looking for something bigger."

Hunter lifted a cigar from the pocket of his striped pink shirt. Stripped of its wrapper, the cigar hung loosely from his lips. He didn't light it. That would be rude indoors, even for the highest paid eccentric on the staff. "You're getting the idea pretty quick. Have a specialty?"

"No, sir. Like I said, I'll write whatever I'm told to write."

"Uh huh," he said, nodding and chewing on his cigar. "That'll change. Give it a couple months. You'll get into a groove, find something that meets your needs as an individual. And the more stories you do on a subject, the better writer you'll be regarding that subject." He paused. "Besides, you'll find Big Boss Lady likes the grunts to have a hobby."

"Why a hobby?"

"So you'll have something to work on late at night, like tonight for example, when everything's quiet, nearly all the rest of us have gone home, and all you have to do is listen to the endless monotony of the police scanner, hoping for a fire or a major traffic accident to help you pass the evening."

"I see your point, but I'm too new at this. I've got no contacts."

"Don't worry. When you've been here long enough, everything falls into place. Whatever your interests are, you'll find a way to work them in one day. Then it'll happen for you. You'll excel. Personally, I've spent ten years trying to excel, but all I know's politics. Nobody excels at politics."

"That's why you're a columnist."

"Exactly my point. I'm a columnist because I'm highly opinionated and I can put those opinions into clever phrases and cynical sentences. Some people may not agree with everything I have to say, but most of them listen. Ninety percent of the folks who read this paper read my column, and if a few bullheaded old geezers would kick off, that might jump right up to ninety-one. In any case, the vast majority *do* read it. They may hate it, but they read it anyway because I know what I'm talking about. What more can I ask out of this business?"

"How can you be sure they read it? So many people?"

"Easy, kid. I know from experience, as will you. You'll know because they'll write you letters. Nasty letters most of the time. They'll call you up to chat and occasionally even to offer praise, but mostly they'll call to yell and scream and do what the public tends to do. That is to say, they'll bitch and moan on topics about which they have no idea, they've considered very little, or they have very valid opinions that are just plain wrong. If you're unlucky enough not to be here, they'll call your answering machine and converse with it for two hours about how evil you are because you support this candidate, that proposal, this radical new idea. You know, I tried to program my answering machine so it'd limit the time on all my messages to two minutes. Would you believe those crotchety old bastards would call back over and over to resume their soliloquies as if they'd never been interrupted? Some would go as far as to pick up with whatever the next word would've been in their previous sentence."

"People like that are out there?"

He nodded and pointed his cigar at me. "That's not all, kid. Folks will stop me on the street, at a restaurant, even while I'm standing at a urinal in a public restroom, just so they can argue with me as if I had no world outside this paper. Tell you the truth, I had a lady follow me around the grocery store watching what brands I picked up so she wouldn't get caught choosing the same ones. We've got a hundred thousand readers, kid. Believe me, they let you know when you strike a nerve."

"I see your point, Mister Delaware…"

"Hunter, kid."

"Yes, sir. Anyway, I see your point, but I don't understand how that applies to me. I'm not a columnist. There's not much room for opinion in a police blotter or a story about pumpkins."

Still pointing his thick cigar at me as if an extension of his index finger, Hunter said, "You'll see. I take a lot of flak because I'm a columnist. It's the same with the editor and the editorial board. That's why we're paid so much. But you'll get tagged, too—for stories you've written that folks don't like, and for my opinions, none of which have anything to do with you."

"It's that bad?"

"It's that bad. And what's more, people will call you about the most trivial things. They've got nothing better to do. Sometimes you'll get sworn at by pure chance for the misfortune of being the one who answered the phone." He paused. After a long breath, his eyes began to gleam like a madman's. "This is a true story, kid. You wouldn't believe it if someone else told it, but it's me, so you'll know it's true." He laughed. "It was all the way back when Conway Twitty kicked the bucket. He was an old country singer. You know who I mean?"

I nodded. "I'm familiar with him."

"Well, he'd had some problems, and he'd been in the hospital for a few days. We'd been running the wire stories, keeping people up to date. When he died, he had the bad manners to kick off in the middle of the night, or around midnight, maybe. Whatever it was, it was after we'd gone to press. So whoever was on the news desk that night had the bright idea to stop the presses, pull some minor story, and insert the *Associated Press* clip about Conway Twitty's death. Out of a hundred thousand papers, the story made it into five or six thousand. In other words, it slipped into a handful of papers from the final edition. You see where I'm going?"

I shook my head.

"Okay, this was on a Friday night, if I remember, or maybe it was Saturday night. Whatever. Well, my bad karma kicked me in the head. I got up early the next morning to come in here and work on my column. When I got here, the phones were ringing off the hook. I was the only one in the newsroom, so I had to answer. I took these ridiculous calls all morning, over and over, and basically, they went like this: *'Hey Buddy, I want to know why my neighbor gots Conway Twitty in his paper and I don't!'* Time after time, the same thing: *'Hey Buddy, where's Conway Twitty? Somebody forgot to put him in my paper.'* One hick even called in without ever saying a thing except expletives, punctuated off and on by the words 'Conway Twitty.' I swear to you, kid, it's true."

I cracked up, doubling over in my seat and holding my side.

"I'm telling you straight. It was nothing but *'Gawdammit damned piece of shit Conway Twitty motherfucking bunch of pussy Conway Twitty gawdammit!'*"

I felt like a piñata smacked too many times in the gut. I was laughing so hard I thought I might collapse from exhaustion or lack of air.

Hunter didn't help matters much. Every time I started to get the fits under control, he'd say something like, *"Hey Buddy, Conway's not dead, 'cause he ain't in my paper,"* or, *"You all killed Conway Twitty, and now you're trying to keep it from me."*

Before I regained my composure, it seemed like I was the one who'd died. "Are they all that bad?" I asked, not so sure I wanted to know the answer.

"No, not all of them. The vast majority, but not quite all. Kid, some of them might like you. Might even write you poetry."

"Poetry?"

"Yep."

"Bad poetry, I'll bet."

He propped his cigar between his stubborn, grinning lips. "Now you're catching on. Like I said, I think you'll fit right in. You just have to learn not to expect anything from anybody, and you have to figure out how to deal with a whole world of crazy people."

CANTO THREE

Sex or Something Else?

She exposed herself on stage: lavish with emotion, energy. All the passion, the joys and sorrows, loves and hates, ups and downs of the human condition—she experienced them and shared them with every word as if reliving the events that led to each flowing, heartfelt refrain. I heard a crackle in her voice during certain high notes at the peaks of sad subsections in her songs. The shrillness and intensity of these parts forced me to feel the things she felt, to know what she knew, to share her life. When she sang of heartbreak, I felt crushed. When she sang of loneliness, I was alone. When she sang of regret, I wished I'd done things differently. Then, toward the end when her tone transformed and she finally sang of love, I accepted it, unable to breathe and knowing I was hopeless. There's no subplot to this story. There's only a vision of her staring down, eyes shaded, head haloed from backlighting, hands gripped tightly around the microphone, lips singing "I love you" in a minor key. The caressing of nylon strings on a classical guitar, the brutal bashing of steel on the twisted body of a neon green B. C. Rich Warlock, the echoing rattling roar of sticks slapping skins—I listened to every sound her band's brushstrokes painted. From the audience, feeling the notes, I lived.

By the time December sang her last song, my brain had cleared away the drugs and booze. I felt normal except for the ringing in my ears. Yet I stood there staring as if buzzed, feeling my head swim from adrenaline and desire. I'd heard more than my fair share by then, but I hadn't heard enough. When the final discordant chord sandblasted every nerve in back of my neck, I shivered. And when the clapping ceased, I sighed.

I nearly made it out the door when the voice stopped me: "Hey, Collin! What'd you think of the show?" I turned to see Nick Knox several feet away, leaning against a cigarette machine. He centered a line made by two college girls. I could tell from his tone he was playing the proud club owner, hoping to play another game with one or both of the girls. I looked at my watch. Just past 2:30 in the a.m. Didn't have to be at work for twelve hours. *What the hell*, I thought.

Living my strut, I walked toward him. "How's it going, Nick?"

"Good," he said, grinning. "*Real* good. Girls, this is Collin. He's with the local press, here for a story on the band. Collin, my friend, say hello to my new comrades Nell and Lena."

I nodded, making eye contact with each. "Hello. Hi."

They returned the courtesy, and I kept a close watch, studying their expressions, trying to predict which one wanted me. They both looked about the same. Dyed-blond hair with black or brown roots, petite faces with eyes like Siamese cats, thin bodies dressed in tight black tops and plaid miniskirts—they were made up so similarly I figured them for sorority sisters. I focused on their gaze, the arc of their smiles, unintended softness in their voices as they spoke their greetings. The *left* one. It was definitely the left one. Lena, I believe. She had an extra bit of emphasis on "Hello."

Knox heard the same thing, conveying the message with a discreet nod in her direction. Not letting on to these suitor tricks, he repeated his question. "So, what'd you think of the show?"

Embellishing, I said, "I thought I had a ticket to the theater of the soul: *'For madmen only!'* I'm still in the afterburn from an emotional orgasm."

"So, you liked it?"

I shrugged. "Yeah, I guess you could say that."

Lena grinned. "The band *was* pretty good."

Knox stood up straight, draped his arms around both young ladies, and looked from one to the other. I sensed he was fighting back sarcasm. "Sure enough. It was a *pretty good* band."

"So, you're a reporter?" Nell said.

"That's right."

"What do you report?"

Knox said, "He tells mothers where their bad little girls spend all their time."

"Right," said Lena.

"No, really," said Nell.

"Really," I said. "I cover the *scene*."

"The scene?" both said.

"The *scene*. The music scene, the club scene, the singles scene, the neo-Beat underground subculture scene. Everything you see, hear, enjoy—that's my job. I also cover crime, traffic, courts, weather, and the other general this and that of a day in the life of the city, but it's the *scene* that calls to me, teases me, entices me out at night."

They didn't know quite how to take me. I spoke to them in the language of dreamers. But they understood the rapture. They felt it in the flow of my words like the rising action in a four-star flick, building and growing, keeping the shortest attention span attentive until the climax. They were eager for that climax: there for me to woo to, to sing playful love songs to, to address eager lips to, and they wanted me to know it.

We talked for a while. The words didn't matter, only the hand on my shoulder, fingers running up and down my tie. Lena sent me signal after signal, and I sent back signs.

Knox helped, encouraging her to seduce me or to be seduced. Why he needed me, I'm not sure. Perhaps my facade worked too well. Maybe he couldn't see through masks I wore into the timid lines that marred my face. But I played along, making a game of it with him.

Nell and Lena played along too, perhaps finding a sport of their own. We talked and touched and were friendly-like, digging one another with words and sensations. Before this experiment ended, my eyes fell through each of theirs, searching inside them for a spark. It was a script played out in dangerous dialogues between four unredeemable characters.

But the ending hadn't been written.

A female hand caressed my neck from behind, catching me by surprise. Even before I turned, I could tell by the look in each girl's eyes that they'd lost me. I thought I heard one sigh.

The dark goddess whose touch blessed me could've owned me with a word. Had she commanded me to cry, I would've plucked out both my eyes to force the tears, or else I would've thought of her in absence. "Hello, lover. How did you like the show?"

"December…" I said, but got no further.

"Great show," said Knox. "You mesmerized the crowd."

The young ladies put in their compliments.

"Good," said December. "Pleased to know I pleased you." I could hear the innuendo in her tone. "What about you, Mister Reporter? What message did our music send you?"

"I heard the inner struggle of mankind," I began.

"Womankind," she said.

"Humankind."

"Okay."

"I heard the inner struggle of *humankind*," I began again, "as soul and spirit progressed from birth to death, existence to essence, being through becoming. I felt virgin insights growing wise, anxiety giving way to confidence, carnal lust metamorphosed into passion, hopelessness becoming hope and finally success. I heard Beethoven applauding from the heavens, and Bon Scott singing along from his cherished spot in hell. What message did I receive from your symphony? It's hard to say. I can't seem to find the words."

"Sounded like a lengthy speech to me," said Knox. "Words aren't your problem."

December met my thoughts with a grin. "You described everything I felt."

I smiled back.

"Glad to know *someone* understood."

Those words enticed my newly tense shoulders to relax. Usually the old Art Critic routine doesn't work so well. It tends to add an element of snobbery. This time, it made me out to be a charmer. "That's wonderful," I said. "Then all my interpretations are accurate, and all your songs are profound."

She smiled wider. "Listen, the band's having a private party at the hotel—just the four of us and a few new friends. Why don't you tag along?"

I considered her offer. A private party, a chance to be in with the band—I've been there. But it seemed different coming from her, as if this were more than the typical sex-and-drugs after-bash.

Uncertain how to react, I glanced around at Mugwump who was shaking his head as if to say, *You're breaking a canon of the Uniform Sexual Code of Etiquette if you back out on a co-op deal to split the proceeds from an evening's efforts.* But I was no stranger to broken rules and bad ethics. I looked at the girls, imagining the taste of their lips, the feel of their skin, picturing each naked in bed, or more likely, on a gritty sofa in another of Club Zero's hidden rooms.

I wanted more. "It's casual. Let's go."

"Killer," she said, using it as an adjective.

"Hey, wait up," said Mugwump. "What's the deal?"

I avoided his gaze. "Sorry, Nick, ladies. It's my job to mingle with the bands, to try and get inside the musical mind. Maybe I'll see you around."

"Maybe," said Lena.

"It's cool," said Nell.

But it wasn't cool, and I knew I'd closed that door for good.

CANTO FOUR

The After-Party

The stranger pulled out a tiny red-black ball in a plastic
baggy. He waved it around. His eyes were glossed over,
heavily dilated, yet he still looked hungry. He wore blond
stubble like scars, his clothes just as ragged from tattered
reddish orange shorts to a concert tee on which the band's
logo had long vanished. "Who's he?" I whispered to December.

"Haven't got a clue."

B.J. leaned in close to us. "Just some sewer rat that
dug itself out of the garbage in time for the gig. But he had
product, no charge and no setup. Just liked the show and
wanted to hang out for a while. He's cool. We already saw
him do a couple hits."

I scanned the hotel room. Worn blue carpet, two
large beds with dirty off-white covers, a red vinyl chair,
generic TV, two cheap wooden dressers, a window-unit air
conditioner—it was typical. Heather and Justin were lying
arm in arm on the bed, apparently long past intimate on
their current tour. B.J. sat lotus-like behind us, while the
stranger sat in front, legs crossed and long, thin arms

stretching out to work the little red ball. There were two other unknowns, both men—one in a corner, the other resting up against a near wall.

The stranger fondled a long-stemmed brass pipe, removing a portion of his treasure from the baggy. "Amazing grace…" he sang off key as he transferred opium into the bowl and mixed it with tobacco, "how sweet the sound, that saved a wretch *like* me…" All of us found him odd. His hands shook and his teeth chattered. "Who wants to go first?" he asked, rushing a frenzied glance around the room.

B.J. spoke up: "You go ahead. Looks like you need it."

He nodded several times, so fast that his face blurred. "That's good." Displaying a box of matches, he removed one stick and struck the tip against the strip. The smell of sulfur filled the room, followed almost immediately by a sweeter scent from the lit pipe. After he took a hit, he passed the pipe to the nearest of the unknowns, and it made its way around the room from there.

When it came to me, the fire had dimmed to embers, so I lit up and inhaled, but not too much. The last time I tried opium I went crazy and took so many hits I ended up vomiting, then blacking out. I didn't want to do that around December, so I held back. Still, almost instantly I felt a jellied spine and numbness like bare skin in saltwater. I wanted to lie back and melt.

The party faded in a couple hours, but not the sensations. B.J. collapsed on the bathroom floor after vomiting fits. The lovers were petting underneath the sheets, moaning to remind us they were alive. The stranger and the unknowns split. I would've left, too, but December wouldn't allow it. "Stay a few. Hang out. I don't get much conversation on the road."

I couldn't refuse her. We'd been bullshitting each other with our chaos and calamity stories, and every time there was a lull, I'd find myself saying, "What should we talk about?"

"What do people ever talk about?" she replied this time as every other. "There's either you or me. Anything else is gossip."

"Never looked at it like that."

"Right," she said. "So, what's it to be?"

"Definitely *you*."

She sighed, smiled, sighed. "I should've known. The reporter likes to listen and observe."

"You make me sound like a peeping Tom."

"Close enough. Same family tree, different branch."

I limited myself to a shrug and a handful of words: "You may be right. But enough about me. Tell me about you. What are your negative impulses?"

"You don't want to know."

"Sure I do."

"If I showed you my dark side," she whispered, "you'd pity me or turn in disgust."

"Somehow I doubt that," I said. "No matter. You show me yours, I'll show you mine."

"Is than an offer or a fantasy?"

Despite my playful banter, the directness of her innuendo intimidated me, breaking through the confident Well-traveled Wayfarer routine. I felt my face flushing, so I turned away from her gaze. I said nothing, thoughts hazed with the stray gray of a drug-trip fadeout into real time.

"Oooh," she purred. "That's a reaction I didn't expect."

I reattached my eyes to hers, stroking a line from a dry throat. "That's how it goes. When you're trying to be cool, there's only so much heat you can handle."

"Heat?" she said.

Uncomfortable silence. I eased back to my original tone. "Tell me a story," I said.

"About what?" Coy.

"Anything you want. A scene from your life. Tell me something I don't know, something that makes December Leigh the poetess and leader of a discordant micro-culture."

"That could take all week," she said, "or at least the rest of the night."

"I've got time."

There was something seductive about her hesitation. She turned away and looked at the ceiling as if attempting the perfect pose. I could've spent hours there admiring the aesthetic beauty. "Okay," she said, ending the pose though far from ending the beauty. "I think I've got one." She lay back, stretching out on the dirty floor, using her arms as a pillow. Her nipples pointed skyward through the fabric of her tee. I caught a glimpse of tight white skin around her lower abdomen where her shirt ascended her belly as she raised her arms. Three quarters of her navel peeked out from below the last inch of black cloth. The indentation, the tiny galaxy spiraling down into her body, seemed more erotic than other inward passageways I imagined. I thought of running my hands around that small fragment of her hidden world, kissing her there, tickling her with a warm, wet tongue.

Arousal struck me in the back of the head like a lead pipe in some dark alley. The blow could've fractured my skull or killed me outright with embarrassment. Luckily, she didn't witness the wound. Crossing my arms to cover the arc in my slacks, I smiled and continued to stare at the patch of skin above her waist. It was far too tempting, and I couldn't look away.

Then, out of the blue, she said, "My stepfather raped me."

"What?" I stopped examining her body and watched her face. It wore no readable expression.

"I was fourteen. He was in his thirties."

"My God."

She broke her self-induced trance and lifted her head to meet my stare just long enough to say, "This is between you and me. No scoop, you dig?" When I nodded, she relaxed her head and continued. "My mother was out of town for a week, and he came in and did it. He might've been drunk. I don't remember. It lasted about ten minutes, if that. He came into my room while I was watching videos on MTV, and it just happened."

I didn't know what to say—what she *expected* me to say. I mumbled something trivial.

She ignored me. "It didn't hurt."

"No?"

"I wasn't exactly a virgin. All the same, I didn't find it amusing." Her words struck me as cold, calculated, absent the poetry pain brings. "It pissed me off more than anything."

"How many times?" I forced myself to ask.

"What's that?"

"How many times? How many times did he…?"

"Oh," she sighed. "Just the once. I made sure of that."

"What'd you do?"

She flinched. "Stabbed him in the leg with a carving knife. But don't ask me how. I was aiming for his chest."

"No."

"I would've killed him, but the damn knife got stuck." She started to laugh, transforming her tragedy into a black comedy and reveling in the noir.

"What then?"

"Nothing," she replied, serious again. "He went to the hospital and didn't say a word. Made up some excuse about falling down the steps, bumping into a door or, I don't know, juggling knives for his circus act. I kept my mouth shut, too. It was over. As far as I was concerned, we were even, and believe me, even's the most anybody can hope for. Even equals justice in a fucked-up world."

"Any resentment?" I asked, prying like a good reporter.

"No. Can't change the past. I'll save my sorrows for my tomorrows."

"That's a healthy attitude. Most of us spend too much time looking at the past, especially our failures and inadequacies."

"Valuable insight, Reporter Man. But it leads to an inevitable conclusion."

"What's that?"

She winked. "It's time to pay your debts. Tell me a bedtime story."

"Okay. How about a fairy tale?"

"Very funny, but it won't get you off the hook. We made a deal. You owe me."

Slowly I laid myself parallel beside her, facing her from less than a foot away. Using my elbow for support, I rested my head on the palm of my hand as if I were great Caesar seeking grapes. It gave me a sense of leverage, a hint of authority over her. I was so close, yet I looked down from a bird's-eye angle like a hungry falcon swooping. My prey refused to run, however. She faced me as if to stare me down. Then, when I opened my lips to speak, she gave up and returned her stare to the ceiling. "Before I spill it, I have to set the scene. You need to know a little more about me."

"Like what?"

"The kind of person I am." As calmly as I could, I told her, "I'm a *Mask*."

"A what?"

"A *Mask*," I said, "a face atop a face. Actually, one face beneath several. I don't fit in so well with any group, so I try to fit in with them all."

"You're a conformist," she quipped. "You don't seem like…"

"I'm not a conformist. It's another mask. I'm as much an individual as you. I have to be. If it were possible,

I'd be like everybody else, but I just can't. It's a hopeless cause. I wish I could sin the group's sins, but I tend to sin my own."

"So what are your *sins?*" she chided playfully.

"Pride, greed, lust, envy, you name it. I've done them all. I adapt to whatever character flaw I need to move the moment along. I'm as capable of overconfidence as I am of cowering under the bed. That's what I mean when I call myself a *Mask.*"

"I'm not sure I buy into it," she said. She glanced my way without turning her head, shifting her eyes and producing an eerie effect. "You haven't played the masquerade with me."

"Oh, but I have. It's just that many of my faces have similar sides."

She rolled over and traced an outline of my jaw with her right hand. Her touch sent static signals to my brain, renewing the euphoria. I closed my eyes to keep the room from spinning. When I opened them, she'd withdrawn her hand, although the path her fingers followed flared up in a thousand tiny orgasms exploding under my chin and around my cheeks. She smiled as if our lips came together. "Feels firm enough to me. What face are you wearing now?"

When I regained my composure, I said, "Who knows? I must have worked a hundred routines since walking into the Zero. Whatever it is, I hope you like it."

"That sounds like a line."

"Are you biting?"

She groaned a slight rejection, but not an unredeemable one. "Now I see it. You're projecting another you. All of a sudden you're devious, coming on strong without actually coming on."

"Really?" I said, surprised. I hadn't realized I'd slipped into my Subtle Cyrano routine.

"Really," she said.

"Well, it's like I always say, lover, I've got more faces than the devil, only what I offer won't cost you your soul. Maybe."

She looked up, judging my intent. Uncertain, she grinned and returned to her previous position, lying on her back and stretched on the carpet. "Maybe?" she said.

"Maybe."

She closed her eyes and sighed a heavy sigh. Before all her calm escaped, she drew another breath and sucked it back in. "You were going to tell me a story?"

"Whenever you're ready."

"Go ahead."

I adjusted my position until I mirrored December, arms interlocked behind my head, eyes pointed upward. "Mine's a little more romantic," I began, "but it ends somewhat less than even. I was twelve, I think. Maybe older. My parents took me to this posh little resort at Hilton Head."

"Nice place. I went there once."

"To be honest, I don't remember. I was a kid, and to a kid, one beach is the same as another. Anyway, I was a loner, experimenting with my first masks to get attention. I was hanging loose by the pool, working a rudimentary version of the old Diving Daredevil routine, trying to impress young chicklets bathing in the sun. I spent the day improvising crazy stunts, clumsy back flips, comic book crash dives, acting like the coolest fish in the water, all the while scared to death I'd crack my skull on the board, the bottom, or someone else's head. Didn't happen though, and somehow I came off as casual. By the end of the day, I had the other kids dancing on the diving board, risking their lives to imitate my stupid, trivial kicks."

"Somebody got hurt?" she asked, trying to guess the plot.

"No, thank God. Be a *wonderful* thing to look back on. I could've been scarred for life."

"So, what happened?"

"The routine worked. Well, sort of."

She rolled over again, this time taking the advantage and looking down at me.

"The point of acting's to entertain. Any star or starlet tells you that. It's also to focus attention on the actor. Follow me?"

"Yes, but what happened?"

"You're in a rush, aren't you?"

"Tell me."

"All right," I said defensively. "I'm getting there as fast as I can."

"What happened?"

"A young girl followed me home."

Her jaw dropped as if I'd told a horrible joke. "I don't believe you."

"It's true. Or it's sort of true. She followed me back to the motel room without me catching on. My folks weren't back from shopping, so I stripped, toweled off, threw on a tee and shorts, then sat down to watch *Battlestar Galactica* reruns. A few minutes later, I got the call."

"The call?"

"The call. She got my room number and contacted me through the switchboard."

"How romantic," December sighed. I could see *her* mask faltering—the Headstrong Rocker fading into the Familiar Fan, the lover of soap operas and trashy magazines with titles like *Teenage Lust* or *Handsome Stranger*. I liked this side of her. "What'd she say?"

"I was cute."

"Cute?"

"Hard to believe, I know, to see the haggard creature I've become."

"I wouldn't say that," she said.

"Gee whiz, missy," I joked, playing the Ever Child routine, "you're embarrassing me." She giggled at my sarcasm as if she were that little girl. It intimidated me, and also it attracted me. *Will you follow me home?* I thought, hoping she might pick up my signal.

After a long breath, December asked, "What did *you* say?"

"I said, 'Thanks.' What'd you expect?"

"That's it?"

"No. Of course not. You're getting ahead of me. We talked a bit, maybe half an hour. She told me she was thirteen. I lied and said I was, too. She said she saw me at the pool, and I said nothing in reply, flashing back to the setting, hoping to find her image. I drew a blank."

"What was her name?" December was getting more impatient.

"I don't know. I forgot to ask."

"You're kidding."

"Keep in mind, I was twelve years old. What did I know about relating to people? What did I know about girls? It's lucky I didn't freeze up and go silent."

"So, what *did* you do?"

"Nothing. She handled the particulars. She arranged a tryst for breakfast the following morning in the motel restaurant. She asked if I could get away. I said yes, so she said, 'Good,' and let me know where and when, what she looked like, what she'd be wearing, everything I needed to know except that she forgot to tell me her name. I agreed, and it was all set."

"It didn't happen, did it?" Her smile took a downturn.

"No, it didn't."

"Why not?"

"My parents."

"They wouldn't let you go?"

I shook my head. "They didn't know. They picked that morning to look for souvenirs, to get up early and walk along the beach searching for shells and starfish and stuff. They woke me up at sunrise saying, 'Let's go, son,' as if it were a happy morning ritual. My breakfast date was snatched away from me, and I never heard another word from the girl."

"Never stand a woman up," December said.

"I know that now," I replied with friendly sarcasm.

"So sad," she said.

"And sappy," came my retort.

"I think it's charming."

"Well, maybe in your eyes. Like I told you, I ended up less than even."

"Sounds like you got a surplus to me."

"I lost more than I gained. My first fling fizzled before it formed, left neither a name nor a face to complement nostalgia. It's not the death of a childhood romance that marks that time in my mind. It's the abortion. It wasn't a valiant loss."

December kissed me. She didn't speak or allude to her intentions. She simply bent down and made contact, sustaining for an epoch or an era as far as my numb, lax form could figure. Then, after pulling away, she said, "There. Now you're more than even. If you would've kept your date, you wouldn't have had that story to tell, and I wouldn't have rewarded it."

"Good point. Still, you can't revitalize the dilapidated past. You can only brighten the future frame from which to view it. Besides, this story serves a better martyr sealed in its tomb."

She leaned down and kissed me again, allowing her tongue to linger on my lip.

My senses shot in all directions. This time, I opened my mouth and zealously kissed her back.

Minutes later, satisfied with kisses, I whispered a warm farewell and closed the door.

CANTO FIVE

Blood

Sprayed across one concrete wall, drying: evil's art sold well on the open market, the open air of Market Alley. Careless splatter and careful meandering streams covered up obscenities, tags, slogans, other true graffiti. Small leaf piles were sticky from the excess, as were torn trash bags and heaps of junk. A tortured, one-armed rocking chair eased back and forth as though the victim sat there moments before being shot three times in the chest.

A witness saw it happen.

For drugs, the cops said: a fourteen-year-old shot by a gang of five teens too young to drive but old enough to grip curved triggers of unregistered revolvers.

This would be my first major headline. Saturday near midnight, I sat in a swivel chair, yawning, listening to the scanner, watching the opening monologue on *The Tonight Show*. The rest of the staff had dwindled, leaving sports writers, copyeditors, and me: a bored police reporter. One moment, I had nothing to do. Then the scanner sent a banshee's death wail through the newsroom. I was startled but not concerned. Those signals blared often for fires, petty larcenies, and sometimes just for tests. This alarm sounded like the rest, except when qualified by solemn words: "We have a possible homicide. Respond to…" The first thing a young reporter learns about police scanners is to ignore them if possible. The second's that whenever a dispatcher says, "possible homicide," it means *"Holy Jesus, we've got a corpse!"* Before the siren faded, I was out the door, notebook in hand.

"Who are *you*?" asked a black police lieutenant guarding the block.

I was first on scene, and my youth concealed my intent. Attempting my best Woodward and Bernstein routine, I flashed a press badge. "Collin Hearst," I said, voice shaky. "I'm a reporter for the *Domestic-Chronicle*."

"You new?" said the lieutenant. He looked me over suspiciously.

"Yes, sir."

"How long you been with the *Domestic*?"

"About three weeks."

He shook his head. "This is a hell of a way to get used to the job."

"You're not kidding. What have you got?"

He looked around, making sure none of the other cops were near. When we were clear, the lieutenant told me, "Fourteen-year-old boy." He said it without emotion.

"Murder?"

He grinned. I almost expected to see him laugh, but when he spoke, his voice remained austere. "Yeah, murder. Three gunshot wounds to the chest. Kid was dead in minutes."

"Any suspects?"

"Not officially," he said, with a nod to indicate that unofficially names and faces were known. "Got a witness. It won't be long."

As he talked, I kept straining to look around him while trying not to be obvious about it. The lieutenant pretended not to notice.

"Kid was a drug addict. We picked him up a couple dozen times for possession, once for delivery. Probably got needle tracks up and down his arms and burn spots over both hands. He's been in juvie, but that didn't change him any."

"So, this was drug related?"

"I didn't say that. It's too early in the investigation to be sure."

That wouldn't be *'official'* information for another twenty minutes when the lead detective could make his speech to the fully assembled media. By then, I planned to have enough info to write the story and get it in a few thousand copies of the final edition. "What's the kid's name?"

"Can't say. Family has to be notified."

"Well, what else can you tell me?"

"Like I said, we got a body, a witness, and a lot of work ahead of us."

I wrote down every word in my usual cryptic scrawl. "Thanks for your help. Uhm, last thing. Would you call this a tragedy?"

He grunted. "This is off the record."

I nodded.

"The tragedy's that somebody close to him didn't kick that kid's ass into next week. Nobody cared enough to get him in shape. And since his family wouldn't do it, it's twice a tragedy that the state of Pennsylvania didn't step in to fill the gap. On the record, it's always sad to see a kid get killed, whatever the reason. It's a dangerous world. I wish folks could learn to live in it."

Sunday, as was his custom, Hunter Delaware came in on his day off. He intended to work on his next column but spent most of the time twiddling his thumbs, chatting with friends, chewing on an unlit cigar, and only occasionally pausing to type an inspired line. "You were lucky," he said when I told him about my conversation with the lieutenant. "You're new, so you got to see a side of that officer most old-timers never do. Cops are like that. They love you at first. But wait until they get burned a couple times. You'll never be able to catch a crafty line. Once they get to know you and you get to know them, they'll remember it's best to stick to facts. It becomes a game to see how much information you can extract and how much they can conceal."

"That so?"

He rubbed meditatively at his bristly black beard. "That's so, kid. They're all opinionated. Every now and then, they'll ramble off a diatribe about whatever irks them or how the public views this and that in our fair city. You'll get a story out of it. The editor'll pat you on the back and circle your byline during the evening news meeting. But after that, you'll be cut off. The higher-ups at the station will find some gripe with the story, something trivial, and they'll yell at the officer dumb enough to tell you the truth. From then on, it's a black ball when you call that cop for a scoop. You'll get the facts in a bland wrapper as if you were reading them off the police report. It happens one by one until nobody with a shiny badge and a uniform wants to hear your name."

"Can't be that bad," I said.

"Trust me. No, don't trust me. You'll see. It'll happen to you sooner rather than later. When it does, remember what old Hunter told you. Then you'll know."

"Know what?"

"That you're one of us, kid. You're part of the family. You're a cub until you're snubbed. When you sit at a table with the rest of us, grumbling in your beer, you'll know you're a pro."

"Uh huh."

Hunter whipped out a cigar, stripped it of its plastic, and began to chew on the end as if sharpening his teeth on a grindstone.

"Now, don't misunderstand me, kid. Sometimes you still get good stuff. Ask a cop about his theories, it's open mouth, insert foot. They love to speculate. It gives'em a chance to show their detective skills, to become the criminal and solve the crime for an eager reporter."

"Are they good at it?"

"Extremely. Remember, kid, good cops have criminal minds. Otherwise, they'd never make an arrest."

"I've heard that one before."

"J-school?" he asked.

"One-oh-one."

CANTO SIX

"Hello!" Voice gruff, unforgiving. First Monday in November, after 9 p.m. Alone in my apartment, I lay stretched out on the sofa, naked except for black cotton briefs. My left hand gripped a plastic cup as if a holy plastic grail filled with grape juice, ice, and vodka. Eyes stared attentively, focused on the television. Steelers playing the Dolphins. I never missed a Monday night game when the Steelers played, and I hated to be bothered in the middle of the game.

"Hello. May I speak with Collin Hearst, please?" Female voice: soft, seductive.

"Speaking."

"How are you?" Energetic yet delicate, tempting without trying.

"Who is this?"

"December." One word whispered as an invocation.

I sat up, trying like hell not to spill my drink all over me. "Hold on," I said. Balancing the phone on my right shoulder, I reached for the remote control and pressed the mute button. The grunts and groans, hard hits and the

70

tired voices of announcers continued on without me. "December Leigh?" I asked, momentarily stunned.

"How many girls named December do you *know*?"

"Only one. How'd you get my number?"

"Wasn't hard. Called the newspaper, and some lady was nice enough to look it up."

I shook my head in disgust. "No respect for privacy," I mumbled.

"I didn't think you'd mind."

"I don't. I'm happy to hear from you. I just can't believe those worthless fucks gave out my number. You could be calling to make death threats—or worse, to whine about typos in my last article. People do that, you know. Staff numbers are hush-hush."

"I told them I was your sister," she explained.

"They believed that?"

"Apparently."

I sighed. "Anyway, it's wonderful to hear your voice. To what pleasure?"

"We're playing Saturday. You *told* me to call for an interview."

Saddened. Spirit crippled. For a moment I thought… oh, I don't know what I thought. It was wrong, whatever it was. "I have to apologize again. I'd forgotten."

"Yeah? Well, I remembered. I have a feeling about you. You seem to know what we're about. I'm sure you'll tell it straight and make us look as good or bad as we deserve."

My face burned to embers. If she were there in person, she'd rib me for my embarrassment. My timidity was evident. It's hard to work a good routine while speaking over a phone line. "I'll do what I can," I said. "Can you hold on while I grab some paper and a pen that works?"

"Better yet," she said, "why don't we get together?"

"That might work," I replied, not catching her meaning. "Will you be here the day before the show?"

"I'm here now," she said.

"You're in Pittsburgh?" My voice crackled and I had to clear my throat.

"Yeah," she said. "We're on our way to Cumberland, Maryland. That's where we're playing tomorrow. I talked the others into spending a night here. Did I make the right call?"

I felt as if I'd won a sweepstakes or been nailed with a surprise birthday party. There was a moment of something close to fright, an adrenaline rush leading to excitement, then a numbing sense of awe. "Sure," I said. "Where are you?"

"I'm at a Burger King down the street from your newspaper building."

My voice trembled. "When did you get in?" Rapid breathing. Palms beginning to sweat.

"About two hours ago. I would've called earlier, but we were driving in circles."

"Lost?"

"You know it. We get lost every time we come through here. This is without a doubt the most confusing city in America, except maybe D.C."

"It's a common complaint. I'd be lost too if I hadn't lived here all my life."

"Well, we're found now. Do you want to get together?"

I paused, uncertain. My plans included a couple relaxing drinks and watching the football game. Asked by anyone else, I would've explained that leaving my apartment would be impossible because it'd require prying apart the contact cement sealing my butt to the couch.

She sensed my hesitance. In an erotic whisper, she seduced me. "Come on," she said, "I'll buy you a burger." The feathery touch of her voice chilled my spine.

I glanced at the television. The game was breaking for a commercial and the score flashed across the screen: Steelers 7, Dolphins 6, early in the first quarter. *Ah, fuck*, I thought. *It'll be a blowout anyway.* "Make it a cup of coffee and you've got a deal."

"Done. I'll be right here."

"Give me twenty minutes and I'll be there, too."

"Don't take long. It's cold in here and I need to be warmed up."

"I'll be quick," I said.

"I'll be waiting."

Before the ripples and tiny waves settled in my grape drink, I was up, dressed, and locking the door behind me, with lights and TV unaltered and still burning off the watts. I had no time to gather up a colorful costume, to build a facade. It's tough to set up a preplanned routine when you start off in your underwear and have to be on the road before your drink settles. I wound up in a ratty white sweater and a pair of blue jeans, covered up with a trench coat to keep me warm on a frigid November night in Pittsburgh. I gave myself to the moment, face unshaven, hair tangled, eyes glassy and wide.

As I lurched into the Burger King, I saw her sitting at a booth in a far corner, her appearance as haphazard as mine: gray sweatshirt, sweatpants, leather coat. The only light and life emanating from her person was a neon orange ball cap on her head, glowing against her deep black hair which draped down behind her in a crude ponytail. I might not have recognized her were she not the only patron. She had a newspaper spread out on the table in front of her. As I approached, she looked up and smiled.

"Great story," she said.

I sat opposite her. "Thanks," I said as I tried to remember what I'd written. Something sympathetic about sick kids getting a visit from their favorite pro wrestler, I thought.

"You have a sensitive side."

"Not true," I said, playing it cocksure. "Only thing sensitive's my ego."

She didn't buy into it. My ragamuffin image came off less than cool. She made eye contact and imposed her opinions with a forced, focused gaze. My resistance crumbled and I had to look away. She said, "It's good to see you. I've been thinking about our last conversation. When you left that night, you left me revitalized." She tapped her fingers on the table. I could almost pick up the rhythm of one of her songs. "It's been a long time since I shared myself without it being sexual."

"Glad to know I helped," I joked. "Of course, I'm not licensed as a psychiatrist, so I can only charge minimum wage for my counseling."

"Very funny."

"I'm serious."

"Yeah? Well, you can bill me. I'll make sure the check gets put in the mail."

Laughter by both of us. Then quiet.

She said, "Let's get on with business. You wanted an interview, so fire at will."

"Okay," I said, and began to search the pockets of my trench coat. "Shit!"

"What's the matter?"

"In my rush to get here," I groaned, playing the Pathetic Goofball routine which, now that I think about it, wasn't so much of an act, "I forgot to grab a notebook."

"You're kidding, right?"

"No. I feel like an ass."

"So, what do we do now?"

"Well, three options. You talk and I'll try to remember everything you say."

She shook her head. "I don't think so. You'll misquote me, and I'll be pissed. I don't want to have to be pissed at you yet."

"Then we could forget about the interview entirely."

"No way. You're contractually obligated."

"Not really. I didn't get that cup of coffee yet."

"*Tisk tisk*," she replied.

"All right. So we split this spot and head back to my place."

"*Collin Hearst*," she said, feigning indignation, "are you trying to get me in bed?"

I think I blushed. I wanted to return the favor, so I said, "The thought crossed my mind."

"Collin!"

But I couldn't play the Hungry Dragon routine for long. I also had to be the Brave Knight coming to rescue a damsel in distress. "But not tonight. My intentions are good."

She gave me this sly look, as if to imply, *Good intentions pave the way to hell.*

"It's just business. We'll go to my apartment, hang out for an hour or so, have a drink, talk about you and the band. That's it, I swear. Trust me."

She kept the evil eye on me as she said, "It really makes me nervous when people say, '*Trust me.*' It always sounds like a scam. Why should I believe you?"

"You shouldn't, but you do."

"Oh, really?"

"Really. You hardly know me. What you do know isn't good. I'm an admitted manipulator. You should run like hell from the plot I laid down."

She took her time responding. After sipping from a giant soda, she straightened up the collar of her coat and stood up, all in one fluid motion. "You're worth a risk," she said. "I feel lucky. Besides, you don't have snake eyes."

"Thanks for the vote of confidence," I said, standing. "Someday I'll show you my seedy side and we'll see if you still agree."

"Not tonight, I hope."

"No, of course not. Tonight, you can rest at ease. Besides, you can probably kick my ass anyway if I try anything." I walked toward the door.

She followed, snickering at the thought. "Wait," she said. "What about that cup of coffee? I wouldn't want it to be a deal breaker."

"Forget it," I said. "You can owe me next time you're in town."

Her smile didn't falter and I knew she liked the idea. "Where are you parked?" she asked. "Mine's back at the hotel."

We opened the glass front door and stepped out into the chill. Bitter winds were whipping around the city streets, shed by the Allegheny, Ohio, and Monongahela rivers. They lashed out like vipers, slashing with fangs of frosty air. I shivered from head to toe.

December didn't seem to notice. "The others took the van and left me here alone to wait on you. It's a good thing you didn't back out."

"That's cool," I said. The wind was molding my hair into random poses. "I'll drive you back to the hotel when we're done."

"I don't think I like the sound of that," she said.

"Trust me."

Clothes scattered across the floor, a four-foot leaning tower of old pizza boxes stacked in the corner like an abstract sculpture, unwashed plates and dishes occupying coffee tables and stands, a half empty bottle of Absolut and another of warm grape juice on the carpet by the sofa, lights on, TV running—safe to say my apartment failed to impress. December surveyed the damage as if preparing a report for an insurance agency, no doubt a form that would read *Claim denied.*

"See what I mean? Attempting a seduction, I wouldn't have brought you *here*."

She showed no disgust, nor did I detect pity. Off and on, she laughed as she scanned the room. Eventually, she focused on my library: a pile of books discarded in the floor beside the television. She bent down and sifted through the pile, coming back with a handful of texts. "Albert Camus, Clive Barker, Carville Carsons," she said, referring to well-worn copies of *The Stranger*, *The Great and Secret Show*, and *Sorority Bondage Bimbos*. "Quite a combination."

"My different personalities all have different tastes."

She thumbed through one of the books, pausing every now and then to read a line, a paragraph, or a page. "I remember this one," she said, showing me the deep blue cover of Camus. "I borrowed it from a bookstore last year during the tour."

I laughed at the way she phrased it.

"The guys never let me drive the van. They're afraid I'll black out and smash the Cancermobile into a telephone pole, or maybe an invisible wall. I'm always high or drunk or tripping. Can't help it. On the road, I got to stay out of my head. But they only light up after a gig when they're nice and snug in a hotel room. Safe motherfuckers."

When she said that, describing her condition, I couldn't help but think she hid it well. But I was wrong. From then on, I kept a careful eye out, and I soon realized she *didn't* keep it hidden. In fact, she was extremely obvious about it.

"Anyway," she went on, "I'm usually alone in the back of the van, stretched out with the equipment, drums and amplifiers smacking me in my head every time B.J. takes a fast right turn. I get bored. That's why I read a lot. When I'm sort of sober, I like to have something to do."

"Can't go wrong with a good book," I said.

"Well, I scream too much to play with a vibrator and I'm not nuts enough to talk to myself, at least not for long periods of time. What else is there?"

"That's cool. You've got good taste in books, too."

"Not really. It was on a rack out front. I read whatever I can get my hands on, so to speak."

"That's not so bad. You get surprised sometimes."

"Sometimes. But often it's a load of crap."

"What about Camus?"

"I thought it was odd." She smirked and then smiled. "Entertaining, but odd."

"That about sums it up," I agreed. "Camus lived for absurdity. Imagine the circumstances that might lead you to an accidental homicide, with bright sunlight in your eyes and thick, gray clouds in your head. Then you go to trial and find yourself convicted, not because of the act but because you showed no sorrow at your mother's funeral weeks before. *That's* absurd. What's more, it's possible. You could be that killer, or I could."

She nodded as she tossed the book back into the pile. "Maybe I'll have to read it again. Still, it was a bit too existential for my tastes."

I took off my coat and draped it over the back of a chair. After clearing off the seat, I sat down. "You're not a fan of the existentialists?"

"Not really." She paused long enough to walk across the room to the sofa. She sat down without removing her coat. "Existentialism's a way to look at the world, same as any philosophy. But I don't like to let it mingle with my novels. It's too depressing."

"I think that's the point. Life's depressing sometimes, so we make of it what we can."

"I know. Yes, we all suffer from our anxieties. Sure, we feel alienated and alone. That's the way our insignif-icant lives go. I just don't want to read about it. I read for the same reason I do drugs: oblivion. I want to escape. I get my kicks and free myself from the same world that brings us things like existentialism. Life is quite depressing enough without reading about other people's despair. It's just not my taste." She reached down and palmed the Absolut bottle, staring into it as if looking for a message.

"How about some ice?"

I slapped myself on the forehead, mocking my own ignorance. "I'm sorry," I groaned. "I'm not the best host in the world. I'll get you a glass, too. A clean one."

"Thanks," she said.

I worked myself out of the chair and plotted a course for the kitchen, maneuvering around the clutter, across the floor, directly to the fridge. It was a top-bottom model, so I opened the top and grabbed a tray of ice from the freezer along with a chilled burgundy glass. With a familiar crack-pop-hiss, I bent the tray, releasing cubes. "Here you go. Care for anything else? Sprite, cola, passion fruit juice?"

She accepted the cold cup with a curt nod. "No, thanks. Grape's fine. I'll settle for what you got." She un-capped the vodka and tipped it. "What's the trick, Collin? A chilled glass?"

"Pretty suave, eh?" I joked.

"You go all out to get the ladies in bed."

"Maybe I do, but not with the glasses. Most chicks don't make it this far."

"That so?"

"Bank on it. True's true, Dee. I don't play the Soph-isticated Bachelor routine except with a select few, and when I do, it takes planning. There's a certain class of women subject to that scam, and I don't spend much time around those types." I reached down and grabbed my plastic cup from earlier in the evening. It was still half full. Swilling warm grape cocktail in my mouth, I scowled like a sick kid taking his medicine, finally swallowing. Picking up where I left off, I said, "No, sometimes I just prefer cold glasses and cold drinks."

December added juice to her glass and smiled as she drank. "I'll tell you this much. If you *are* playing me, it almost seems like you're going out of your way *not* to give me a line."

I glanced at the TV, still flickering in silence from earlier. The game hadn't ended, but the score flashed across the screen, showing the Steelers up by something like eight hundred and eighty points or so with a solid ten minutes to go. I kept my attention focused on the beer commercial that followed in order to avoid making eye contact with December. "I'm working. I have to be professional."

She slammed her drink. Her craving not satisfied, she reached down and mixed herself another. "Why don't we get started?" she said. "Waiting makes me uncomfortable."

I pretended to cough. "Again, apologies. You probably think I'm a fool or a fake."

"It's my fault. I caught you unprepared."

"I confess, you were the last person I expected to see today, except maybe Jesus Christ or the president of Nigeria. Doesn't matter. I'm a reporter. I should be able to get it together in a rush." I sighed. "I'll be back in a second."

I lurched into the bedroom and rummaged around in a desk drawer until I found a half-empty notebook and a pen. "That'll do," I said. The warm drink never left my hand, and I downed the last of it as I returned to my chair. I sat the empty cup on the floor. "Let's begin." I tapped my pen on the notebook three or four times before touching the tip to the page. "Let's start with something simple. Tell me about the band's name. Where did that come from?"

She turned her head, staring at the TV screen. "Nothing special there," she said with a heavy exhale, seeming to relax. "It's not a big story. Maybe I should have you talk to B.J. He could recite pages and pages of lies and embellishments to give your readers an interesting tale. He'd tell you about dark visions of a withering orb haunting some apocalyptic sky. He could build up a mood that's so wonderfully melancholy. Of course, nothing he said'd be true."

"What's the truth?"

"The truth? We're Cancers. Everybody but Justin. He's a Virgo. The rest of us were born within days of each other. Heather and I were July first, and B.J. is a stars-and-stripes baby.”

“Odd coincidence.”

“We almost went with Three Cancers and a Virgo, but it sounded too doowop. Couldn’t call it Cancer. That’d sound like a punk band. Add the word ‘Moon,’ and there you go.”

“Interesting.”

She shrugged.

“Out of curiosity, were you in other bands before this?”

“Me? No. I had nothing going except a heroin habit and a lousy job as a stripper in Columbus. I was nineteen. I had no hope and no future as anything but a hooker or a housewife. That was three years ago. I met B.J. and Justin on the job. I was hired with two others to table dance a private gig for a frat party. I did a lot of those. Anyway, Justin and B.J., along with some old guy whose name escapes me, were the band that night. They played seventies rock covers of Black Sabbath, Blue Oyster Cult, Alice Cooper, Bad Company. Sounded like shit, but don’t tell’em I said that.” She paused. “Well, halfway through the show, they stunned me. Started playing something so out there most folks wouldn’t even recognize it. It was Queen’s ‘The March of the Black Queen,’ off *Queen Two*, one of my favorite songs. It’s about the most erotic work of vocal art I’ve ever heard. Problem was, the old guy, the singer, had a voice that could scare off a pack of wild dogs. Nasally at times, scratchy at others. It made me sick the way he ruined the song. So I started singing. And that’s it. Although it helped that I took classical guitar and violin in junior high and high school.”

I scribbled down every word. When a page filled up, I flipped it over and started on the next. “Do you enjoy playing music or would you rather be doing something else?”

"There *is* nothing else. I dropped out of high school in the eleventh grade. I was seventeen. Music's my savior, and I give it all my love and adoration."

That bewildered me. Her style, her energy, her manner of expressing herself in words and song lyrics… Maybe she was self-educated, I thought. "Aside from that, what do you enjoy most about what you do?"

"Talking to reporters," she jabbed. "No, that's bullshit."

I laughed. "Best be straight with me. Reporters make tough enemies."

"*Yeah, yeah, yeah.* So, what was the question again?"

I reworked it, saying, "What's the magical element in your rock'n'roll fantasy?"

"My God, that sounds corny. Uhm, I love the energy. Nothing thrills me more than looking down at a group of fans up front slam dancing or headbanging or whatever the hell kids do these days. To see a bunch of drunken college students going crazy and losing themselves in the moment, trying to become a part of the rhythm of the song, it satisfies me, makes me feel like I've accomplished something. Who knows? Maybe I have."

"You have a different style. How would you describe your sound?"

December took a long drink. "Our bio sheet that we send to hacks like you describes it as *humanistic thunderangst.* B.J. wrote that, though like I said, he's a world-renowned liar."

"*Humanistic…*what was it?" I said.

"*Thunderangst,*" she said. "*Humanistic thunderangst.*"

"What exactly does that *mean?*"

"I think it just means that we're passionate, emotional, expressive. Our songs encompass an array of images ranging from a porno flick soundtrack to a funeral mass. I've always got a song in my head. Wherever I go, whoever I meet, they're all independent melodies to me. I observe my surroundings and put them into words in my head.

Then I sit back in a shadowy spot and compose a masterpiece to remember them by."

"Seems like you'd have an awful lot of tunes."

"I do," she said.

"How many?"

"Thousands, tens of thousands, hundreds of thousands, millions. I don't know. There are songs I love and songs I've forgotten, songs I've mingled and merged together, songs I never play for anyone but myself. At times, I hear them all as static in my head."

"I take it you're referring to private songs rather than the type on your album?"

"For the most part," she said. "I offer maybe one in ten to the band. We use maybe one in five of those. Our disc has twelve songs on it, out of about fifty we play live, varying our set list from show to show. Occasionally I'll get up the nerve to play a solo piece from my private collection, but not too often."

"Do the others write songs?"

"No. Justin has no talent for lyrics or melody lines, and Heather only writes pop songs that don't mesh with our style. B.J. has talent, and his stuff sounds good, but his lyrics are way out there, somewhere between a punk rant and a religious sermon. He does a lot of screaming, a lot of rambling, a lot of improvising... He had a big Suicidal Tendencies influence, and believe me, it shows. His songs never make it past the development stage. He's got a timid streak a mile wide that keeps him from singing, and I couldn't begin to tackle his crazy vibes. For the most part, Cancer Moon's songs are my songs. Does that answer your question?"

"Let me see if I've got it straight." I hesitated, planning my words carefully. "You write all the band's songs, so this *humanistic thunderangst* must come from inside *you*?"

"Never thought of it that way. I might have to go kick B.J. in the ass."

"So, does it?"

"I guess so."

Shuffling pages. "Bear with me. I want to explore that. I need to get inside you."

"I beg your pardon?"

"I'm trying to figure out what makes you tick."

"Oh, that's all?" Sarcasm evident.

"Listen, we've got this obscure concept, this living storm of a neurosis that comes from inside you. In order to define it, I have to start by trying to define *you*."

"Sounds like a challenge."

"I'll manage," I said. "But I need your help. Talk to me. Tell me another story. Show me a side of you people never see."

"You're asking too much," she replied.

"Better believe it."

She finished her drink and mixed another, swirling the glass around. She didn't ask for more ice, and I didn't think to offer. A sip. A swallow. "Now how about a road story?"

"Too traditional. Road stories tell where you've been and what you've done, but they say nothing about *you*. I'm looking for something personal, something that will make the readers drop their jaws and say, 'Holy motherfucking shit! That's the most amazing thing I ever heard.'"

"What makes you think I'm willing to reflect so deeply? For the sake of your story?"

"Sure."

"Why would I want something like that in the morning paper?"

"I'll tell you why, and it's a fact. Good press sells shows, and good press clips help sell bands. The better the story, the more propaganda slaves you'll see lined up outside the club ready to fork over a four, a five, or a ten-dollar cover to come see you play. You wouldn't believe how many bands have signed their record deals or been picked up by bigger labels because of clips filled with praise and admiration from reporters like me. My clips have helped sign at least five local bands to small labels. Take it straight, Dee, I know what I'm doing. Trust that. Trust *me*."

"There you go again," she said.

"What's that?"

"'Trust me,' you say. Trust, trust, trust me. Isn't it a federal offense to keep saying that?"

"Since when are you concerned with an infraction here and there?"

"Good point," she said. For a moment, I thought she might give in. I misread her. Instead, she kept silent, staring at the television and sipping warm booze from her glass.

"All right. If you won't play it that way, I'll ask you more direct questions."

She didn't even look my way. "Ask," she said, with a somewhat chiding tone that seemed to add in an unspoken echo: "*…but that doesn't mean I'll answer.*"

"What was the first record you listened to?"

She turned toward me, hesitating. "I don't remember exactly. I think it was Queen's *News of the World*, but it might have been *Two* or *A Day at the Races*."

"You're really into Queen, aren't you?"

"Hell yeah! Freddie was the greatest. Even dead, there's no other corpse that matches his range, his style, and his sheer talent. Few musicians I know of, alive or dead, can sing brilliant harmonies with themselves. Roger Waters when he was younger, and maybe Axl Rose in a whiny kind of way, but Freddie kicked their asses. He had balls, too. I remember an article where he said all these crazy things. I don't know if it was true or more lousy reporting…" She grinned. "…but I liked what I read. It was the early eighties during the initial AIDS paranoia. He said he didn't care about the threat of death, and he intended to fuck as many people as he could. Safe sex be damned, he said. If it killed him, it killed him. That's balls. That's attitude."

"It *did* kill him."

"True," she agreed with a sad sigh. "That's the blemish. Now people look back and say, 'He got what he deserved.' But I don't accept that. He just gambled and lost. He placed a risky wager, and it didn't pay off. But it could've."

"Does that mean you share views like his?"

"Similar views? Yes. A similar lifestyle? I don't have the guts to say 'I know but don't care' all the time. I've messed up some in the heat of passion or under the influence. So far I've been lucky. But it's not the same. It's just something that happened. Not once have I squared my jaw and said, 'Today I'll roll the dice.' That's not me. I can't change who I am. I'm a child of anxiety, filled with fear. I had this crazy friend who said all my problems came from millennial transcendence. She told me just to keep healthy and not burn out too quick, because all my troubles'd soon be over."

"You believe that?"

She shrugged. "When it comes down to it, I'm afraid."

I didn't know how much of her speech I'd be able to use, but I scribbled it all down. "What about your song lyrics, or your performances? Do you emulate Mercury there?"

The question seemed to cheer her up. "On occasion. I've never done a show in a bath towel, if that's what you mean, but I try to be daring. I've played shows in costume, dressed up like a cop, an astronaut, a pirate, a hooker—though people often tell me I look like a hooker anyway, so that's not much of a stretch. I've used hair dyes and body paints, wigs, leathers, lingerie, and I even did one gig dressed up as a fat man in a purple tuxedo. It's perpetual Halloween for me on stage. Every few shows, I'll go crazy and do something unique for that performance. It keeps the crowd interested. It keeps *me* interested. As for my songs, I do try daring things with melody lines, harmonies, and rhythms, but not the lyrics. Can't have trickery with words. They're personal. I can't go for mimicry either, even for my idols. No matter how much I'd like to live someone else's life, I can't." She sipped her drink, and closed her eyes. "Far too much of my stuff is really personal. A lot of it comes from old lost love that lingers, a feeling that never fades expressed in a song I never play. It's just another song."

"You were in love?" I pried.

"Many times. Love and loss—they're the two great redundancies of life. Been done and redone, undone and overdone. Remember, there are basically three types of songs: love songs, unloved songs, and transitional songs written by tired people in between the two. Love songs are cheesy, unloved songs are depressing, and transitional songs are poetry. Transitions catch the world on fire, touching on relevant topics while speaking with giddiness and despair of the lover between."

"What types do you write?"

"I've written them all. Right now, thankfully, I'm stuck in sort of a transitional mode."

More in my head than on paper, I took note. Then I opened my mouth to press the issue, but I'd hesitated too long.

"Next topic," she said in a firm, direct voice that left no room for interpretation.

"All right, Dee. Back to the band. You say you joined three years ago? How long was the band together before you stepped in?"

"A year. Maybe two."

"So, you're no small part of the band's success?"

"I guess you could say that. No album without me, that's for sure. We did a demo and sent it to Candescent Echo Records. There were about thirty songs in all, some of our best material. They signed us on the spot and produced the disc. We didn't even have to go into the studio. Our demo was solid, so they just lifted twelve tracks, digitally reworked them, and that was that. Next thing I knew, we were getting undressed for the album cover."

"That's the way it is these days. The major labels like to see an album or two before they'll sign a band, and small labels don't have the funds to record and produce that much."

She nodded in agreement.

"A band's best chance is to have a lot of ready work."

"Ain't that the truth. Best way to become a recording star's to supply the recording and let someone else supply the star. We didn't know that then, but we know it now. We're on our way."

"Cool. So, how are the records selling?"

"I'd like to say they're selling better than I could've imagined, but that'd be a lie. Nothing beats my expectations. I'm so vain that mirrors refuse to look at me for fear I'll shoot the messenger if I see a blemish. Truth is, I expected our disc to be in a second pressing by now."

"Oh?"

"The label pressed five thousand copies. We've sold maybe three or four thousand."

"That's not too shabby for a first album."

"Could be better. We don't make any green until the second batch. As a band, we've been paid exactly one thousand dollars so far to give our label the right to record the album. Our royalties don't kick in until number five thousand and one. Then we get a dollar a disc."

"So, safe to say you're not where you want to be?"

"It's safe to say we're not billionaires yet," she replied.

"Then tell me, where would you like to be in, oh, say, ten years?"

She seemed to stumble over her thoughts. She bent and sat her empty glass on an old magazine on the table. In exchange, she picked up what was left of the vodka and drank straight from the bottle, gripping the neck with white knuckles.

"Relax," I soothed, playing the old Family Friend routine. "It's a common question."

"Doesn't mean it's an easy one."

"I see," I said. "Think about it for a minute or two. I'm in no rush."

She took a long swig from the bottle and then, apparently finding the taste too bitter, she chased it with another. Her eyes wandered around the room, returning at last to me. Not comfortable with that view, she averted her gaze again. Shaking her head, she drank more. Dee looked helpless when she was frustrated. That was encouraging. It told me I was doing my job well. Nonetheless, I had to fight off a growing urge to take her in my arms and comfort her, to caress her shoulders, kiss her on the forehead, and whisper, "There, there," as if that meant something. Finally, after another quick liquor fix, she said, "Ten years. Where would I like to be in ten years? How about singing the Canadian national anthem at a World Series game?"

"Seriously?"

"No, *not seriously*. I'm not even Canadian, you fool."

I might have cracked a smile. "What, then?"

"Well, I'd like to be famous, but that's standard. I don't know. Maybe I'd like to be respected like the Dead or the Beatles, as if I'd really contributed something to the world. People who are into our kind of music may or may not like that idea, but no one can question the kind of influence cats like Garcia and Weir or Lennon and McCartney have had. That's what I want. Folks can love us or hate us, but I want them to appreciate us either way."

"That's good. What else?"

"I'd like to own my own recording studio, maybe help other bands starting out."

"Anything else?"

After a good-sized swig, she said, "I'd like to be able to walk down any street in any city in any state in America and have some faceless fan recognize me as if I were a kissing cousin."

"That's cool. What about…"

She interrupted, waving the empty Absolut bottle to get my attention. "We're out of booze," she said. "It's time to bring this interview to a close."

"No problem. I just need a few more questions."

"As long as they're basic…"

"Trust me."

"There you go again."

"What? Oh, sorry. It's a habit."

"Ask your questions."

"Okay, back to the album. Tell me about a couple of your more popular songs."

December took a deep breath. "That's better," she said. "I enjoy talking about the music. Okay, I guess we can start with the title track, 'Touched.' That's sort of a soft concerto, with some pretty heavy undertones. It's about a girl I knew several years ago, another stripper. A lot of people hear that one and think I'm referring to insanity." She sang part of the chorus:

> *I'm touched in the head, and*
> *touched in the heart,*
> *touched by visions of angels' wings…*

I remembered the song from when I saw Cancer Moon play live at Club Zero. How mesmerized she looked as she savored the words on her lips and tongue. It was as though she were sucking on chocolates, making love to sugar. Even without music, she looked that way now.

"Beautiful," I said.

"I think so. Kids hear that song and they presume my friend went nuts. That's not it. The song isn't about insanity. It's about religion. She found God and walked what for her was a straight path. She was *touched* by religion. The song's a metaphor, I guess you could say. When she gave up the naked life, she started singing for a Methodist choir. She was really quite a girl."

"What about the other songs?"

"Uhm," she said, bringing herself back to reality. "I think my favorite's 'Evening News.' It's got all the important elements. There's a hook, a catchy rhyme, a little bit of tension, and a story line. It's about the one time we were on the news, the local telecast for the NBC station back home. There were stories about war, police brutality, a few rapes and robberies, a murder, and somewhere toward the end of the telecast, a thirty-second soundbite of us playing 'Touched' at a benefit. It was our only time on TV, and it was ridiculous. That disturbed me, so I wrote about it."

"Any others you want to talk about?"

"There's 'The Snowman.' That's about drugs. 'Deep Pockets' tells the story of this high-school rich kid with a prostitute fetish. He was quarterback of the football team. Not too stupid. Far from ugly. All the girls wanted him, but if he didn't have to pay for it, he wasn't interested."

"True story?"

"True enough. Yeah. What else did you want to know?"

Trying to fill the holes, I said, "How many times have you been to Pittsburgh?"

"Three. Well, this will be our third. Of course, we've driven through here a lot, but we've just had the three gigs. We played here once when we were nobodies. Last month, we came back with a little more confidence. And here we are again. These folks down at Club Zero really dig our sound, and that feels good, you know, to get respect from folks."

"What kinds of responses have you gotten?"

"They all love us. Alternakids and thrashers, punkers and metalheads, pop brats and acidics, they all dig us. We've got something for everyone. We're just a musical circus, hoping for hundreds to come and ride the rides. Who knows, maybe folks will leave with something sugary sweet to eat, or something soft to cuddle with and take back home to bed."

"What might that mean?"

"Well," she spat with a facade of indignation, "cotton candy and a giant teddy bear, of course."

The laughter overtook me like a surprise high—sudden, numbing, powerful.

"What'd you expect?"

"I guess I'm just a pervert."

"Oooh," she purred with a hint of seduction. "We should get along *real* well."

"Why's that?" I asked.

"Come over here. I'll show you." She was serious.

CANTO SEVEN

Introduction to the Music Scene

Thursday. Eight months after I got my start at the *Domestic-Chronicle*. Michelle, the regular late cops reporter came down with a severe hangover—that is to say, the flu—so I filled in for her. The evening went by slowly—no major crimes, no fires, a few minor traffic accidents not worth more than a brief. I sat at my desk, listening to the scanner and reading the day's edition yet again. My attention span had shortened, and I spent the evening staring into space.

Kathryn Carter entered the newsroom from her executive office in the far corner. She bombarded the room, firing off damnations at everyone but me. She cursed Gray for mistakes in several obits. She reamed Agatha with a verbal strap-on of abuse for lame headlines and improper typefaces. She almost murdered poor Eric Engles, the new city government reporter, in a fit of passion over his libelous remarks about the mayor on page one. I thought Kathy's head might spin wildly while her eyes shot flames. She scared everybody.

Well, not *every*body.

After listening to a long tirade on his recent column, Hunter Delaware—grizzled veteran that he was—stared the editor down and said without a trace of malice, "Fuck you, you crotchety old biddy."

The ice queen met Hunter's gaze for a stressful moment, then began to grin. Her lips curled up in that rarest of her expressions, and she let out a tiny giggle.

No one knew how to react. Several seconds of catatonic silence passed before anyone relaxed. Then, finally, the tension broke and the rest of us joined in with laughter. But not too much—we didn't dare. So, Kathy spoke again with a calmer, friendlier voice. "All right, settle down. I've got a story that needs done. Who wants it?"

Papers shuffling, drawers closing, keyboards *click-click-clicking*. All eyes turned away.

"Come on, guys," Kathy said, trying to sound excited. "This is a good one." She scanned the room, somehow overlooking me. I was the only one not avoiding her gaze, but somehow she never saw me. "Eric, you owe me after that fiasco today."

"No way."

She snarled at him.

"Look, I've got controversies out the ass with this curfew deal in council. I don't have the time to take on another project. Get somebody else."

"Gray? I know you need the work. It's after hours tomorrow night. Plenty of overtime."

The obit clerk seemed interested but a bit skeptical. "What's the subject?" he said.

"Local rock band: the Tube Socks."

"That's important?" he said.

She scowled but ignored the comment. "They're playing at ten sharp over at Simone's Spot, then going back for seconds Saturday night. I need you there tomorrow so you can hurry back with a review-slash-preview for a Saturday hole. Cozy assignment. You'll love it."

Gray seemed to mull this over. He shook his head. "I don't think so."

"Why not?"

"I don't know the first thing about rock bands. The only music I listen to's gospel."

"Christ," exclaimed Kathy. "Hunter, how about you? I know you like rock'n'roll."

"I like *good* rock'n'roll," that widely-read and just-as-widely-hated columnist replied, thumbing his black beard. "The operative word is 'good.' Never seen a local act qualify."

"Come on. You're always bragging about all the Rusted Root shows you hit."

"That's different. I'm not exactly sober."

"Tell you what. I'll give you a ten-dollar expense account for drinks."

"You sure know how to appeal to the animal in me," he joked. "But I can't. Got two columns and a special section piece on the school bond to spit out by tomorrow night or I'll be stuck in here all weekend." It was an odd thing to say. Hunter almost never went home.

Kathy groaned.

"So, what's so special about this one, anyway?"

"The publisher's nephew plays drums," she said, a touch of mock helplessness in her voice.

The staff let out a chorus of oohs and ahs, understanding.

"It's the first gig, so the old man wants a write-up. You know how it goes. He tells me, so I tell you. He says I do, so I say you do."

"But I don't," Hunter corrected.

"That's the problem." She calmed before the storm: "Fuckety fuck fuck fuck! Shit, shit!"

Hunter seized the opportunity to not so much rub salt in an old wound as cut the scar open while using a salty knife. "Why don't you hire someone to replace Elsbeth?" he said. "It's been more than six months. Then you wouldn't have this problem." Elsbeth Jordan had been half of the *Domestic-Chronicle*'s *Life* staff, covering music and the arts. She quit a month or so after I came aboard, leaving Dorothy McGuire, the other *Life* writer, swamped.

"Can't afford it," Kathy said. "We're in a recession, you know. The old man's not hiring."

"Well fuck him, too," said Hunter. "He won't put up the cash, he don't deserve the special attention for his sweet little nephew who probably can't play for shit anyway."

More laughter made its way around the room.

Not from Kathy, not even a smile. "You've got a point," she said. "Put a hat on it."

Hunter didn't reply. I think he was shocked like the rest of us.

"Okay," Kathy tried again. "There's got to be one of you future welfare recipients ready to step to the plate and swing a bat. Just think about it. Free drinks, overtime, a chance to impress the old man and maybe even get on *my* good side for a couple hours."

"How about Hearst?" Hunter said.

The boss turned, flinching when she saw me as if I were a ghost.

"He doesn't have much going on."

"That true?" she said.

"Yeah, I guess so."

"Praise the Lord. It's yours."

Inside, I began to glow. From the first mention of rock'n'roll, I wanted to be the one. But I was still so unsure of myself and afraid to speak up. I'd sat there anxiously like a kid in the principal's office—guilty, but looking meek. "Sure," I said. "Love to."

"Praise the Lord," Kathy said again. "You know where Simone's Spot is?"

"I've been there a couple times."

She exhaled a pleasurable sigh. I thought she might have an orgasm. "Excellent. Now if you just tell me you know something about music, we're in business."

For the first time as a reporter, my timidity transformed into arrogance. Cocky, I slipped into a free-willed *Rolling Stone* routine and said, "I know *everything* about music."

Kathy forked over a ten spot, with her only instructions that I return what I didn't use and fill out an expense account with the total listed as "various necessary fees." I did as she said and, when I turned in my form, I taped a single coin to the page and left it on her desk. The night of the show, I drank three fat screwdrivers in a little over an hour. By the time I made it back to the newsroom, I was sloshed. I had twenty minutes to type the eight-inch story, but my eyes couldn't focus on the screen or keys. To write the piece, I closed my eyes and let my fingers employ techniques they'd learned from so much college training. I composed the story in my head and left my hands to do the rest.

"You're drunk," said Hunter as he caught me staring vacantly out the fifth-floor newsroom window. "Good for you, kid. You'll make a fine reporter one of these days. Care for a cigar?"

"No, thanks," I said, without inhibition. "I rarely smoke…tobacco."

"Too bad. Can't beat a good cigar for an evening of booze and bad assignments." As if to prove this to himself, he withdrew a half-smoked butt from the pocket of his plaid shirt and began to chew on the unburned end. "So, how was the band?"

"The Tube Socks? Smelled more like an old jockstrap."

"That bad, eh?"

"I wouldn't say bad, exactly. I've seen a lot of bad bands and I wouldn't want to insult these *kids* with that kind of label. I think a better description's *painfully average*."

Hunter spent a few chuckles. "That's the same thing I said about my last girlfriend. Well, tell me the story. I don't want to have to read the paper tomorrow. Did you torch 'em?"

"No."

"Why the hell not? No balls?"

"I don't like to write negative things about kids trying their best."

Hunter growled.

"If the they were so dreadful, if I truly thought, you know, these guys are just pathetic, trust me when I say I'd casually forget to write the story, then deal with the consequences later."

He grunted and groaned as if from painful indigestion. "Maybe I was wrong about you, kid. How can you expect to be a success if you don't run the cheese grater up and down a deserving spine? Niceness goes against the true spirit of American yellow journalism."

I grinned, my mad-looking lips reflecting in the window, hints of moonlight or an arc lamp or something outside making my face seem jaundiced and truly demonic.

"Come on. Piss somebody off. Be a man."

"All right, Hunter. You're ugly and plaids don't help."

He snarled and, for a moment, I thought he might lunge for my throat. Then his expression faded into a mischievous smile as he leaned his head back groaning great, sickly guffaws. When he finished, he cocked his head toward me and said, "I think you've been hanging around *me* too much, kid. That could be an occupational hazard."

I agreed.

"Anyway, if they're no good, and you won't be mean, what'd you write about?"

"Easy. With a lousy act, there's only the lousy to work with. Not so with an average band. There's usually a little good mixed in with a whole lot of bad. I can pick out the good and write about it using words like 'potential' and 'young,' along with lengthy quotes from the band."

"So, you faked it?" said Hunter, cutting to the heart.

"Well…"

"You faked it. Fess up."

"Okay, I faked it."

"That's devious, kid. You worry me sometimes, pulling stuff like that. You could have my job by the end of the year. The publisher's bound to fucking love you."

"Maybe so," I agreed. Turning my hand into a gun, I pointed at Hunter and pulled the trigger. "Then again, where would I be without your advice?"

"Good point, kid."

"Besides, they can't fire you. Need you to cover the night-cops beat once I'm in your chair."

Saturday, I staggered into the office around three, grumbled hellos to several colleagues, and grabbed a copy of the day's edition. Slouching low in my chair, I opened the paper and skimmed through it until I found my article on the *Life* page. It had a color centerpiece photo, with the whole package hairline-boxed. I would've felt giddy if not for one of those I-swear-I'll-never-drink-again headaches.

"Tube Socks to get the feet tapping," the headline read, summing up my eight inches of bullshit.

I smiled softly, but it turned into a groan.

I got my assignments from Allison Fredericks, who filled in as city editor when Arnie had a holiday. As usual, there wasn't much. So, I headed for the police station to read incident reports. After scribbling down facts about a rape, a handful of burglaries, and a collage of stolen car briefs, I packed up my pens and notebook and went to dinner. When I made it back, the staffers were watching me, gauging some aspect of my character. They glared at me with a cross between keen interest and the evil eye. Then the compliments began.

"Good job," said Agatha.

"Congratulations, Hearst," said Rick Dunlap who shouldn't have been there—Rick always had the same days off as Arnie, though Arnie was smart enough to stay home. His voice crackled out a second "Congratulations" in that hoarse Marlboro voice of his.

"Hey, Coll," said Gray, "nice work. If I'd known the benefits…"

"Thank you…" I said repeatedly. "I appreciate it. Thank you very much." I had no idea what they were talking about. "What's the deal, Allison?" I said to the frantic city editor as she rummaged through her desk in search of a facsimile she'd lost.

"You haven't heard?" she replied.

"Heard what?"

"Your name got mentioned in the news meeting," she said.

"In the news meeting? What for?"

She sounded very excited for me. "Kathy circled your byline."

I shrugged. "So? Is that abnormal?"

Allison had to look away. As she spoke, she barely kept a straight face. "Kathy's a bitch," she said. "Unless your story's about the National Organization for Women or the Earth Mother cult, she usually has nothing but scorn."

"But everyone talks as if a circled byline's common when you do good work."

"Just a myth," she explained. "It's something we pass around to make ourselves feel better when a bunch of us get yelled at. It's something to strive for whenever we're doing a story or a layout. But I've been here three years. I've seen it five or six times, and never for a *Life* piece."

"I see," I said, though I'm not sure I did. "Why to-day? What does it mean?"

"It means the publisher himself must have called."

The Morning After

The morning after perfect sex, there's such an easy spirit and a sense of repose. The morning after I interviewed Dee for the story on her band, the morning after she kissed me—her invitation to delight, her offer I accepted with my lips—I gave myself over to tranquility just like that. I woke up in bed, having skipped so casually through a deep, safe sleep—the kind I wouldn't have enjoyed without her in my arms. But I achieved such a restful night and its morning-after serenity without even a moment's penetration. We forgot to fuck, have sex, make love—whatever term would've fit. I'm sure we intended to do it. Definitely. It just sort of slipped our minds like a meaningless holiday.

We spent time on the sofa, working each other, escaping from our twin hells of need. Kissing, caressing, we engaged in all the rituals. Sometimes steady, gentle, while at other times as frantic and unfocused as cowboys dragged behind a horse, we both burned inside and out: lustful, eager, ready. Then we moved our traveling carnival into the bedroom. Once there, we mellowed, felt no need to push the limits of desire. We lay back on the bed, content to talk.

She told me another story: this one about her grandfather—how much she loved him, how he played piano and sang decrepit, old songs that sounded wonderful to a child, how he held her close at her father's funeral and explained the tricky business of death, saying, "It's a time to make amends for all the traded wrongs and to remember all the shared joys," and how she rejoiced in that same wisdom at *his* passing. She paused just long enough to fall asleep.

I paused from listening just long enough to follow.

When I opened my eyes in the morning, Dee was gone.

Moon rocks!

Alternative band in town to spread infectious strain

By Collin Hearst, Staff Writer

Three out of the four were born under the same star sign. Together, they transcend astrology, offering only a sign of the times: a pure, driven mantra made up of rock'n'roll.

It's an odd coincidence, admits fiery lead singer and rhythm guitarist December Leigh, who fronts the band Cancer Moon. "We almost went with Three Cancers and a Virgo, but it sounded too doowop. We couldn't call the group Cancer. That would make us sound like a punk band. Add the word 'Moon,' and there you go."

No, Cancer Moon isn't a punk band, nor are they into '60s-style harmonies. Perhaps the band's sound is best described as alternative rock, though alternative to what, one cannot say too easily.

The group's songs employ a wide variety of styles ranging from classic rock to classical music, with plenty of screaming, hissing and assaulting the ears to add a modern touch.

"Humanistic Thunderangst," said Leigh, trying to describe the band's style. "I think it just means that we're passionate, emotional, expressive. Our songs encompass an array of images ranging from a porno flick soundtrack to a funeral mass."

Cancer Moon will perform at 10 p.m. today at Club Zero on 20th Street. Admission is $5. No one under 18 will be admitted.

The rest of the band consists of B.J. Brown on lead guitar, Justin Criss on drums, and Heather Cave on bass.

This show will mark the band's third trip through Pittsburgh, its second since the release of its debut album, "Touched," available during and after the show on compact disc.

Well worth the $12 cost, it features such instant classics as "Deep Pockets" and "Evening News," not to mention the title track, which Leigh describes as being a soft concerto about a stripper who finds religion. Leigh said, "Kids hear that song and they presume my friend went nuts. That's not it. The song isn't about insanity. It's about

[continued on page *D-6*]

Part Two

Brief But Sweet Refrain

CANTO EIGHT

The Chuang Tzu Routine

Chuang Tzu woke from a long night of opium and dreams having seen through a butterfly's eyes, caressed his wings across the wind, soaring over canyons and a stream. With delicate stained-glass wings, he saw fairy tale forests and foreign lands. High in the air, as high as he could climb, he danced a jig. But later, with his human eyes straining in the morning sun, Chuang Tzu thought he still lived a butterfly's life. He couldn't be sure if he were a man dreaming himself a butterfly, or a butterfly dreaming himself a man.

Those were simple times, when every existential crisis could be countered with a few puffs on the hookah. My life was more complicated. The world didn't sort itself out for me. I felt so lost that I slipped a gear and fell into an unexpected Chuang Tzu routine with no one around to see.

For me, four nights passed.

From the first instant until I saw that wonderful girl again, I spent each hour of every night alone in bed in darkness, dreaming intimate moments with her, or some faceless apparition I presumed was her. She beckoned, tempting me with pleasures I'd missed when the real Dee was here. I fell in love a hundred times each night, only to wake with heartbreak when I found myself alone. I dreamt the vicious cycle of love and loss, lust and unfulfillment over and over until it left me weary, worn, confused. I didn't know if I were the lonely man dreaming of perfect love or the lover sadly dreaming himself alone.

I'm not a butterfly, so the Butterfly routine won't play. Neither am I Chuang Tzu. So why, I wondered, am I dreaming his dreams, weaving myself a web with his philosophy?

Damn it to hell, Chuang Tzu! What's the answer? How did you solve the paradox of your opium-dementia, you crazy bastard? Somehow I missed the ending on whatever day it was one professor or another told the story about the butterfly dream. I must have fallen asleep in class, dreaming myself a student who cared enough to pay attention and take notes.

The Brush-Off

Head down in a humble, priestly pose, hands pressed into pockets—I struggled against the cold witch casting her spells on November. Trench coat, leather gloves, scarf, fedora—I walked the streets of Pittsburgh heavily armored against the chill. Wind attacked me from all sides, plunging icy spears into my face, ears, and fingertips. An early snow, though nominal, left sidewalks slippery and damp. Chilled water pricked me through my socks. I countered every strike with a ritual shiver.

Nick Knox wasn't so humble in the cold. I found him standing outside the front door at Club Zero, leaning casually against the building. He was talking to a heavyset man, a bouncer, who paced back and forth in front. Nick wore neither coat nor gloves, not even a long-sleeved shirt. He had on the same clothes he'd worn the day we met, the one with 'Mugwump' written across the chest. Despite the bitter cold, sweat dripped off him. The bouncer, by contrast, wore a heavy black parka with red lining visible inside the hood, and he was freezing.

Mugwump didn't recognize me—all bundled up and with my head bowed just enough to hide my face in the shadow from my fedora's brim. I could see him clearly, but to him, I was just a blur. As I approached, the bouncer turned. He grumbled something too soft to understand, to which Mugwump grunted an inaudible reply. Then the bouncer pulled his hands from his pockets and stood in what looked like a defensive stance. "Five dollars and your driver's license," he said.

I lifted my head slowly, trying to bring my sardonic smile into the light for a second or two before my eyes were visible. "I beg your pardon?"

Mugwump's eyes, redder than his hair and narrow from some drug or other, lit up and expanded. "Holy shit," he exclaimed. "Collin Hearst! How the hell are you?"

"How's it going, Nick?"

"Friend of yours?" said the bouncer.

"He's cool. He gets in free."

"No problem," said the bouncer.

"He did that article in the paper today, the one the band was bragging about."

"That was you?"

"It was," I replied.

"*Wicked.*"

Mugwump slapped a sweat-soaked arm across my back. "Great story, dude," he said. "Great fucking story. Thanks a lot."

"No big deal," I told him, laying the Apathetic God routine on thick. "It's what I do."

"Yeah, right."

"Would I lie?"

"Right," he said again.

"So how's business?"

"Considering the shitty weather, we're doing fantastic. We've already outsold the last show."

"Glad to hear it."

He slapped me on the shoulder a couple times and said, "We owe you. Your story did it. Not for that, I bet we'd have an empty house."

"Publicity's king."

"Abso-fucking-lutely!"

"Well, Nick, if you'll excuse me, it's cold as fuck out here."

"Oh," he said. "Sorry, man. Go on in. I'll join you."

The bouncer grabbed the door.

As I stepped across the threshold, I understood Mugwump's queer state of undress. A blast of hot air smacked me in the face like a wall of fire, melting clothes to skin. "Jesus," I said, wheezing as I gasped for breath. The air seemed to have burned away like rocket fuel.

"Ain't it the truth? I turned up the heat earlier. Didn't know if it'd kick in or not."

"It did!"

"Fuck," he said. "I know it. Nearly killed me. I had to change clothes."

Empathizing, I stripped off my gloves and scarf, sliding them in my coat pockets. I was already starting to sweat. As I undid the buttons on my trench coat, I glanced around the club. "You should crank the heat up more often," I said.

He took a quick look. "Don't I know it." More than half the crowd had stripped down to near nakedness, holding wads of clothes under glistening arms or waving articles around like flags. It was scandalous. College kids were down to the barest essentials: from fishnet stockings to boxer shorts painted with lame patterns of hearts, kittens, and hundred dollar bills. Patrons had given themselves to the night, nearly unclad and almost as uncaring. They were drinking, dancing, pressing the flesh. Of those still in all their clothes, few looked close to comfortable. Fewer still were dancing or enjoying the moment. For the most part, they were scattered around the bar or seated at tables. "Now I'm horny as a long-stemmed rose."

"Got a plan?" I said.

"Working on it."

"I see."

"The chicks love me." He stopped. "Speaking of which, here comes one now."

A woman emerged from the mass of gyrating bodies and made her way toward us. She was older than I would have expected, maybe in her mid to late thirties. Bundles of fake blond hair hung down from her head, and she had several of what people might call "character lines" in highly visible spots around her face. She wore a flowing black skirt that extended from her waist to her ankles, though aside from that she'd stripped to nothing but a red satin brassiere. She spoke as she neared, sounding flighty and unreal like a teenage groupie. "There you are, Nicky. I've been looking all over the place for you. Have you got any more of that *stuff*?"

"*What* stuff?"

"You know, the *stuff*."

Mugwump's face turned an ugly shade of red. He raised a hand as if to strike, but he didn't hit her, instead punching the palm of his other hand. "Are you insane?" he screamed, his voice quickly trailing to a stern whisper. "You want me to get busted? Could be cops around."

"Shit, Nicky. I'm sorry. I didn't mean to…"

"Fuck!"

"I'm sorry," she said again.

He sucked in a breath, forcing himself to relax. "It's all right. Looks like there's no harm done. Just don't do it again, okay? Think before you say shit like that."

"I'm *so* sorry," she said, repeating it a couple times. "Let me make it up to you." She licked her lips in a way that, done by anyone else, would've been sexy.

Mugwump got the point. His leftover anger fizzled like a cigarette butt left to die on an icy Pittsburgh street. "Angel, you do know the way to my heart."

"Gee, Nicky, I try," she said, laying it on thick.

He smiled at her. "Listen, Angel, why don't you go wait for me in front of the box. I've still got a few words left for my good friend here. I'll be right over."

"All right, Nicky. Not too long or I might change my mind." As she turned to go, I saw rows of stripes across her back—some old and white, others freshly scabbed in reddish brown.

"She's a tough one," Mugwump said, as if answering my thoughts. "Kinky to the core. Likes pain. You got to use your fingernails or she'll get up in the middle and go home."

"Her name really *Angel*?"

"Guess so. Fuck if I know for sure."

"What did you give her?"

"Just a little powder. Nothing special."

I nodded.

"Well, as you can see, I got to move along. Listen, man, thanks again. I'll catch you later if you're still here. In the meantime, I'll tell Cliff to feed you drinks on the house. That cool?"

"It's cool," I said, reveling as always in my bad reporter ethics.

"Thought so," he said. "That case, I'm off on another adventure."

I reached out and grabbed his oily arm as he turned away. "One thing first," I said.

"Eh?"

"Where can I find December?"

The band was rocked, or maybe wrecked, long before I spotted Dee. Mugwump had loaded everyone up with pot or coke or smack or crank or whatever it was. Dee Leigh and the Cancer Moon crew were off in another realm. Strumming disharmonious chords and singing out of key in chorus, the four musicians sat scattered around the club's back room, playing unplugged. If they weren't so out of sync, I would've thought they were practicing—or else a military invasion. All four were dressed in olive green combat fatigues and caps.

"Collin!" screamed December when she noticed me. She waved her arms to end the song, convincing everyone to stop except Justin who, like Animal on the old *Muppet Show*, kept hammering away at his drums long after everyone else gave up. I could tell by the look in his eyes that he was *gone*. To get his attention, December tossed a shot glass straight at his head, only missing by inches. The glass hit the wall behind him and shattered with a pop, leaving a whiskey residue sticking like ectoplasm to the bare white wall.

"What the fuck?" he bellowed, barely understandable.

"It's Collin," said December. Her words were slurred and, despite her excitement, the expression on her face had the ashen character of oblivion. "Collin, come give me a hug."

I obliged, eager for her touch.

Her arms wrapped around my back, and she kissed me, holding me there immobilized. Then she pushed me away as if I'd encroached on her personal space.

"Hello," I said. "Good to see you."

She ignored my introduction, saying, "Thank you *sooooo* much."

"What'd you think? I'd scam you?"

"I was worried you'd torch us. You'd print a bunch of crap and blame it on your editor. We've had that done to us before. But you really came through. Thanks, Collin. Thanks." Her rant poured out at full speed, exhaled on a single breath. After she took in a fresh supply of air, she continued with a new tirade. "All week we were nervous. Isn't that right?"

Her friends said nothing.

I knew what she meant. I'd been nervous, too. When I'd interviewed her, she'd made an unspoken promise about tonight, assuring me I'd be rewarded. More bad ethics on my part, but I didn't care. I was as fascinated by her as if she were a real superstar and not the lead singer of a traveling club act. Her black hair, her sleek eyes and chin, her tiny frame—I wanted to devour them. And her singing voice! Good God! It gave me tremors just to hear it on the CD. Then to have her play it so sweet and friendly at the interview, well…

"We kept talking about you. Every night on the road, before a show, in the van, in the motel, and just everywhere, man—that story was all we thought about." She grabbed me by the striped tie that dangled outside my unbuttoned coat. Pulling me to her, she kissed me again, parting my lips with her tongue. I almost thought she might want to pick up right now and go. But she shoved me away again, pushing hard. I couldn't make any sense of her mixed messages.

Next thing I knew, there was an arm around my shoulder and my lips struck a different target. It was Heather, the bassist. I guess she wanted to keep up with December. She wasn't as forceful though, offering a tiny taste in gratitude. I didn't really know her, and I wasn't interested. But it was over before I could pull away. As she finished, I heard the drummer laughing in coarse, choppy bursts like an overworked mule.

That's when Dee gave me the brush-off. Stepping in front of Heather, she shoved me toward the door. "Thank you again. You'll have to excuse us now. We got a gig to get ready for."

I didn't know how to react.

"Let him stay," the drummer said. "He's not bothering us."

"He's bothering me," Dee said. "He's a distraction. I can't concentrate." It seemed so cold, so malicious, as if she were saying, "I got what I want, now take a hike."

Perhaps it was the dry, seemingly unemotional tone of her voice that sold the lie and convinced me to take her blunt words at face value. Or maybe it was the drugs that left her expression so numb and uncaring. Wounded, I vanished into the crowd.

I knew this night would be a painful one, whatever went down from then on. I shook my head, already lonely, aching, sad. "Jesus," I groaned. "At least the drinks are free."

Booze for Beverly

I sat at the bar, taking my frustrations out on a steady stream of free booze. Cliff kept dishing out drinks, and I kept accepting. "What a perfectly glorious night," I said as if in denial. "The heavens have opened and shown us perfection, leaving us to dance our twisted jigs beneath embers of the earth, deep in the inferno." As if to verify this, I took a cocktail napkin and toweled off pools of sweat from the shoulders of my trench coat, following that with a wet pass over the waterfall of my brow. "There's no cancer to eat away at this soul. I've had my chemo, my radiation, my drugs. The doctor's packed her black leather bag and headed on her way. No more house calls, thanks. I'm cured. I'm healed. I'm alive."

Cliff couldn't understand me, but I'll wager even money that he recognized despair, the gut-devouring virus of lost love or the plague of a love that never was. In that carrion depression, I worked my Eccentric Madman routine while Cliff kept plying me with drinks. "Here you go. Try this."

"What is it?"

"You'll like it. Drink it."

"What is it?"

"I call it a Shaved Twat," he said.

"A what?"

"A Shaved Twat. Drink up and I'll tell you the secret."

I shrugged. "Fair enough." Tossing my head back, I choked down the whole hideous concoction. I felt phlegm melting away in my throat and heard my sinuses open with a pop. My ears burned as if I'd been eating spicy Italian food. Worse still, Cliff's elixir tasted like spoiled meat and left a rank aftertaste. I grimaced. "What the fuck? That was terrible! What was it?"

"Get this, and don't ask me how I came up with it. It has three active ingredients."

"Sounds like you're building a bomb."

"Maybe I am. Now shut up and let me finish." He nodded and looked over his shoulder nervously as if he were about to offer to sell me a watch. "Like I was saying, it's got three active ingredients. There are a few other minor ones, but they just add character. Primarily it's the three. There's cheap tequila—and I do mean cheap— bubblegum flavored Schnapps, and milk."

"Milk?"

"I wouldn't lie to you."

"Shit," I said. "That's disgusting. Give me another."

He held his arms out bent slightly at the elbows like a sorcerer casting a spell, pointing all ten fingers crookedly in my direction. "Man, you make a bartender sing. I feel like an artist."

Going along, I said, "So, paint me a fucking picture."

Grinning, he said something, but it was drowned beneath fresh screams of electric guitars from the club's stacks of speakers. "What?" I asked, but he'd already gone.

"That's a good sign," a strained female voice said loudly in my right ear. I turned to see a girl, maybe nineteen or twenty, looking me up and down. Most of my features were hidden because I'd refused to remove my fedora or coat despite the Club Zero heat. The same couldn't be said for her as she made her play. Dressed down in the casual manner of the crowd, her tight, trim body beckoned from beneath a plain white bra glowing purple and a pair of rolled-up gray jeans, though the cold of November that waited outside was still reflected in her heavy socks sticking out of black Doc Martens.

"What was that?"

"It's a good sign," she said.

"What is?"

"That song."

I listened. "It's just old hair-metal."

"No it's not," she defended. "It's 'Is This Love?' from Whitesnake." She shook her head, finding me silly for my lack of observation. "You don't know, do you?"

I shook my head.

She giggled. "Means Mugwump got laid." She paused, not sure if I understood. "Do you know Mugwump? Nick Knox? Owns the bar." When I nodded, she told me, "Well, that song means he got some. He plays it when he's done."

I have no idea how I reacted or what expression I wore. "You know from experience?"

"Hardly," she replied with an indignant roll of her eyes. "*Every*body knows. It's just a fact. When Mugwump plays the Whitesnake song, it means he came and he's back in the box. But don't get the wrong idea. To say that I would...with him? I don't think so. He's not my type."

"So, what's your type?"

She fed off the line as if she'd set me up. "Buy me a drink, and maybe I'll let you know."

I winked at her, but I don't know if she saw it with my eyes still in the shadows of my hat. Turning, I waved for Cliff, who forced himself away from a gorgeous brown-skinned girl at the end of the bar. "Sorry, man," he said as he approached, shouting it loud enough to be heard atop the music. "I got distracted. You know how it goes. I'll make you a Shaved Twat right away."

"A what?" said the girl.

"Excuse me," said Cliff, acting embarrassed. "Didn't mean to offend you."

"Forget it," I demanded. "I'll take that drink and bring her a…what was it?"

"*Corona*," she said.

Cliff leaned over and spoke in a whisper I barely heard with all the screaming heavy metal. "I don't know, Man. Mugwump might not approve."

"Too young?" I said, playing innocent.

"Not that. It's your tab, man. Nick said to give *you* free drinks 'cause you're a reporter and a cool cat, and 'cause you wrote that story about the band and all. She's not on the menu, if you know what I'm saying."

"Is that all?" I said, pulling away. My voice came out like a dagger. Leaning back, I added in a respectful whisper, "Give her a drink. It wouldn't be right if I didn't buy it for her." I whipped out a ten and dropped it on the table. "In fact, bring her two and the rest I'll call a tip."

"You got it, bud," Cliff said as he slapped his hand onto the ten spot, absorbing it with his palm. "Be right back. This time, I promise I won't get sidetracked."

The girl said, "What was that about? My age?"

Seeing a chance to lay down the classic Highbrow Big Shot routine, I winked at her from my left eye, trying to make sure enough light caught it, and told her, "Don't sweat it. I've got everything under control."

She smiled. I sat there and watched as she grooved to the dying Whitesnake chords. Her skin seemed to radiate with artificial tan from the black-light glow. Her short golden hair beamed like a halo. As she danced, still sitting on her stool, her body slithering and tight, she got my blood pumping. I wanted to touch her, to wrap my arms around her waist and pull her to me. But I turned away, keeping an eye on Cliff as he put the finishing touches on my drink.

"Enjoy." He dropped our drinks on the bar. "I'll be back in a sec."

"Thanks," I said. Turning to the girl, I lifted my glass in mock salute.

She did the same with one of her bottles. "Tasty," she said. "How's yours?"

"Not so tasty."

She giggled but said nothing.

"This sludge oozes like a dying sea snake," I said, ranting again, "though it tastes like it's already dead. Some evil force made up this concoction, intending to release it to wreak havoc on an unsuspecting world. But the creator made the mistake of tasting his creation and passed on. The world was saved for a moment. Still, like the black plague, this thing refused to fade out forever. I'm sad to report—rather, it's my *duty* to report—that our good man Cliff behind the bar rediscovered it. Now it's spreading around the world as if carried by rats."

My tirade amused her. "If it's so bad, why do you drink it?"

I leaned back and flashed her a doleful grimace. Reaching up, I pushed on the brim of my soggy fedora, tilting it back on my head as if a sombrero or cowboy hat. My lungs spoke in a long, resigned sigh. "To save the world," I said. "I have to hunt down every last one, so I can be sure the species is destroyed. The only way to destroy one is, well, you got to ingest it. It's painful. Oh, damn, it's painful. But I'm the last hope. Without me, mankind's surely doomed."

"Uh huh," she said, trying not to laugh. "So, what's the real reason?"

"You don't believe me?" Smiling, I explained my scam to her. "Bartenders love guinea pigs," I began, telling her the tale I'd told so many girls. "It's free. I'll try anything that's free."

"I'll keep that in mind," she said.

"I'm sure you will." I slammed the rest of my drink with a wince.

"You look grim."

"My life," I said. "Besides, to be a tortured artist, one must be properly tortured."

"You're an artist?"

"In a sense. I'm a journalist who writes about artists." I extended a sweaty hand. "Collin Hearst, with the *Domestic-Chronicle*."

"Really? The *D-C?* Did you write that story about Cancer Moon?"

I suddenly felt a hundred percent better. "Sure did," I said.

"That's why I'm here."

"How do you mean?"

"I was at the dorms. Don't live there, mind you, just visiting a friend. Anyway, he had a copy of the paper. Me, I didn't plan on doing jack-shit tonight. I figured, with the snow and all, I'd be spending another boring Saturday at home. Then I read about Cancer Moon. That's why I came out."

"Glad to hear it," I said. "What's your name?"

"I'm Beverly. Bev."

"So, Bev, was it the first time you heard of Cancer Moon?"

"Nah. I saw 'em once. Right here, I think. They played here a couple months ago."

"Last month," I agreed.

"Maybe. Hard to say. So many bands that come through Pittsburgh."

"Anyway, you liked the show the last time?"

"The band was all right," she clarified. "That *girl*, though...she has a beautiful voice."

"Yes, she does," I agreed, trying not to sound infatuated or let on how that *girl* was the reason I felt so miserable. I didn't dare tell Beverly I'd come here hoping to fall in love with the band's lead singer, only to have her brush me aside like a gnat. Beverly didn't need to know my situation. The details wouldn't get either of us what we wanted, wouldn't have either of us playing our private Whitesnake songs for the rest of the night. So, I said, "Let me ask you another question. Why are you here alone?"

Her lips arced up and she leaned closer, building privacy between us. "I'm not," she whispered, or rather spoke at a normal volume which came across as a whisper beneath the noise from whatever rap or rock song had just begun to blare. "I sort of came with Derrick."

"Derrick?"

"He's my, uhm, friend from the dorm."

"Not a very bright boy, leaving you alone like this. You might get accosted by some pervert who'll take you off and do unspeakable things to you."

"Oooh," she sighed. "Promises, promises."

"I see. Where's old Derrick now?"

She shrugged.

"Really, it's never a good idea to leave your beautiful date by herself too long."

"Well, Derrick's not exactly a good idea for a date," she said. "You know how it is with freshmen. Don't know much, haven't seen much, aren't experienced. Turns out Derrick isn't even eighteen. Couldn't get in the door."

"Too bad for Derrick, but a break for some lucky bastard."

"Could be," she replied. "But like I told him, I came all this way in the freezing cold, so I'll be damned if I leave without seeing the show just because a man turns out to be a boy."

The bartender passed our way, grabbing my empty cup. "Another?" he said.

"Tempting, but no. That's all I can stand for now. What else you got?"

He leaned on the bar in a thinker's pose, thumb and forefinger massaging short hairs on his chin. "Let's see.

How about an Electric Espresso? No…shit. Our espresso machine's busted. Have to save it for another day. How about this mix I worked up with some Green-label Jack Daniel's, Vladimir vodka, Amaretto, Grenadine, and pineapple juice? I call it a Rusty Enema."

"*Fuck* that," I blurted. "Maybe I'll just have an Absolut Screw."

He looked hurt.

I told him, "I got a lot of balls, but I don't think I'm up for some asshole's dirty bath water. I'll save that for another day, too."

"Fair enough." Pausing to grab the Absolut bottle, he asked, "You want ice, or you like it straight up? I forget."

"Ice," I said.

He dropped a couple ice cubes in my cup, topping them off with a stream of vodka and a couple squirts of orange juice. "Here you go, man. Don't get too far gone on me." He turned toward Beverly, opening his mouth as if to ask her what she needed. Seeing she still had a bottle and a half, he thought better of it. "Kids," he muttered as he turned away.

Facing Beverly, I grinned wickedly. Or perhaps the alcohol did.

"What?" she said.

"Just getting to know your face so I can remember it after."

"After what?" she said.

"Whatever," I told her.

"Ooh," she moaned. "I like the sound of that." This time when she reached for her drink, she took a harder swig. We both knew where we were headed, what the night would bring.

We watched from the dance floor, as close as we could get to the stage. Standing behind her, I held her close, enshrouding her in the trench coat. My slippery arms kept a difficult grip around her stomach and waist while my hands occasionally slithered up, fingers easing under cotton. She never resisted or pulled away. Exactly the opposite, it was as though she struggled to get closer. Whenever the band played an alluring song, Bev slid her hands behind her. I felt them rubbing on my leg, my thigh, teasing my zipper. Each time, I bent to kiss the back of her neck or suck at an earlobe's dangling fruit. She countered with soft groans, clenching her fist around the fabric of my pants.

No one in the crowd seemed to notice, though we stood out like stone men in a house of wax. Black hat, black trench coat—I could've been the Phantom of the Opera with his unwilling lover or grim Death hovering over a kill. We were hidden in plain view. The nearly nude partiers paid no attention. Some watched the show, while others played their orgiastic games.

One person saw. Several times I looked up from a kiss in time to catch December's staring, glaring gaze before she turned away or closed her eyes. Her voice kept singing, her fingers focused on strumming chords, but her thoughts weren't with them. Her eyes swore she suffered, though it could've been from the passion of a song. She put on a hell of a show, pushing herself to extremes.

Cancer Moon played one set. It lasted barely over an hour. Then December coughed a dreadful "good night" which echoed through the P.A. speakers. She looked weary, defeated, but I figured it was the heat. Another day, she'd tell me I injured her, to which I'd reply she'd injured me. Such a simple misunderstanding for two misguided people. But that night, I couldn't see…

From the crowd came chants of "Encore, encore!"

It wasn't to be.

As the revelers who braved both cold without and heat within for one good show caught on, the catcalls and applause died out, fading into a groggy rumble and a barrage of boos. People ambled back to the bar or to find their warm clothes and heavy coats in whatever shadows they'd stashed them. It didn't seem like anyone was happy.

The last thing I heard was a hateful voice shouting over weary mumbles from the crowd. Must have been Mugwump. Sounded like him. "No! Keep playing! Do another set!"

But December Leigh and her crew put down their instruments, took no bows, and vanished quickly from stage and sight.

"Goddammit, get back up there!" that voice cried out in a panic. "I did acid for this show!"

CANTO NINE

The Trouble with Two Women

Sunday morning with bruises, I showered, shaved, and readied for work. I chose a blue suit to highlight my mood. I frowned at myself in the mirror.

Sometimes the morning after makes me sad.

I survived Saturday night, waking up with a beautiful woman naked and peaceful beside me. She looked so serene I just wanted to watch her, and that felt good for a while. But there's more to a morning than joys of the moment or the night before. I saw the sunrise raging with orange, bending through a tear in the corner of my eye—a tear for December. But I take that back. I woke up well past time for the sun's ascent. So, not sunrise—it was little more than a pretty array of lights seen through morning-blurry eyes. And maybe that wasn't so much a tear either... Maybe it was...

I watched Bev awhile longer, giving my head time to clear. Then, bending down, I kissed her as she slept. "Hello," I said when she finally stirred, returning the gift. "Good morning."

"Morning," she replied with a rumble.

"Sorry to wake you, but I have to go to work."

I didn't give her my number, and she didn't offer hers. Neither of us asked. We understood each other. Beverly didn't expect anything more last night when she went looking, and neither did I from the moment I'd been found.

She kept up the facade for a while. She kissed and touched and kissed and said nothing without innuendo. She savored the con, and I loved her for that, for playing her part to the end. It reminded me of someone I'd seen in a mirror. I dropped her off about three blocks from the dorms. It's what she wanted: more of her make-believe. I let her out far enough from school to imply she lived in an apartment somewhere near there, but close enough for her to walk back to her dorm. She held on to her routine as long as she could.

The monotone voice told me I had three calls. One came from a reader who liked the piece on Cancer Moon. The other two, somehow not a shock, were from December. One excerpted fairy tales and fables in her tone. The second seeped effluvia from deep pools in the underworld.

"Collin," spoke the first, "this is December. Thanks so much for the story. The band loved it. *I* loved it. It was ideal. Listen, we're hanging out at the hotel right now, unloading some personals and stuff. Room three-sixteen. Call me if you can. If not, please, *please* come to the show. I'd like to thank you personally. See you later." It soothed me to hear her warm voice, and what it seemed to promise. At the same time, it didn't. I would've cried, but the Weeping Willow routine didn't mesh with the Impenetrable Fortress I tried to be.

I sucked up my emotions and listened to the other message. I slumped back in my chair while December spoke again, poisoning me with her sorrow. Or with mine. "It's Dee," the tired voice exhaled. "Sorry we couldn't get together. Maybe another time. It's like…oh, this sounds stupid talking to a machine, but I was afraid I'd *disturb* you if I called you at home. Anyway, it's a shame things didn't work out. Well, I'll see you. I hope so, anyway. Goodbye."

The click that canceled her message could've canceled me. I didn't bother to hang up. I sat lax in my chair, ignoring the robotic voice telling me in polite terms to *please get off the fucking line*, and then the subsequent dial tone that must have hummed a full five minutes before I got myself together.

Hunter Delaware stumbled in and sat across from me at his desk. "Kid, you look worse than I feel. What's the matter? Bad night?"

"You could say that."

"Hangover?"

"Surprisingly, no. I'm fine."

"That's a shame. If you had one, I could show you the proper empathy. Mine won't go away. I've had it since about nineteen seventy-one." When I didn't laugh, he added, "It's worse this morning. Must have been that glass of wine."

"Could be," I said with a shrug.

"Either that or the two cases of Iron City Beer that Rick, Kathy, and I downed last night." Getting no reply, he said, "So, it's not a hangover, you say? Well, what is it? Women troubles?"

I nodded.

"I'm familiar. Tell me about it."

"I'd rather not."

As an award-winning journalist, Hunter knew better than to give up. "Girlfriend?"

"Ehr, no. Guess not."

"Lover?"

I had to think about that. "In a way, I guess."

"So, did you get laid last night or not?" The bluntness cold-cocked me.

"Unfortunately, yes," I replied.

"Ah, now I understand. I used to say the same thing when it happened with my ex-wife." He said it in such a matter-of-fact tone that I almost thought he was serious. "Okay. Stop moping around, kid. Spill it. Tell Doctor Delaware what's wrong."

"There's this girl," I explained, hesitantly.

"We've established that. You've recently enjoyed her company."

"No," I corrected. "Not that girl. It's a different one."

"Ah ha! Now we're getting somewhere. You played around with a lucky lover, but you blew it with Lady Love."

"That about sums it up."

"Tisk tisk," he censured, shaking his head. "That's a crime in some states. God knows, I could've been convicted many times. Back in my youth, of course."

"I can imagine."

"So, tell me about it while I indulge my habit. This definitely requires a little help." He leaned back in his chair, propping his feet up on the windowsill beside his desk. Reaching into his pocket, he withdrew his fat, brown cigar, uncovered it from the plastic, and bit the tip off, spitting it into the wastebasket. Then he stuffed the unlit stogie in his mouth.

I resigned myself to the old Manic-Depressive Patient routine, spilling out my sad and sappy tale, editing out the parts about my bad reporter ethics. "The thing is, I don't even know what happened. Everything seemed to be going well. Now, I don't know. I'm terrible with stuff like this."

"Hmm. Strange case. Possibly a mix-up, a misconception by you or the lady?"

"I don't know. Maybe. I hope not. If it was, I fucked up."

"Kid," he said, "remember this and take it to heart. Never hesitate and never look back. Learn from your mistakes and move on so that when history repeats you're ready. That's the best advice I can give you. If you want more, you'll have to pull old columns from my file."

I nodded with resignation.

"Good," he said. "Now ignore everything I've just told you and you'll probably be okay. As usual, I do hope I've been absolutely no help whatsoever."

It took a moment for his words to sink in. Then, finally, I laughed. Hunter was so absurd he could have been a character from Camus. "Actually, you've been a big help."

"Really?" he said. "How's that?"

"You confused me so much I forgot what the problem was."

"Hey, kid, any time you need a rabbit punch to the head, remember to look me up."

CANTO TEN

*The Country Singer Wants to Die,
and That's What I Like about Him*

In two years after my first local-band feature, I wrote a hundred stories for the *Life* page on rockers, rappers, punks, alternakids, jazz acts, orchestras, gospel groups, and even a barbershop quartet. National acts stopped by to chat or their managers called me up with quotes, but mostly I shined a spotlight on the wannabes, up-and-comers, small bands reaching for success. I wrote about the destined, and often the destined to disappear. In Pittsburgh, it didn't take long before I was better known around town than many of the bands I covered.

The editor filled my mailbox with letters and leaflets, cassettes and compact discs. I started slowly, doing a story every week. Then two, three, four. Next thing I knew, I turned in a piece and realized it was the tenth in an eight-day stretch. In that period, I'd only written four crime stories and taken one general-interest assignment. The music scene had become my primary job.

It was mostly an office gig at the time. I listened to demos and wrote reviews, found phone numbers to call for fifteen-minute interviews. I rarely attended shows or got up close and personal with a superstar. The Billy Ray Rose story changed all that.

Rose was the kind of guy not even sleazy, late-night barroom babes would sleep with were his songs not in heavy rotation on the radio. Just another one of country music's Billy Rays, he struck me as a typical backwoods heavy breather who caught a break. Receding hairline, fat jaw with diminished chin, gold fillings in tobacco-yellowed teeth. He dressed in straw cowboy hats, fake leather boots that glistened like plastic, unfaded jeans in deepest shades of blues and blacks.

Billy Ray Rose wore the term 'redneck' as if it were his given name. 'Hick,' to him, was a synonym for 'friend.' He could've stepped straight out of a coal mine or a hole-in-the-wall after-hours juke joint in some tiny, isolated Appalachian town. He came from about three hours south: Charleston, West Virginia—not a giant city, but that state's largest. The way I understand it, he made perfect grades all the way through school until his senior year when he slid to the middle of his class. At nineteen, he headed north to Morgantown, about an hour or so from Pittsburgh. He attended West Virginia University, majored in physics, minored in classical music, and completed three years before being kicked out—so the story goes—for racial slurs in class. At twenty-one, Rose moved to Pittsburgh and formed his first band: Sparky Plugs. The name soon changed to Big Red Bug Guard, and finally to Billy Ray Rose and the Reds. He was the star of the band, after all—or so *he* said. Rose's group played dives and pool halls throughout eastern Pennsylvania, hitting every hole-in-the-wall town his drummer-slash-manager could find on a map. That helped Rose build his reputation some, but he didn't need much buildup around here. In Pittsburgh's lifeless country music scene, his band was a happening act.

Billy Ray got his break when a friend of a friend of a friend's cousin got in touch with an old girlfriend who happened to be a producer in Nashville. She came to town at her ex-lover's request, caught Rose on stage, and fell in love with his sound. She signed him right off and flew him to Nashville, leaving the band behind. She liked Rose. The Reds weren't that lucky.

Rose recorded his first album, "Too Young To Give Up Drinking, Too Old To Forget." It had one original song and nine by young writers with no future in the business—that is, aside from raking in some of the cash that Billy Ray made. Rose took borrowed songs and made them hits. His back-up performers over-performed, his producers overproduced, and his marketing team over-marketed him and his record until, within a year of moving to Nashville and by age twenty-four, Billy Ray Rose was a name known to almost every country music fan in the U.S. His album sold five million copies, and his first single, "Even Bartenders Cry," went platinum almost overnight. He made a video for that goddamn annoying song which set records for requests, then went on his first national tour, opening for one of country music's *other* famous Billy Rays. After two more singles, "Lost Love, Where Are You?" and "Someone Stole A Page From My Little Black Book," he headlined small venues, relying on *his* name to sell out shows.

Billy Ray Rose became a superstar. That's what I know about him. It's what he is—or was—to millions of fans. It's not what he is to me. Not even close. No, to me he's a bad guy who made my life a little better just by being his usual annoying self. He's an interview that made me famous in Pittsburgh. Or infamous. But, like I said, he's just another one of country music's Billy Rays.

I met him at the peak of his fame, days before he released his second record, the flop that stalled his career. Rose was playing a Monday night gig at Star Lake, with the new disc due in stores the following day. For publicity, old Billy Ray had to suck up to hacks like me. He wasn't very good at sucking up. In fact, he'd been an ass to reporters several times over the last couple years. He challenged one reviewer to a fist fight, and he once asked a critic, "Why's a black guy cover country music in the first place? Don't know enough boutcha own music?" My interview wasn't quite that bad. Still, he had a way of getting under my skin.

It was Friday evening that found me working in the newsroom. I sat at my computer, mostly reading the day's wire copy about crazed rock'n'roll singers being arrested, getting in fights, causing riots, or whatever it was they'd done that day to keep their piece of the ever-shrinking attention span of the average American teenage compact disc buyer.

Arnie waddled over from the city desk, skin sagging from age and a newspaper man's hard life—like it was back in *his* day, anyway. He wore the most bedazzled look on his face. It was like he'd seen Death across the street slipping coins into a parking meter. "Collin," he said.

"Yeah"

"Do you…?"

"Uh huh?"

"Do you know…?"

"What is it, Arnie? Spit it out, man!"

"Do you know who Billy Ray Rose is?"

"Billy Ray Rose," I said. "Country singer. Real dumb-ass. Got those annoying songs that make canaries kill themselves. What was it? 'Bartenders Cry in Their Beer' or something?"

"Yeah, something."

"Why, Arnie? What's up?"

Arnie twitched, a little unsure of himself.

"Come on. I've got work to do." It was a lie.

"He's on line three."

"You're shitting me!"

"No. He's on line three. Wants to talk to our music critic."

"He wants to talk to the…?"

"Music critic."

"We don't have a music critic," I said.

"That was my reaction at first. Then I thought, well, that's sort of you. I mean, ain't it?"

"Oh, thanks," I told him, heavy on the sarcasm.

"It's your area," he said.

"I know, I know. Line three, you say?"

"Line three," he said.

"I'm on it."

"Thanks." He slapped me on the back as if we were old pals.

I put aside what I was doing, grabbed a pen and a clean notebook, and reached for the phone. "*Domestic-Chronicle*," I said instinctively. "May I help you?"

"Buddy," said the phlegm-filled voice, "who am I talking to?"

"Collin Hearst. What can I do for you?"

"Well, hell," he said. "This is Billy Ray Rose callin'. Get it? Billy Ray Rose callin'? Collin, callin'. See?" He coughed, or blew his nose, or something crude disguised as a laugh.

"What can I do for you, Mister Rose?"

"What you can do's get up off your ass and get over here'n get this interview done with." He pronounced it *innerview*.

"Interview?" I said, annunciating the word just to be rude. "What interview?"

"You're supposed to interview me about Monday," he said.

"Don't know what you mean. When was it schedule-ed?"

"Right now," he demanded. "I'm scheduling it right now. Get here. I'll have security let you in the back way."

"That's short notice. I'm not sure I can…"

"Won't take no for an answer, Buddy Boy. You get here. Right away." The bastard hung up before I could get more than a breath out in reply.

"Fuck," I said.

Jilly—the staff photographer I took with me—skittered around the room, completely speechless as she shot the pictures. I guess she was a Billy Ray Rose fan. Who knew? Even so, I think Rose intimidated her. If not him, then maybe his reputation. He wasn't known for being nice to women. Or anybody else for that matter, now that I think about it.

"What makes you special?" I asked, challenging him, trying to seem tough—a hard-edged journalist rather than a feature writer who loved bands and free booze.

I almost expected him to lose his country cool. Instead, he answered with a somewhat despondent tone. "I'm not special," he said. "I'm successful."

"How do you mean?"

"Listen, Buddy Boy, anybody can be successful. Practice, hard work, a little luck—they all lead that way eventually. I mean, if you stick with it. Garth Brooks, Charlie Daniels—they's just plain successful. Worked the circuits, did what they had to do, put their whole lives on hold for the music and, you know, to build their careers. Seems to me they got what they wanted. They earned it, you know? But, Buddy Boy, then there's fellows like Elvis Presley and Johnny Cash. They's the ones I call special. Hank Junior, he's successful. Hank Senior, now that man was real special. Right? You get what I'm telling you? See the difference?"

"I think so," I said. I hated to admit it, but I agreed with his logic.

"I want to die successful," he went on. "I want to die dead certain I put all of what little I got into making my music. You got that?"

I nodded, a voice in my head joking, "So, he wants to die successful, eh? Fair enough. Sounds like a good deal. Why don't we get on with it?"

"That's good, 'cause a distinction needs to be made. Billy Ray Rose is successful. Billy Ray Rose ain't special." For the briefest moment, I accepted his humility as a sign that an actual person existed inside the crude shell of a man. But he had to keep talking, the dumb bastard. "What the hell. I never wanted to be special. I just wanted to pick up chicks. *Heh heh*. Now I'm famous. I got first pick of the litter any time I want. Shit, yeah. If that's the payday, I'd take being successful any day."

By editorial consensus, that last part of Rose's tirade got omitted. It didn't find its way into print despite my argument for burning him at the stake by showing off the *real* Billy Ray Rose to the world. Of course, I was still young then, and kind of naive. The world already understood the *real* Billy Ray Rose. At that point, folks didn't care. What mattered was what folks *wanted* him to be. Everybody had their expectations.

In a way, those expectations are why the interview made me a celebrity for a while. I asked him typical questions, and he answered typically. But then I asked the most basic question in a reporter's arsenal, the easiest softball pitch for him to smack out of the park, and one with no malice whatsoever implied or, as far as I could imagine, even possible. I said, "Tell me, Mister Rose, where do you think you'll be ten years from now?"

"I'll have sold ten million each of ten records, with ten million left in a bank account to show for it. I'll lounge around my heated swimming pool nearly naked, with girls scattered everywhere, you know, fulfilling whatever fantasies I have left. I'll be lean and tan, with bulging biceps and triceps and them other muscles. I'll be head-to-toe perfect, by God, and the best-selling artist of all times. I won't be able to leave my house without fighting back an army."

The editors wouldn't let me use any of that either. I had a feeling they wouldn't, but I wrote it down anyway and went on to the follow-up: "So, you think your fame will keep growing?"

"Buddy Boy," he replied, "come ten years, I'll have my own religion."

Reminded of words on the statue of Ozymandias, I inscribed Rose's quote at the base of my article, and the editors for some reason didn't edit it out. I like to think their eyes were tired after all the other bad shit Rose said that they found and decided to cut.

Anyway, that story made me news for a while. Several reporters from major newspapers and magazines called me at work to make sure I'd gotten Rose's quote right before they ran it, knowing the impact it would have. I told them the truth: I left out the words 'Buddy Boy' as on all my Rose quotes so I didn't lose six full inches of copy. That satisfied them, though none of them found it nearly as funny as I did.

I won't say it's that quote that *began* Rose's downfall. He'd already made enemies. After all, he'd let his mouth drive from day one, but he never bothered to teach it to read the STOP signs and speed limits. Personally, I think he should've put it in park just that one time. There are some things not even a successful man can say.

CANTO ELEVEN

Second Encounter with Billy Ray Rose

When I came face to face with country singer Billy Ray Rose the second time, I almost felt sorry for him. In the two years since my story on him ran, his career went downhill so fast it would've made an ideal subject for a country song. I read all the wire stories about the many ways he continually stumbled and fell. I took careful note of every failure, setback, and inch Rose traveled up Shit Creek: how his second album sold less than two hundred thousand copies; how his agent dropped him, his manager dropped him, his label dropped him; how he spent two months in an Arizona jail for punching a lady cop before a show in Phoenix; how radio stations refused to play his songs after on-the-air racist jokes; how he spent three weeks in a local hospital because he made similar comm- ents on a public street in Youngstown, Ohio; and how he served two terms in rehab for powder. I also kept up with his recovery: a rumored course in sensitivity training; the two-million-dollar judgment he won against his record label for breach of contract; how he used all that money to clear up problems with the IRS, then spent what was left to self-produce a third album, distributing it himself; and how the first single, "Back from the Badlands," was slowly getting airplay on stations not afraid to "test the waters."

Despite Rose's new luck, I was surprised that first Saturday of the new year when I heard his voice on my telephone. He didn't have a critical following these days, and no self-respecting reporter wanted to talk to him, not even just to call him a freak or shout, "Fuck off!"

Needless to say, I took the call.

Rose had a gig at some hole-in-the-wall redneck joint called the Black Dog, the Big Dog, the Dead Dog—something like that. It was south of Pittsburgh near Morgantown, West Virginia, where Rose spent a few years in college. It'd take me an hour and a half to get there, which was a good reason to say no when Rose asked me for another interview. But he did *ask* this time, which intrigued me. *Why'd he choose me?* I wondered. *What could he say that I'd find worth the ink it takes to quote him?* Perhaps he thought I owed him one, or maybe he remembered me well enough to know I'd be fair despite my personal distaste for him. Anyway, it took balls for him to make that call. That deserved some small measure of deference. The least I could do was show some balls myself.

"I'll be there," I said, and headed for Kathy's office to convince the Queen of the Damned that Billy Ray Rose, one of the all-time ugliest people inside, deserved a listen.

"Get fucked," was her response. "Billy Ray Rose wouldn't merit an obit in this paper if he died saving a drowning puppy in a hurricane."

Even with her dislike for Rose, it just took a touch of the old Logical Philosopher routine to change her mind and send me off to Morgantown. "Look at it this way, if the story doesn't pan out, we trash the interview. Nobody'll know we considered it. You lose nothing but mileage expenses and my time—a few hours I can spend on the road doing what I do best or back here at my desk doing next to nothing. But what if there's a scoop? Suppose this nutball has a tale to tell that no one else will touch. We can win big, can't we? It's a gamble, but it's a small one—more like a dollar on a lottery ticket than a day's pay at the track."

"Interesting concept," she agreed, though still reluctant. Her crooked grin had grown from an equally crooked grimace, and I knew she found me aggressive and ambitious today. Kathy approved of aggressiveness. She respectted ambition.

"Trust me," I said, "it's a sure thing."

She stared down at her right hand unconsciously toying with a red company pencil. She wanted to say yes, but she had to let the business and news portions of her brain fight it out.

"It's a Saturday night. What else do I have unless there's a murder, a rape, or a riot? You can pay me to hang out by the telephone, chatting it up with secretaries and deputies. I might get a brief about purse snatchings and prostitution stings. Or, pay me to do what I do best."

"Get going," she said. I was out of my chair like a whirlwind and heading for the door of her office when she called after me. "Take the Keg and the Cups," she said. "If you get anything, mix us an Electric Cocktail. Otherwise, give us a call and tell us you've *sobered up*."

"No problem," I said, as I closed the door behind me.

The Keg was intraoffice jargon for a cheap Japanese laptop bearing the obscure trademark of the Kigami Corporation. Our publisher purchased this toy computer eight months earlier. It was only slightly less complicated to use and nominally more sophisticated than a block-plate printing press with carved potatoes for letters. The Cups were two rubber cradles connected by a short cord which, when plugged into the Keg, served as a crude modem. This modem worked by placing the receiver from a standard telephone firmly into the Cups, thereby allowing the story, or Electric Cocktail, to be sent across phone lines by a cacophonous series of sonic bleeps and crackles directly into the main queue in the newsroom. It always came *mixed*, meaning completely backwards with the first letter on a newsroom terminal being the last letter typed on the Keg. For some reason, the Cups transmitted from bottom to top, sending every story across the phone lines inversely. So, frustrated editors would have to work through a long series of complicated computer codes to get the story straightened out, or else have a part-time staffer type the whole thing from scratch after sifting through all the backwards tripe. Either way, it took about the same amount of time and effort. That's why the editors despised the Keg and Cups—that is, all except Kathy who considered them useful. Needless to say, those who actually dealt with mixed Electric Cocktails preferred that their story-drunk reporters *sober up*—which is to say, that they admit they have a problem and quit the story cold turkey.

I was a drunk. In several months of mixing Electric Cocktails, not once had I sobered up. I drank my fill. True, every now and then a story I sent wouldn't be worth printing, but I sent it just the same. Whether I was covering campaign speeches or county fairs, improv poets or doom-saying street preachers, my copy always arrived on time. I drank and drank, and the Keg was always full. I left decisions about sobriety to the editors. They knew that, so every time they saw me lugging the Keg at my side, my colleagues wanted a drink. A real one.

A wreck just after the switch onto I-79 south backed up traffic, so the trip took more than two hours. I wasted another twenty minutes finding the club. I stopped at three gas stations and a Dairy Mart before I met anyone who could give directions. This is partly my fault for inquiring about the Dead Dog when, as I later found out, the actual name was the Angry Bulldog. I finally asked an old man at a Chev-Elev who corrected me and guided me on my way.

The Angry Bulldog's owner must have been more fond of being anonymous than making profits. At the Chev-Elev, I scanned a phone book searching for enlightenment but found none. I even bought a copy of the local paper which turned out to be useless in my quest for an address. Resigning the newspaper to my passenger seat with the Keg, I drove around until I found the bar which, I realized, I'd passed at least once along the way. Not that I would've recognized it. How could I guess the club playing host to a former country music superstar would be a graying wreck of an old barn with a dirty glass door on one side, marked only with glued letters *A-N-G-R-B-U-L-L-G?* I expected a glowing neon sign with a big-breasted cartoon mascot, or at least a picture of some filthy mongrel snarling at the passersby.

I pulled into the gravel parking lot, empty except for one rusted heap of an old van. I guessed *that* was what remained of the Billy Ray Rose Traveling Circus. I knew I had a story even before I heard a single word from Billy Ray. For anyone else, a gig at a bar this small wasn't worth a two-inch brief. For the former Grammy winner for Best New Country Artist, a booking in this rat trap was the fifth act in a Shakespearean tragedy, the point where the hero's character flaws finally bring him down. And Rose had many flaws.

I got out of my car and walked toward the door, lugging the Keg along like a heavy bucket of cow's milk. The door was unlocked, so I went in.

This dive was one large room with a worn red-orange carpet, semi-round tables, a raised stage in one corner, and a well-stocked whiskey bar along an entire wall. The place stood empty except for a golden-haired young man with a matching thick blond beard. He was wiping down the bar with a wet rag. As I approached, he looked at me and grinned.

"Hey there," he said. "What can I get you for?"

I plopped the Keg down on a barstool. "How's it going? I'm Collin Hearst, a reporter with the *Domestic-Chronicle* in Pittsburgh. I'm here to meet Billy Ray Rose."

He nodded. "Said you might hightail it up here. Said he could count on you. I guess ole Billy Ray still has a little magic left after all."

"That's what I'm here to find out. Is he around?"

"He's in the back. Be out in a minute. Get you a drink?"

Alcohol sounded agreeable. "How about an Absolut Screw?"

"Sorry, buddy. We ain't got Absolut. Got Gilbey's, Popov, Vladimir…"

My stomach churned. "Make it a Jack and Coke."

"No problem," he said, reaching for the bottle. He poured the whiskey into a short glass, then opened the icebox looking for soda. Groaning, he shook his head. "I'm afraid we're out of Co'cola. We got RC, or you can have it straight."

"RC's cool," I said, just wanting the damned drink.

He pulled a two-liter bottle out of the icebox and filled my glass to the rim.

Can't even afford a soda fountain, I thought. *Billy Ray Rose, you're going places.*

As if in response, I heard a long series of sneezes followed by an oath: "Sheeit!" I recognized the voice right off. Rose appeared from behind a curtain to my right. He was dressed in fake cowboy clothes including white chaps with pink stripes and frills, a pair of dirty white boots, and his traditional straw hat. He looked more like Roy Rogers than Clint Eastwood.

The bartender dropped my drink on the counter. "Buck fifty," he said.

"Good price," I replied, dropping a couple dollar bills on the counter. Then I took a sip as my eyes filled with tears. That was one hell of a strong drink. "Real good price," I coughed.

"Hey hey," said Rose when he saw me. "You made it." His voice sounded more nasally than I remembered, and he sniffled a lot as he spoke.

"Same old Billy Ray," I said.

Throwing me a puzzled glance, he shrugged and said, "Listen, Buddy Boy, I'm glad you came. I've got a lot to tell you. I'm on the comeback trail, the road to recovery, the highway out of the old town into a big, bright city. You know, this time I think I'll do okay. I won't let the slum lords and sewer rats stop me. You know what I mean?"

Actually, I had no idea what he meant, though there was a vague impression in my mind of Rose's previous racist comments and his habit of espousing them in front of television cameras. I figured he was spouting off another coded epithet. Looking back, I don't think that was it.

"I learned my lesson," he said. "I'm a changed man, and you can print that!"

"What do you mean by changed?" I asked.

"I'm different. Just look at me."

I did, but I saw the same crude shell of a person I'd seen two years before and on so many trashy talk shows and gossip programs since. "I need details, Rose. I'm not your P.R. man. You've got to make me see it, understand it, believe it. Otherwise, you're wasting my time. You won't make the paper, not even a brief on the back page. Pretend I'm your priest. Confess, repent, and then we'll see if the world thinks you're worth forgiveness." I said the world as if as many people would see *this* story as had seen the first one two years ago. But the world wouldn't care. Not this time. Still, my world was the Pittsburgh music scene, and I could at least promise him my world would decide whether he should be forgiven.

If I'd said what I said two years ago, the interview would've been over. Rose would've shown me the door, or he might have hurt me. But our roles had changed. He sighed noticeably and dropped down on a bar stool. "You're right," he said. "No playing it cool. The fact is, I'm lucky you're here. Damned lucky. I called up a whole shit pot full of reporters this time around, and I couldn't get past hello before they hung up on me. Buddy Boy, most papers won't even list my name with the upcoming events when I'm in town, and they'd do that for *any*body. Satan playing a banjo could make the upcoming events list. So, I got it. I owe you. That ain't no lie. You tell me what you want, and I'll give it to you."

"I don't want anything. I'm just a storyteller. If it's worth telling, I'll tell it. If not, I'm out of here. I can just go home and get some sleep. Remember, you called me."

"Where do I begin?"

"Well, you said you've changed. Most of America isn't prepared to believe that. I doubt I will either." I downed the whiskey, gasping as it burned my throat. After slapping the empty glass on the bar, I reached into a coat pocket for my notebook. "Convince me."

He closed his eyes and his face tensed, making him look as if he were wishing on a pitched penny. When he relaxed and opened his eyes, he cleared his throat with a cough. "I guess it's best to get it out. That's what they told me at the clinic. Course, that was the snortin' and boozin' and stuff. This is different. Well…here goes." He paused for a breath. "I'm a bigot."

His last sentence set my hand in motion. "Go on."

"A bigot," he said again. "My daddy was a bigot. My granddaddy was a bigot. All my brothers and sisters, too. When I was a kid, my friends were bigots—every last one. Hell, more than half the folks I grew up with, you know? And all this time I didn't reckon that meant a thing to nobody. Figured it was just normal. Never stopped to think about it."

"You're saying you don't think it's all that normal now?"

"No," he replied. I misunderstood at first, thinking he meant, "No, I'm not saying that," until I glanced at him and, just for a second, saw this sort of deep, numbing sadness in his eyes. It was a look that couldn't be faked— not by a professional actor, and sure as hell not by a moron like Rose. In that instant, I understood what he'd intended: "No, it's not normal at all."

"What changed your mind?"

Hesitation. "Rushanda," he said, a word he pronounced "*Rush into.*"

"Say again?"

"Rushanda. Rushanda Johnson. She's the colored girl … sorry … the African-American lady that's been teaching me what nobody else ever did."

"Can you spell that name for me?"

He did, adding, "I think that's right."

"Okay. Now, she's been teaching you what kinds of things?"

"Been helping me to understand where I come from, where she comes from, the differences between us, and the similarities."

"That's good," I said, encouraging him. "How did the two of you meet?"

He massaged his chin nervously while he stared at the floor, but he resumed eye contact before he said, "She wrote me a letter after she saw me on the TV. About six months ago. Don't even remember what I said, you know. Just talk. Lot of folks didn't see it that way. Must've been pretty mean. I got a lot of letters. I always do after I chew my toenails on TV. This time wasn't no different. Folks cussed me, threatened to bust me up again. This girl, Rush, she wasn't like that. She didn't act like those folks. She just wrote letter-type things. You know? 'Hello. How are you? Hope all's well for you.' Then, on the last line, she wrote, 'Why do you hate me so much?' like she was one of my old girlfriends."

I wrote down his words so frantically that my hand cramped. I didn't pause to shake it, knowing I could profit from the pain.

"She didn't ask why I hated black folks. I probably could've answered that'n. I had lots of reasons. Not *good* reasons, but they were the ones I heard since I was in powder and Pampers.

"No, she asked me why I hated *her*. But I didn't. Truth is, I didn't hate nobody, 'cept maybe my manager and those pricks at the record company. Some of you guys, too. No offense."

I grinned and kept writing.

"I was confused, and a little lost. So, I wrote her back, telling her what I just told you. Sent my number, too. She called me up just a few days later to say she understood."

"That's touching," I said with all seriousness.

Rose either didn't hear or flat out ignored me. "The two of us met for lunch. Since then, we've been talking a lot, hanging out. She's been explaining things."

"So you're not a racist anymore? That what you're saying?"

"No, sir," he said. "I'm still like I was. Probably be a bigot the rest of my days. But with Rush's help, I'm trying hard to fight it. She's teaching me to see how other folks feel when I say things like I said in the past, when I act the way I acted. Don't know if I'll ever *not* be a bigot, sure as sunshine. The best I can do's try not to offend folks, not to make'em sad, and hope to somehow get past my roots."

Sarcastically, I said, "You blame your family?"

"That's not it," he replied with a tired sigh. "I'm just like'em. I'm a bigot. I said that. I learned it from my daddy, sure. But then on, it's my mouth talkin' and my brain that won't make it stop. Besides, that's only part of it. I'm also a druggie. I learned that one all on my own." Rose went on to chronicle his journeys through addictions, having gotten intimate with heroin and crack before falling into the outstretched arms of his current love, powdered cocaine.

He went into explicit detail, describing the pleasures, problems, related illnesses and recoveries, sharing each scene as if it were unique. There's something about a man who admits his flaws and takes responsibility for them that merits a little sympathy. Rose wasn't trying to hide his problems. He wasn't trying to lie and say, "I'm clean, Man. Look at me. I've been through treatment so many times there's nothing left to treat." I felt like Rose didn't want to manipulate me, to pull the wool over my eyes. He seemed more concerned with truth than publicity. He didn't waste time convincing me of his genuineness, and that made his words seem genuine. It may have been a con, but if so, it was the best I ever saw. "Don't know that I'll ever clean up," he said. "Don't know if I want to."

"I see what you're saying. You don't like who you are, but you're afraid if you change you might like yourself even less."

"Buddy Boy, I got a lot of problems. May never get rid of them suckers. Point is, I'm trying. I'm trying like heck to just stop and think before I talk, and I'm trying just as hard to catch on and apologize real quick if something stupid slips out. With tons of help, somewhere along the way I might be able to give up the drugs. If I fall back from time to time, it's still fine and dandy. I'll have a friend right there to straighten me out. Folks might read your story and say, *'Well, hell. Old Billy Ray just wants to sell his tapes. He ain't different.'* That's okay with me, honest to God. It ain't important if they get it or believe it or whatever. It just ain't."

"How *are* you different?" I said.

Smiling for the first time in a while, he looked me in the eye. This time I saw hints of peace inside that stare. Without pausing to consider his words, he told me, "I have a friend."

I wrote that in my notebook in big, bold letters, underlining it seven times for effect. That wasn't the end of the interview, but it *was* the end of the story. For twenty minutes more, I questioned Rose, collecting more basic information. "What about the new album? Where will you be playing? What are your plans?" These asides were filler for the real story: *Billy Ray Rose has a friend!*

Rose was testing his equipment and running through a handful of new songs getting ready for the gig. I sat at the bar, sipping more whiskey and typing a twelve-inch story into the Keg. It didn't take long and, when I completed the piece, I packed up and headed for the Chev-Elev to find a pay phone so I could transmit my article. That meant twenty minutes of down time while the crotchety Kigami whizzed and whirred. I leaned back against the brick wall and thumbed through the local paper. Then I saw it: a small ad in the bottom right corner on the last page of the last section. "Agamemnon's," it read. "Drink specials. Pocket Pizzas. Live tonight, Cancer Moon. 8 p.m. to midnight. $2 cover." I looked at my watch. Quarter to eight. I could make it.

When the Keg ran out of juice, I gave the newsroom a call to make sure my story came through. Rick answered the phone. He bitched and moaned as soon as he heard my voice—it was the same as an affirmation. I didn't care. It was a good story. He'd see that when he got it right side up.

After Rick calmed down, I told him, "Don't think Rose's story's a hoax, but I think I'll stick around a bit. If he's fucking with me, I'll call you back and tell you to scrap the whole piece."

"Do it quick, gawdammit, before we waste an hour cleaning up this mixed-up crap."

"Will do," I said. "See you tomorrow, Rick."

"Hearst, if this story sucks, don't bother showing up."

CANTO TWELVE

Lame Club, Lame Gig

From Pleasant Street in the middle of Morgantown, Agamemnon's flashed glitz and glamour like a big-city bar. It invited attention with postmodern murals across the gray cinderblock walls and a billboard on the roof with the club's name atop a seductive-looking elegantly-dressed chick holding a really big axe. It wasn't a small bar from the outside. Inside, however, it was just one room cluttered with tables, chairs, and cheap replicas of toga-clad Greeks and Romans from Socrates to Caligula. There wasn't a bar actually *in* the room. Instead, big-breasted waitresses in short, tight black outfits wandered around from table to table taking orders for booze, pizza, nachos, or whatever other generic crap was served.

I couldn't imagine Cancer Moon playing here. Agamemnon's seemed better suited for a rotary club meeting or an accountants convention than a rock concert. There wasn't even a stage. The band's equipment had been set up haphazardly on the floor in a far corner of the bar. *How are they going to play in that mess?* I thought. *There's hardly room to breathe.* There was far too much light for a concert. Rows and rows of tubes—all white, all bright—traced parallel and perpendicular paths up the walls and across the ceiling. From beside the door, a plaster Apollo's eyes projected spotlights across the room, building two great circles on the phony stage. *December will be pissed*, I thought. All around me, students and hipsters wore sunglasses to mute the glare. *I wish I hadn't worn my contacts today. Jesus, it's bright.* I squinted and tried to drink away the coming headache.

I ordered a Long Island Iced Tea and began to flood my system as soon as the waitress handed me my glass. Drinking it down like water, I felt myself relaxing. I wanted to sit, but Agamemnon's was packed with people. I had to wander around in circles until a table opened up near enough for me to grab it. Even then, I had to share it with a couple college boys who invited themselves to join me.

When I first saw December a few minutes before the show, she didn't recognize me. Why should she? She had no reason to suspect I'd be here. Besides, the lights were too bright. She probably couldn't see me clearly. I left her alone and tried not to draw attention to myself.

She was every bit as beautiful as I remembered. But she was different. She'd highlighted her jet black hair with silver streaks, adding life to her typical somberness. She came guised in a black fishnet body suit beneath which could be seen a rainbow halter and baggy pair of black men's boxers. To top it off, God help us, she actually wore four-inch platform shoes and silver glam-rock glitter paint over her lips and around her eyes. She looked like something out of the sparkling seventies—that, or a highbrow strip club.

Once the band started playing, she stepped to the microphone and did three sets with her eyes closed tight to avoid all that horrible whiteness in front of her. All the while, her painted eyelids flickered like two disco globes beneath the bar's burning incandescence.

While her image gave her a new vividness, a new energy, her sound came off poorly. Chords and melodies merged into maddening strains pouring from a Peavey P.A. turned up too loud. Some of the band's heavier progressions distorted out as sound waves bounced off walls and patrons, grumbling back in a collage of noises. The amps fed back. The instruments were poorly mixed and sounded out of tune. One of the guitars went dead halfway through a song.

Adding to the mayhem, between songs some old drunk in the audience kept standing up, shaking his fat ass, and screaming, "Hey, baby, play 'The Twist.'"

I could tell Dee was into the music. Yet she came across as little more than a mad wolf baying at the moon. With her mic too quiet, the lyrics were inaudible most of the time. When they *could* be heard, Dee's voice sounded flat, whining and crackling like a young boy's.

By the time the show ended, the crowd had dwindled to a dozen hardy drinkers, the old Twister who'd passed out in his chair with his head down on a table, and me. All the madness, all the mayhem, all the passionate frenzy exploding from inside Dee and her bandmates—they were there but not the same. They came across in miscues and backfires, a brutal unmasking.

Then I saw the first real tension flare up between Dee and the band as she assailed them with trifling gripes and an obloquy of scorn. "Fucking prick," she screamed, labeling the thunderstruck drummer, who scowled back at her with a grimace of his own.

"What the fuck did I do?"

"Prick," she repeated, with all her scorn pouring out. "Fucking prick!"

"What?" Justin appeared to be totally at a loss.

"Can't you keep a simple rhythm, you son of a bitch? It's only four-four time. Can't you *handle* four-four time?"

Justin shook his head, disgusted.

"You're high," he said.

The lead singer didn't react like her senses were slowed by dope. With a quick reflex motion she side-armed her microphone at her unsuspecting drummer. The projectile sped toward him like a baseball, coming within inches of his face before the mic cable caught on an amplifier and bounced back like a bungee cord, pulling the metal missile backward, too. The mic crashed loudly through Justin's cymbals and dropped to the floor with a heavy thud.

Justin looked stunned. His eyes widened and his jaw hung.

Heather turned around just in time to the see the missile miss its mark. "Jesus Christ, Dee! What's the matter with you? You could've hurt him."

"I could've killed him," December corrected, much calmer and more composed. As an aside, she added in a loud murmur, "Fucking prick."

With a resigned wave of her hand, Heather turned and went back to disentangling cables, trying to get her equipment packed up so she and the band could split that Roman *Inferno*.

Justin remained silent, but I could read the concern on his face. He sat there unmoving behind his drum kit, eyes hazed over with fear and frustration, staring straight at Dee.

She returned his gaze with a cruel Medusa mask that might have turned the drummer to stone had he not looked away at the last instant. Having won, she began straightening her own jumbled cords. Picking up the thrown mic, she started wrapping its cable around it one loop at a time. Despite her rage a minute before, she portrayed calm until the final loop, then unplugged the cable from the P.A. and gently tossed the mic into a plastic bag.

I figured now wasn't a good time for a reunion. I was probably the last person she wanted to see on a miserable night like this. I imagined her bludgeoning me to death with a mic stand, or maybe just kicking the shit out of me with her platform shoes. But unlike her bandmates, I was brave. Or maybe just drunk. I stood up, slid my hands in coat pockets, and moved toward her slowly, cautiously.

Dee had her back to me, so she didn't notice me coming. Justin did and, despite his near-fatal mic experience, whispered a warning. "Dee," he said.

"What?" she replied, a bit less spiteful.

Justin gave a soft nod in my direction.

December turned around, and her face lit up. Her frown fizzled into a goofy grin glowing beneath her glam-rock glittering eyes. "Collin!" she gasped.

"Hello, Dee. Good to see you again."

Without a word she lunged toward me and, before I could even get my hands out of my pockets, she had me in her arms, pressing her lips to mine with the force of a trash compactor. The oily silver lipstick felt like cake batter on my skin. "What are you doing here?" she asked, kissing me again before I could reply. "Did you see the show?"

"Yeah," I said, with little emotion.

She understood. "Terrible, wasn't it?"

"I wouldn't say *terrible*. It was just..."

"What?"

"It's this club. Bad scene. The light killed the mood, and the acoustics ruined the sound."

"You think so? It wasn't us?"

"Pearl Jam would sound like shit in here." With anyone else I'd have slipped into my Bitter Critic routine and fired off negative adjectives like darts. With December, I felt stuck in a wrong gear, playing the Infatuated Fan. Besides, I guess it wasn't totally a lie. After all, the light *did* kill the mood, and acoustics in this pathetic shithole *did* ruin the sound. And who knows, maybe Pearl Jam *would* suck here as the singer hid his eyes with a hand.

Dee kissed me again with more energy. When she pulled away, she said, "You're right. I should've known." Releasing me, she backed up. "What are you doing here?"

"Working," I replied.

"In West Virginia?"

"I had a story with a Pittsburgh angle."

"Cool," she said. "How did you know we were here?"

"An ad in the city paper," I explained. "I was in town. You were in town. Had to come."

This time she looked skeptical, folding her arms as if accusing me of stealing the last chocolate chip cookie from her jar. "Are we that good?"

This time, I didn't have to lie.

"As a matter of fact, I listened to your disc on the way down here, even before I knew you'd be playing." With my left hand finally out of my pocket, I traced my thumb around one of the glittery trails under her eyes. "Besides, you have the most sensual..." Long pause for effect. "...stage presence..." Another pause. "... I've ever been lucky enough to see."

She grabbed my head with both hands and pulled me to her, our lips connecting again. I felt the warm wetness of her tongue on my upper lip. When she finished, I looked down at my feet and said, "Listen, I want to clear up that scene, make sure there's no misunderstanding."

She placed her index finger on my chin and lifted my head until we made eye contact. Then she ran her hand through my hair before retreating. "Don't apologize. It's not your style."

She was right. The Repentant Adulterer routine isn't one I'd mastered. "I'm not offering apologies. 'I'm sorry' means I didn't intend what I did. Make no mistake, I meant to do it. I just want to understand what happened before that, what happened between you and me."

This time it was Dee who turned away, staring at her colleagues for several frightening seconds before looking back. "What happened?" she said with a sad sigh. "What happened is you came for me and went away with *her*. What happened is you picked up some porcelain doll and took her home. What happened is, whatever you did to *her*, I expected you to do to *me*."

I was surprised. Not entirely, but enough.

"Really," she said. "I don't think I can express it any better."

"Why didn't you tell me?"

"Tell you?" She sounded indignant. "You're supposed to know. You're not a beginner."

"But I thought…"

"You thought what?"

"I thought…" I couldn't find a polite way to say she'd ripped me apart inside, casting me out in the night to fend for myself like a starving pup. "Never mind," I said. "Doesn't matter what I thought. The message didn't get through."

She poked me in the chest with her finger. Her voice took on a more menacing tone as she said, "Let's make no mistake, this time. Maybe you fucked up, or maybe I fucked up. Most likely, we both fucked it all up. But get this, and don't misunderstand! Okay?"

I nodded.

"I want you to take me home."

I hadn't anticipated her demand, but I'd hoped for it. The anxiety built up in me from her first kiss. My nerves blazed like tiny atom bombs. Now that she gave word, I kept cool as a Strawberry Daiquiri and twice as composed as one of Shakespeare's sonnets. "Who am I to deny a lady anything?" I said. "Where's your hotel?"

She broke out in a silly schoolgirl giggle. "Not my place," she said. "*Yours.*"

"That's an hour and a half away."

"Wonderful. If we leave now, we can be in bed in an hour and thirty-one."

"What about the band?"

"Fuck'em. I'll leave your number, and they can pick me up in a day or two."

"They won't mind?"

Her mild chuckles erupted into mad, sarcastic laughter. "They'll be glad to get rid of me. We've been cramped up in that van for too damned long." She turned and shouted a question at the drummer. "Justin, you won't mind if I take off for Pittsburgh for a couple days, will you?"

"Not at all. Take off!" Justin seemed too eager.

"You'll come and pick me up?"

"Sure we will," he replied. "Well, better ask B.J. It's his van, you know."

"B.J.?" said December.

The guitarist was hunched over an open guitar case shoving a candy-apple red Ibanez into its slot, while both of his other guitar cases, already full, formed a barrier around him. He looked at Dee when she called his name. "Get going," he said. "What the hell are you waiting for?"

"See. What'd I tell you? Of course, if you don't want me to come…?"

"Don't be naive, lover. I can't wait to get you alone."

"Yeah," she said, "but can you handle me for more than fifteen minutes? Can you handle me for more than one night?"

"I'll take whatever time you've got to spare."

"Good," she said. "But don't bet your life on controlling me, Collin. You won't admit it, but you're weak. Understand? Weak. With warmth you could wobble. With pressure you'd bend. With strength, I bet you'd break. And Collin Hearst, my aluminum love, with a gentle touch you could be molded into shape."

"Nice, but I'm used to wobbling, I can only bend so far, and nothing you can do will break me. As for that other stuff, taking your shot's all part of the game."

"Play time's over. I'm ready to go to war."

Naked and Bleeding

We were out in the night and on the road, flying drunk-speed into the abyss of a Pennsylvania interstate in the haunting a.m. Countryside sped around us, hazed over by a fresh dusting of light snow and accentuated by sporadic flickers of moonbeams slipping through the slow-moving clouds. On a slippery bridge-freezes-before-roadway night with alcohol and high speed, we easily could've wound up in a ditch or a creek or a self-consuming pile of our own blood and scrap metal. An errant deer strolling across the highway would've killed us. But we weren't concerned with fears. We had places to go and things to do. Special places. Important things. So, I hit the gas. Several times along the way, December placed her hand on my leg, stroking gently in circles and arousing me for a moment before pulling away and either stretching or playing with the buttons on my car radio in an unsuccessful attempt to find a better song than the one inevitably on. Once, she played the disc suspended in the stereo, but when she heard her own voice blasting through the speakers, she quickly pushed stop. "How can you listen to that crap?" she said.

I grinned and gave no reply.

Otherwise, we spoke little. Neither of us wanted to be the one to break the silence. I kept my eyes on the road ahead, and she kept hers on me.

Just before we crossed the Fort Pitt Bridge, she finally asked, "Are you involved?"

I knew what she meant, but I played with her. "Involved with what?"

"Involved," she said. "You know, in a relationship."

"Odd question at this time of night and under these circumstances. Does it matter?"

"It might."

"You're gambling with the moment."

"Yes, and you're avoiding the question. That makes me suspicious."

"Are you sure you want to know?"

"I'm sure."

"I only ask because if you're not sure, I'd hate to…"

"I'm sure! Now answer the damn question."

I grinned my usual devilish grin, though it might have been distorted by the numbness in my lips. "All right. Don't get all hot and bothered. The answer's *no*. I'm not *with* anyone. I haven't been *involved* for years. That's not to say I haven't been around."

She sighed, almost a commentary in itself. "Lonely not alone."

I smiled at her and said, "I think I like that."

How we ended up naked and bleeding in the closet with the door closed and piles of sweaters and coats burying us alive, I'm not entirely sure. I expected to have sex with her. I didn't expect her aggressiveness. It began as soon as I turned the key.

Now opening doors, like making love, can be handled many different ways. One can finesse the key, caressing it, stroking it, using a delicate touch to hear the gasp as the lock comes to climax with a click, or one can simply penetrate, do the act, and withdraw hastily, impatiently, more concerned with the goal than the getting there. I've been known to open my door in both ways and many others, depending on my state of mind and the circumstances. I had no real preference. December did. She preferred the rape of the lock, assailing me from behind and shoving me through the door which found itself opened by a forceful twist of the key. I fell inward onto the living-room floor, suffering the first stings of scrapes and carpet burns. Dee fell on top of me, but she picked herself up. Yanking the key from the lock too late for classic *coitus interruptus*, she dropped my key ring on the floor and slammed the door with a hammering crack that would've woke my neighbors were they not college students and likely still partying.

"Take it easy," I calmed as I lifted myself from the carpet.

But she was having none of that. Grabbing me by the breast of my trench coat, she rushed me backward into the living room until I lost my footing and toppled over like an old oak tree snapped in half by lightning. My head smacked into a coffee table and I grunted in sudden agony. "It's just a little pain," she said as she straddled me and began to unbutton my coat. "Pain and pleasure are Yin and Yang, always in perfect balance. The greater the pain, the greater the pleasure." As if to prove this, she bent over and kissed me, digging her jagged canines into my lower lip.

"Fuck," I cried out, but she muffled my shout by covering my mouth with hers. I felt her saliva dripping into my throat and across my tongue—an odd exchange of fluids.

Sitting up, she pulled off her parka and tossed it aside before she returned her attention to my winter wear. She finished with the buttons and pulled on both sides of the coat as I slid my arms from the sleeves. From there, it gets sort of hazy. The alternachick turned glam-rock goddess stripped herself slowly, making sure I witnessed every step in the unraveling. I tried to reciprocate, pulling at my tie, but she wouldn't allow it. Gripping my arms with a tiger-like fierceness, she dug her claws into my skin. The sudden stabbings sent me struggling to free my arms. After the initial surprise wore off, I followed her advice and refused to give in to the pain. Seeing my acceptance, she flashed me a sinister smile and let go, saying, "Do what you're told and nothing else. Don't act. Don't react. Don't resist. Don't even move unless I tell you to."

"Whatever you say," I agreed.

"Exactly." She bent down with tongue extended and licked the left side of my face, leaving behind a warm, wet trail to remind me. "You like that?" she said. Before I could reply, she stood up and walked away.

This is insane, I thought. *She's fucking with my head, throwing me off balance, acting crazy to see how I'll respond.* I laughed, somewhat maniacal but soft and subdued, too quiet for her to hear. *All right*, my mind pouted as I lay there alone, *she wants to play, I'll play.*

But my resolve was short-lived. I got tired of waiting, so I stood up and went looking for her. I found her in the kitchen in front of the refrigerator, now open, with the chilled air flowing across her bare flesh. Hunched down like some sort of wild animal, she was chewing on a slab of cold pizza left over from my midnight munchies God knows how many moons ago. She seemed to be enjoying it.

"Hungry?" I said, as I neared her from behind.

Startled, she dropped the pizza onto the floor and then hopped around to face me without leaving her crouch. After a moment's wariness, she lunged, propelling her shoulder into my chest as if she were a football hero making a tackle. All the wind went out of me, and I groaned as I flew back, crashing into the big, green wastebasket, knocking it over and sending soda cans, paper towels, and the remains of my last few meals scattering every which way across the floor. Both of us landed in the compost heap, sticky liquids and unknown lumps assaulting us from all sides, soaking my clothes and clinging to her skin. Normally, the idea of rolling around in a garbage pile would've revolted me, but being there—feeling, smelling, experiencing—added to my excitement.

Regaining the offensive, December straddled me and ripped open my shirt, sending severed buttons to the trash pile. "I told you not to move," she demanded, then bent down and kissed my chest, circling a nipple with her tongue.

I groaned and sighed and accepted everything she offered. Before long, all my clothes were scattered around the kitchen, nothing more than clutter added to the compost heap.

Dee led me back to the living room where we urgently commenced with the good stuff. We started out standing. With one skillful leap she wrapped her legs around my back and roughly forced me inside her. I lost my balance and almost fell backward one more time, but I found a wall and used it for support. "Tell me you love me," she demanded as she moved in a fervor.

"What?" I said.

She head-butted me in the chin, lacerating my lip and drawing blood. I groaned as my skull smacked against the wall, reaffirming my fresh bumps and bruises. That reaction had become redundant. Trying for something more original, I shouted, "What the fuck's the matter with you?"

She did it again, this time catching me below the right eye.

The entire side of my face went numb in anesthetic ecstasy. "Fuck!"

"Tell me you love me. I don't do this with men who don't love me."

"You're insane," I chided.

She lunged forward again, but this time, I jerked my head to the side at the last possible second, causing her to miss. Her action and my reaction finally forced us to give in to gravity and we toppled sideways onto the floor like bowling pins after a strike. Seizing the initiative, I rolled over on top of her, reestablishing our connection. She struggled, not resisting the penetration but merely my control. I grabbed her arms and pinned them to the floor above her head. And all the while she kept shouting, "Tell me you love me, damn you! You tell me you love me, you son of a bitch! You black-hearted son of a bitch!"

I leaned down to kiss her and she snapped at me, trying to bite off my face.

"Tell me you love me, motherfucker! I'll fucking kill you!"

Finally, I gave in and whispered the words. "*I love you.* All right? I love you." At the time, I wasn't sure if I meant it or not. "I love you, okay? I love you." I must have said it fifteen times.

Her body went limp. She stopped struggling, closed her eyes, sighed, and said, "Now, don't you feel better?" From then on, her form lifted to meet my every thrust. We went at it like that until we both died from pleasure, and then we lay beside each other, waiting to be reborn.

When we regained our composure and our breath, we began the ritual all over again—violent at first, then passionate, then peaceful. We destroyed every room in my apartment before somehow winding up entwined inside a dark closet with the door closed behind us. It's there that December decided to fall asleep. With my eyes adjusted to the dark, I watched her for as long as my pupils could focus before I, too, drifted off to the land of dreams.

CANTO THIRTEEN

Columnists Love a Scandal

I didn't stagger into the newsroom until one or one-thirty: three hours late. No big deal. No one came in early on weekends aside from Hunter Delaware, and he wouldn't blow the whistle.

"What in God's name happened to you? You look like death warmed over, kid, almost like you slept with an alligator. Get mugged? In a car wreck? Fall out of bed? What happened?"

"I got lucky," I explained, with a wave and a sigh.

"Oh, yeah. You look like it. Somebody asked me, *What's the matter with Collin Hearst?* I'd say, 'Can't you tell? He got lucky.' And you look like you got *real* lucky. What was her name, kid? Marylou Table Saw? Dolores Fan Blade? Christina Freight Train? You look like hell."

It was true. I'd showered, shaved, and cleaned up as best I could, hiding many of my major wounds beneath layers of winter clothing, but I couldn't hide the cuts and bruises on my face.

"Seriously," Hunter went on, "you've got to tell me about it. It's a federal law, I think. Freedom of Information Act, and all that. What's the scoop?"

"The scoop?" I said as I gingerly placed myself in a chair. "You writing a book?"

"Just curious. Don't leave me hanging, kid."

"I ran into an old friend," I explained, "and we became new friends. On the floor, on the bed, in the closet. What else can I say?"

"Looks more like old enemies to me. She fubarred your sorry ass."

"I enjoyed it. Sometimes you got to let go, fly off the high dive straight into the deep end, race headlong into madness without looking back. The closer you get to insanity, the more you realize just how sane you are. I thought I was already a basket case, Hunter, but this chick showed me I'm Mister Straitlaced by comparison. I act like a lunatic sometimes. She *is* one."

"You in love? Sounds like you're in love."

"Me? I don't think so. Could be, I guess, but I don't know. What's love? It's a label, a stereotype, something to get people pinned down into categories so we can judge them and scorn them if they stray. I'm not sure this fits. The things I'm feeling aren't definable, aren't capable of being classified. Am I in love? Maybe. Am I flipped out over this girl? You make the call."

Hunter broke into one of his long, chaotic laughs, sounding like a jolly old pirate with a fresh bottle of rum. "Kid," he said, "I find you more entertaining every time we speak. Don't change. No matter what happens to you, don't ever change."

Breaking into my classic Rural Slacker routine, I shrugged and whined, "*Que sera, sera.*"

Hunter finished his hardy laugh.

I tried to laugh too, but it hurt.

Changing topics, he said, "Well, I'm happy for you. I really am. You say you got lucky? That's great. With the story you wrote, you deserve it."

"Beg your pardon?"

"Your story. It was brilliant. You took a pompous, foul-mouthed, hillbilly most folks want to lynch, and damned if you didn't make him look almost sympathetic."

After a night with December, one story was the same as another to me, except for the story of our lovemaking. I'd forgotten Billy Ray Rose like a lousy song without a catchy chorus. "You know, this girl tore me up. She erased every thought from my head except the ones about her. I'm not sure I even remember writing that story. You say it came across well?"

"Came across? Kid, I've been here for less than an hour and I've already fielded a dozen calls, all but one of them positive. It's a masterpiece."

"Glad it went over okay. Did it make the *Life* front?"

Hunter's eyes squinted into ominous beads. He glared at me as if I'd just cursed his mother, kicked his dog or smoked his last cigar. "You haven't read the paper, have you?"

"I'm lucky I made it here at all. Of course I haven't read the paper."

He shook his head. "You better take a look before you do anything."

"Why? What's the deal?"

"Kid, you made the front page."

"The front page of the *Life* section?"

"You made the *front* page, A-one, lead-off batter, stripped across the top with a bold headline."

"That a joke, Hunter? Are you fucking with me?"

"It's not a joke. You made the lead atop the first page of the whole by-God newspaper."

"Can't be."

"It is."

"It *can't* be."

"I wouldn't lie to you, kid. Rick was pissed when you mixed that Cocktail last night. Arnie was busy and all the cubs were out on assignment, doing *your* stories as a matter of fact. So, Rick had to type in all the codes himself to get that story straightened out. He was purple with rage. But when he read your article, he almost fell out of his seat. He goddamned loved it. Showed it to me, and I loved it. Showed it to Arnie and Aggie, and they loved it. Then he showed it to Kathy, and I'll be horse-fucked if she didn't love it, too."

"I don't believe it," I said.

"Neither did I. She hates everything. But she told Rick to get it on the front page, and that's what he did. Plan was to stick it in the corner, cut it, and jump it to page two, but it didn't work out that way. The lead story on the school board meeting fell through, and the surprise session with the council petered out. Your scoop was a lifesaver. You wound up with the lead."

"I don't believe it," I said, reaffirming my position.

"You'll see. I wouldn't lie to you, unless you were a woman."

Hunter called it. My story made the front page of the expanded Sunday paper, stripped across the top beneath the banner headline, "Local celebrity confesses evil ways, repents."

The wily old columnist had also spoken true about reactions from the masses. I spent most of Sunday fielding calls from denizens of the 'Burgh expressing everything from joy to consternation about Billy Ray Rose. "It's great to see him overcome his problems," a lady said. "Country music should welcome him back to the fold," said a devoted fan. Another swore, "Listening to the radio hasn't been the same without him." And, "Buddy," said one more, "I got to tell you, he's the greatest thing this side of Johnny Horton." Of course, a few callers chided me just for mentioning Rose's name. "You're a disgrace," said one. "It's disgusting," said another. Some labeled *me* a racist for having my byline on the story. One guy accused me of "being part of the conspiracy to oppress black men in America." When I tried to explain that it wasn't true and that I wasn't even a fan of Billy Ray Rose, he swore at me: "You're part of the conspiracy, you son of a bitch. You and Rose and all your friends in the media." Not wanting to argue, I told him I hadn't heard of any such conspiracy, but I'd be more than happy to look into it. He replied, "You're a bastard," and slammed down his phone.

The call came shortly before five, near the end of my abbreviated work day. "Rowen Rousseau," the warm, friendly female voice informed me. "I'm a reporter for *Musicade Magazine.*"

"*Musicade?*" I said, dumbfounded.

"Familiar with it?"

"How could I not be? Music's my life."

"Good," she said. "So, you're a fan?"

"Not a fan," I said. "I cover the scene. A pro has to keep up with the goings on in his world. I read *Musicade* every two weeks, but it's a resource to me, the same as *Spin, Rolling Stone, Rap Sheet, Metal Edge,* or *Alternative Times.*"

"Good. Better to have your respect than your admiration."

"So tell me, Miz Rousseau, what can I do for you?"

"Please," she corrected, "it's Rowen."

"Groovy, Rowen. What's your angle?"

"What do you mean?"

"Your angle, your story."

"Mine's not important. It's your story that interests me. Your story on Billy Ray Rose."

"I guess I should've expected that. Folks have been playing phone tag with me all day. So, what do you want?"

She wavered a bit before answering, perhaps deciding what approach to take with me. She decided on the direct one. "How would you like to rewrite it for *Musicade?*"

"No joke?"

"No joke," she said.

"I could do that."

"Great. Listen, what time do you get off tonight?"

"Somewhere between six and seven. Depends on whether I get any work done or spend the evening staring at a blank screen and talking on the phone. Right now I'd say closer to six."

"That's perfect," she said. "I'm at the Rainbow Cafe. Meet me here when you're through." I noticed with all good humor that she didn't say "Will you meet me?" or "Can you meet me?" She was in charge. It was much the same way Rick or Kathy might give instructions: *Hearst, do this*, or *Collin, go down to the police station*, and sometimes even, *Collin Hearst get your ass over there or you'll be out of work in the morning!*

"Okay," I agreed. "You'll wait?"

"I'll be here. I'll have a cappuccino or two and maybe a piece of key lime pie. Don't rush yourself. Just show up as soon as you can." An interesting contradiction.

"What do you look like?"

"I'm a woman," she said, her tone as sarcastic as mine. "Are you familiar with women?"

"That's not what I meant."

"I know what you meant. Don't worry."

"Huh?"

"You won't overlook me, and I'll bet I can pick you out of a festival crowd."

"How do you know?"

"I know *people*. It's my job. Besides, even if I'm wrong, you'll be the only one wandering around the cafe with a displaced look on your face like you're searching for enlightenment in the cracks on the walls. One way or another, we'll hook up. Cool?"

"I hope you're right."

"I am," she said. "Accept it."

The Rainbow Cafe was a generic coffeehouse seemingly out of its element in an upper-class business zone in the North Hills. When I say generic, I refer to the cafe's grand design. In ages past, a coffeehouse was a place for aspiring artists to gather and brood over their works, a place poets and philosophers, painters and anarchists could be left alone. They hung out, sipped their coffees, and did their best to create. That is, when they weren't doing the same in the darkened corner of a shady bar. It wasn't the same these days. There were so many coffeehouses and so many would-be artists that one cafe became the same as another, and the artists too. It's as if the muses of the world got together and said, "We've got a good thing going here. Maybe we should start a franchise." Even the chaos seemed routine. Trying to write in one of these cafes was about as inspirational as it would be in a Burger King.

The Rainbow Cafe looked the same inside as any other artificial dive in any other town in America. There were two rows of red vinyl bar stools, a few tables scattered about and bolted down, and an assortment of terrible paintings on the walls, much like the ones that might be found in hotel bathrooms except that these most likely were painted by Rainbow patrons.

I found Rowen Rousseau sitting at a table by the far window, busy scribbling something into a miniature notebook. My first impression was that she looked about my age, though I soon guessed she was a couple years older. Her short hair, elegantly sculptured and straight, had been dyed a dark reddish orange. It hung just above her chin, accentuating pale skin and contrasting her bright blue eyes. She wore a black and blue pseudo-suit half trendy and half professional. At once, she seemed to stand out and fit in.

"Taking notes on my tardiness?" I joked as I approached. She looked up, startled, and let out a soft gasp. After glancing at her watch, she said, "Quarter of seven. You're not late." She didn't stand to greet me. Instead, she offered her left hand, which I shook rather awkwardly with mine. "Rowen Rousseau," she said, as if she hadn't introduced herself on the phone.

"Collin Hearst. Pleased to meet you."

"Pleasure's mine." As an afterthought, she added, "You're in bad shape. You look like a victim. What happened? Walk into a brick wall?"

I shrugged but said nothing.

Not pressing the matter, she motioned to the chair opposite hers. "Have a seat."

"Thanks." I sat down and flashed her a delicate smile. Slipping into my Friendly Inquisitor routine, I said, "What are you working on? Some big scoop us locals overlooked?"

She stared at me blankly before catching on. "Oh, you mean this?" She closed her tiny notebook and made a show of putting it into her black leather purse. "A poem to pass the time."

"Care if I read it?"

"Some other time. Today we have business."

"Okay," I said. "Tell me what you want."

The waitress, an energetic redhead in her late teens with rips and tears in her tee and jeans and a hole in her nose with a fat, gold ring, interrupted us. "Can I get you anything, honey?"

"Go ahead," said Rowen. "It's on my expense account."

"Thanks." Turning to the waitress, I said, "Orange cappuccino. No, make that a coffee."

"One orange coffee," she said, glancing at Rowen. "What about you? Need another?"

"No, I'm fine for now." She pointed at a row of mugs she'd pushed aside—three empty and a fourth half empty.

It was a wonder she didn't have the jitters. "I think I've had my fill."

"Back in a second," the waitress said.

"So, where were we?" Rowen asked.

"You were about to tell me what you're hoping for."

She might have figured that mistakenly for a come-on because she gave me a practiced, cynical glare designed to ward off predators. But she didn't hold the pose for long, mellowing and saying, "I'm *hoping* you'll write us a story. That's the long and short of it."

"How much copy and what's the deadline?"

"The next issue goes to press on Friday. We need it Wednesday at the latest."

"Short notice."

Rowen nodded. "How does five thousand words sound?"

"Sounds like a lot of words."

She grinned. "Seriously, can you do it?"

"I don't know. The story in today's paper was somewhere between twelve and sixteen inches. At a guess, that's maybe about six or seven hundred words tops. Not very long."

"Can you flesh it out? I worked for a daily and I know you don't use everything."

"True enough," I said. "Between surplus quotes and paraphrasing, I can expand the piece. But five thousand words? That's still a stretch."

"Add some background material, some history, maybe a few opinions if you have any."

"Opinions?"

"This is a rag, Collin. It's an infotainment zine, as they call us in the trade. We're not bound by the same standards of objectivity. As long as you're honest and don't libel anyone, you can say whatever you please. Point is, you can put more of yourself in *if you want*."

"That's a different approach from what I'm used to."

"Yes, but can you do it? That's what's important. Can you take a few hundred words and expand them into five thousand?"

I considered the offer during a long silence that burdened the air like dread in a dentist's waiting room. Finally, I said those famous words: "Why not?"

"Wonderful," she said. "My editors'll be pleased."

"I think I can embellish it enough, put some of my personality into it."

"That's fine."

The waitress brought me my coffee. "Here you go, Honey. Be anything else?"

"No," Rowen and I sang in unison, driving off the teen.

I sipped my coffee, laughing to myself.

"What's the matter?"

"It's cold," I said.

"That's why I never get coffee. Espresso's made fresh. Coffee sits around for hours until some sucker comes in for a fix."

"I work in a newsroom. I'm used to bad coffee. I just expected something more."

"That's the way it goes," she said.

I nodded. "So anyway, how did you pick me? I mean, why are you even here?"

"I'm on vacation," she informed me.

"In Pittsburgh? In the middle of winter?"

Defensively, she countered, "Hey, I've got family in Pittsburgh, and I'll take my time off whenever I can get it."

"Sorry. Wasn't being critical. That just surprised me."

"No problem. Well, here's what happened. After I saw your story in the *Domestic-Chronicle* this morning, I phoned my editor and read him the clip. I believe his exact words were, 'Fuck me *gloriously!*' He says that a lot, so don't get too cocky. Anyway, he told me to sign you up."

"Unbelievable. You'll have to forgive me. I'm still absorbing all this. To me it's just a story. I knew it was a good piece, but I would've been satisfied if it made the *Life* front. When I came in this morning and saw it made the lead, I almost passed out from shock. Since then, I've taken calls from deranged hillbillies with their 'Hey, buddy. Hey, buddy,' all wanting to know where they can buy that new CD, or from vigilante minorities threatening to hang me upside-down. Then you come along, and all of a sudden this story gets even bigger. Blows my mind."

She laughed, though I couldn't see the humor.

"What's funny?"

She gave me a wicked, mischievous grin. "You haven't even asked about the money."

"Money?"

"You do get paid, you know. For freelancers, it's twenty cents a word."

"Twenty cents a word? For five thousand words that's…"

"You got it. Ten bills, a grand, a single K."

"That's a lot of money."

"*Musicade* has a circulation of over three million. Our rag appeals to an eclectic population from rappers and rockers to twangers and composers. If it involves music, we cover it. So, try to imagine the rates that we charge for advertising."

"Must be phenomenal. All the same, a thousand dollars for one story?"

"Not as much as *Playboy*," she countered.

"Still outstanding. How much do *you* make?"

She groaned. "Not a lot. Freelancers get the hefty fees. Staffers get the shaft."

"Really?"

"We're on salary. It's a good salary, better than straight news, but not like freelancing."

"Wild," I said.

"I can live with it. Can you?"

"No problem."

Rowen fished around in her purse for a moment before pulling out a neon orange business card. She scribbled something on the back. "Here you go," she said. I took the card. *"Musicade Magazine,"* it read above a drawing of two electric guitars crossed like swords on a coat of arms or the bones on a pirate's flag, "a festival of sounds and celebrities." Below the icon in small letters were Rowen's name and three numbers: phone, fax, and e-mail. I turned the card over to see what she'd written. *"Notice of agreement regarding Rose story, 20 cents per word, approx. 5,000 words, if by Wednesday, Jan. 11."* Below that, she had signed it, "R. Rousseau." At the bottom, she'd written a fourth number for a local phone. "That'll stand up in court if you're worried about getting the check. At least, that's what the lawyers tell me. You're only under a verbal obligation, however. If you decide to back out or don't get the story to us by Wednesday at midnight, the deal's off. No harm done."

"Got it."

"If you finish by six o'clock Tuesday, call me at the number on the back. I've got an eight o'clock flight back to Jersey. If you miss me, you can fax it or e-mail it or read it off over the phone. Just make sure you identify yourself so your story doesn't get shelved. Clear?"

"Crystal."

"Good. If I don't hear from you by six on Tuesday, I'll tell Craig to keep an eye out."

"Craig. That would be Craig…?"

"The editor, Craig Kennebrew. He's a good guy. If you miss me, he'll take care of you. Well, is there anything I left out, anything you're concerned about?"

"I don't think so."

"Then I'll see you tomorrow or the next day. Until then…" Without standing up, she held out her left hand. "…take care of yourself and write a story that kills."

CANTO FOURTEEN

Music Soothes the Savaged Beast

I struggled inside like an amateur musician stepping on stage for the first time. Skin and clothing were soaked with sweat. Heart skipped in unsteady hopscotch rhythms. Muscles tensed, screamed for release as in the fatal moments before orgasm. White-knuckled fists clenched tightly on the steering wheel. I drove at random, feeling nearly mad from prosperity.

Times like that, only one thing calms me. That RX is the same euphoric drug I take for pleasure and to block out needless pain. Music soothes me, saves me, saturates my skin with ease. But it has to be *new* music. While I have no problem listening to catchy hooks and commercial tunes I've heard a hundred thousand times, it's the first time hearing newer music by a newer band that mesmerizes me with the singer's voice, a melody line, or shrill sounds of licks on guitar. The first few times I listen to an album, every song sops up my emotions like a sponge. I become part of the song: a drum beat, strummed chord, stinging assault in falsetto. Then I drift into the cosmos, bonding also with the stars.

After, when I come back down, I've crushed a burden. I've broken the bonds that hold the hurt inside. I believe it was Unamuno who said we only know we exist when we suffer. Or maybe it was Pearl Jam. But Unamuno also points out that the opposite's also true: we forget ourselves when we enjoy ourselves, we get lost in the moment, released from thoughts of our existence. That's the way it is for me. I forget I'm alive and live.

I pulled into the parking lot at Shangri-La Records and I could already feel tranquility coming on. Shangri-La Records was a sort of counterculture music mart where one could choose from the classics and the obscure, as well as the new and experimental. Also, one might delve into other realms of happiness. Part of the store was a pseudo head shop. Hidden by black curtains in a small area in back, shadows grew fat under minimalist lighting from a pair of purple lava lamps. There rows and rows of pipes, hookahs, brass bats, and Buddha-shaped bongs were sold legally as *tobacco* equipment. Shangri-La was a perfect little paradise for revelers.

The store was owned and operated by four neo-hippie sisters who ranged in age from twenty-three to thirty-eight. Ages aside, the four could've been identical twins. They shared the same long, straight red hair, the same average features and plain, unadulterated looks. It was a rare occasion when any of them could be seen without a tie-dyed shirt or skirt or dress or hat or at least some swirling sunspot-stained fragment adorning her pale skin. They were the friendliest chicks, too. They loved all their customers and showed no scorn for anybody, however rude.

Ember and Leela, the two youngest sisters, were working the store Sunday when I got there. It was almost eight, half an hour past closing time. Even so, I knew they'd let me in.

"Collin!" said Ember with a soft, friendly hug. "Good to see you. It's been…what?"

"Maybe a week," I replied.

"Oh. Well, it seems like forever. What are you after tonight?"

"Not sure. I need a quick fix, but I can't decide on a remedy. What would you prescribe?"

She and her sisters knew me too well. They understood my eccentricities and my love for music. When I came looking for something new and hip, they always had an answer. Ember thought about it for a moment, then took me by the hand and led me across the store to where her sister was sorting through play copies of new CDs. "Leela," she said, "put Phlat Top on for Collin. If he doesn't like that, try Doldrum or the Kinetic Cadavers."

Leela smiled at her sister, then me. "Hi, Collin. How you doing?"

"Fantastic. I've got a piece to work on for some big bucks."

"Wonderful," she said, fumbling with the in-store stereo system. "What's it about?"

"Billy Ray Rose, the death of a redneck."

She giggled playfully.

Ember said, "I saw your story on him today. It was touching."

Touching? That was one word I hadn't expected. Still, these ladies could see the good sides of all kinds of lowlifes. Being in the music business themselves, although vicariously as store owners, they were well aware of Rose and his struggles. "Thanks for the kind words."

Ember shrugged as if to ask what other kinds of words there were.

About that time, Leela had the first disc ready. "Here goes," she said, cranking the volume as track one of the new Phlat Top disc began to rumble through the speakers. "This is great," she shouted over the heavy bass and booming drum machine rhythms, jazzy saxophones and clarinets adding color in the background. "It's vibrant, upbeat, turbulent! You'll love it!"

I didn't. It wasn't mixed particularly well, and I could barely hear Phlat Top rapping and ranting in the background, followed by a kind of trite chorus:

Living in the suburbs, da ta da,
living in the suburb-burb-burbs,
with my baby in the suburbs, my my,
living in the suburb-burb-burbs.

It wasn't the vibe I wanted. I waved at Leela to turn it down. "What else you got?"

"Heard the Cadavers?"

"Yeah. Their label sent me a copy. Might be playing in town next month."

"What did you think?" Ember asked.

"Honestly? I thought it was slightly better than a load of crap."

"It grows on you," said Leela.

Her sister added, "That's true. I didn't care for it at first."

"Well," I said in deference, "maybe I'll listen to it again. As for now, what's new?"

"Put Doldrum on," said Ember.

"Okay," her sister agreed.

"You'll love Doldrum."

"Doldrum?" I said with a touch of sarcasm. "Sounds depressing. I don't know if I need that kind of groove. I'm already in the doldrums."

"It's not," Leela said. "Or maybe it is. It's like Pink Floyd. Do you like Pink Floyd?"

"*Love* Floyd."

"Then you'll love this. Give it a listen." She switched discs and pushed play. The next thing I knew, the store filled up with slow, soft, jazzy, acid-trip guitar sounds fluttering down from imaginary clouds and leaving rainbows in their wake. The atmosphere was charged with energy that danced a waltz up and down my spine, buzzing through tense muscles and frayed nerves. The melodies seduced me, enticed me to seek them in the empty air. I tried, but soon as I caught a glimpse of one, reality would shift, leaving me struggling to see another note. Even before the enchantress began her subtle incantation, I knew I'd found my disc. Then, when that voice drifted in on a wisp of wind, the room vanished, the sisters disappeared, and I lost myself as well each time I blinked. I felt nothing, saw nothing, knew nothing except that voice within the song. Another minute and I might have been gone for good.

Silence! Loud and as frightening as my heartbeat.

I felt sensation returning to my fingers, hands, arms. Consciousness came back slowly, wanting to hold out a little longer, to stay with the singer and the song.

"What do you think?" said Ember.

If I'd tried to explain what I thought, it would've taken all night. I said, "I'll take it."

Her Vulnerable Side

By the time I pulled into the parking lot behind my apartment complex, all my nervous excitement had filtered down into a soothing calm. If anyone saw me there sitting, shedding my concerns like static on an old sweater, while sweet music poured its honeydew through my car, my skin, my skull, they'd probably swear my eyes began to glow.

It was almost ten when I closed the door behind me, finally back in my apartment. Every light was on, but there were no signs of activity. The stale air carried an intimidating silence. I thought I was alone, that my goddess got bored and went to find herself another mortal. It wouldn't have surprised me. I'd left her there all day. So, I wouldn't have blamed her.

She hadn't left, however.

I found her asleep, lying face down on the bed. She was naked, and her pale skin seemed haloed by the glow from the overhead light. Her legs, buttocks, back—they accepted their aura, reveled in it. Her hair sparkled too, looking damp. She must have just taken a shower, washing away the glitter make-up and blood. I'd never seen her so vulnerable, so exposed, pure, innocent. Her facade had faltered and dripped down the drain with the water, silver and soap bubbles. She could've been a virgin bride on the eve of her nuptials or an overprotected princess pampered by servants but hidden away unaware of the sins indulged by impetuous lovers.

I needed to touch her, caress her, satisfy my fingers with a dance on her skin. After kicking off my loafers and draping my coat over a desk chair, I slipped into bed beside her, careful not to jar the mattress and awaken her with a shock. I wanted to do it right, to ease her back from sleep with a gentle touch. "You're beautiful," I whispered, "like sunlight through stained glass." With the care used to capture a butterfly but not damage its wings, I swept my hand down her back.

"Mmm," she sighed, awakening. Or pretending to awaken—I couldn't tell which. "Where've you been?" she said warmly as if talking to her dream lover. "I missed you."

I responded with kisses to her back, shoulders, neck.

With each kiss, she arched her body to meet my lips, and soon she was resting on her right side. "That's nice," she whispered. "Oooh."

Her damp hair brushed against my cheek as I climbed to her left ear. I pulled the strands back with my right hand, allowing my lips to continue their advance. My left hand eased around her waist, gliding up across her abdomen until it caressed a tender breast, teasing the nipple. She exhaled with a lingering gasp. December was almost a changed woman as she responded to my strokes. She seemed more the domestic kitten eager for my touch than the fierce, aggressive tigress from the night before, the one who'd hunted me, raging with intensity and carnivorous lust. While I'd enjoyed the beast, the purring pet excited me all the more.

Slipping into my Ethereal Don Juan routine, I whispered into her ear, "To look at you is to succumb to all my weaknesses, to forsake rationality, to cease to exist until your touch summons me back." I smiled to think that I gave her the same weight in my life as music.

Dee didn't open her eyes throughout. Guided by instinct, she tilted and twisted her head until her lips found a match. Then her mouth sang to mine, and I loved her songs as always.

"I tremble at the sight of you, December."

"You're afraid?" she said.

"Only of rejection."

She reached behind her, caressing my knee, thigh, groin. "Why would I reject you?"

"For the sunlight," I said.

"Why sunlight?"

"Because every dream dies at dawn."

Reaching my zipper, she opened it up. The next thing I knew, her cold fingers were inside my pants, working their way through the flap of my black cotton briefs. "If that's the case," she said, "then let's enjoy the night." My emotions came to life in her hand.

An instant later, I was inside her, probing with slow, deliberate thrusts. Working my right arm under her in the groove between head and shoulder, I kept a firm embrace, pulling her tightly, her naked back pressing against my clothed chest. There was no rush tonight, nor rage.

"Enchanter," she said, referring I think to me, although I was the one enchanted. It didn't matter. We accepted whatever magic passed between us. With something less than sleight of hand, I massaged her breasts, each in turn, and then my hand went lower.

I said something to her then—something she wanted to hear—but I can't quite recall what it was.

"I've never been loved like that," she told me, lying in my embrace. "So hushed, restful."

"It's only fair. I've never seen it so maddening like last night."

"We've traded our extremes," she said.

"When you live for extremes, what else have you got to trade?"

She shrugged. I felt it more than saw it.

Slipping into my Good Husband routine, I tried to reassure her. "It doesn't matter. The important thing is that we experienced the moment and let it happen." I ran my fingers through her hair. "No point worrying. Take what comes. May be good or bad, but it won't be stale and lifeless. Why glitter when you can glow? You know? You and I keep glowing. Sure, we've had our glitches, but even those radiate crazy flames the same as you and all your passion."

She mumbled something in reply—something I wanted to hear—but I can't recall what that was either.

Part Three

Disharmonious Coda

CANTO FIFTEEN

Cacoethes

… an insatiable desire. That comes from the Greek word '*kakoethes*,' or wickedness. From the most talented artists to the vilest of suicides, folks who live for the extremes are led by their cacoethes. They follow it down whatever shady path it takes. It might be a form of madness, but this cacoethes is also a sort of consuming addiction like heroin. It nudges a person forward, controlling his life, and if he tries to come down, to break free, it just digs its claws in deeper until he cries 'Uncle!' or just plain cries. There's no point resisting. Best to just relax and follow the madness wherever its crooked grin leads.

For two years, I'd been playing kiss and tell with my cacoethes. It was leading me in strange directions, guiding me to heavens and hells, and I was happy. My work was play, and I looked at my playtime as a job, getting down to the dirty work of being human.

Monday would be *all* work, I swore. I needed to write my article for *Musicade*. It was such a long piece with such a close deadline. I didn't know if I could do it, even though I'd promised I could. The first hint of sunlight peeked in around bare blinds shortly after seven, waking me. I knew it was going to be a beautiful day. I could sense it, feel it, create it in my mind. December slept beside me—face flushed, hair in tangles, eyes sealed shut. I didn't disturb her. Easing from bed, I collected my laptop and notes from my desk and went into the other room to write.

Sitting lazily on the sofa with my computer on my lap, I typed, "Some songs never fade, though the lyrics may change with time." I don't know how often I've said that—far too much, no doubt—but I couldn't think of a better time to use it. From there, the story blossomed into a field of flowery phrases. I typed one sentence after another, not worrying about anything except the rhythm of my tap-tap-tapping. An hour passed before I even paused to check my notes or reflect on what I'd written.

Though Rose's story originally had been nothing to me but words on paper, this time it had a life of its own. I believe it was Hegel who wrote that nothing great's accomplished without great passion. This story came from such a passion, and it had a great potential. So I set out to make it into a great thing. And it was dear old Camus who said all great things are rooted in the absurd. Considering my subject, Camus and Hegel both would agree I was right on track.

December woke just before noon. She stumbled into the living room and dropped herself beside me. Even as the sofa shook, I refused to be distracted. My fingers continued to dance on the keys like star-crossed lovers unwilling to let the moment end. "Morning," she said.

"Morning," I said.

"That a big story?"

I told her to hold on.

She sighed and slumped back on the sofa.

I finished a sentence, then two, then a complete paragraph, and finally a full page before I saved the file on a floppy disk and took a break. Looking at Dee, I saw she was still naked. A ravishing sight. Her body would be a dream to most, while others would plunge knives into backs for a look. "Sorry," I said. "Didn't mean to be rude."

"No big deal." She faced me, connecting our eyes with glue. I felt my skin warming, and just then I wanted to lean over and kiss her less like a lover and more like someone in love. Before I could, she said, "What're you working on? Something important?"

Breaking the bond, I looked away. "A money piece. It's for *Musicade*."

"You're not serious?" I turned back to find her staring, eyes wide and mouth agape, as if I'd just told her I was married or HIV positive.

"It's true. The big M. I spoke to this chick yesterday. She works for *Musicade* as a writer or editor, I don't really know what. She wanted me to expand on a story I'd written, to come up with five thousand words in the next day or two. It's a great gig. It'll really bring in the bucks."

She groaned.

"You don't like *Musicade*?"

She groaned again and then laughed at me, harsh and critical. "To say I don't like *Musicade* is like saying right-to-lifers don't like abortion. It's not that I don't *like* that worthless rag. I *despise* it. Damned bunch of pretentious posers." She made a fist and slammed it hard on the sofa. "Do you read that rag?"

"Sure. I have to stay up to date."

"Then you're familiar with the column called *Open Mic*?"

"Yeah. They review discs from independent labels. You send your tape, and they treat it like the rest of the magazine treats pros." Hearing myself say that, I knew what was coming.

"Did you happen to see the review on our album back in August?"

I shook my head. "I can't say that I did."

"That's the whole point. Nobody did. We sent those sorry sacks of shit a copy fresh off the line, and they gave us the shaft."

"No review?"

"Oh, they gave us a review, all right. Two short sentences hidden on a jump page: *'Cancer Moon, just another alternative folk band. You've heard this one before.'*"

"I guess I can see why you're upset."

"I prefer *'bitter.'* Just hearing you mention that rag makes me want to vomit."

"Sorry," I said, sighing. "I've got to do the story, though. It's money."

She put her naked arm around me and leaned over, resting her head on my shoulder. "I didn't mean that," she said. "A job's a job. Hell, I know that well enough. We've played everything from gay bars to high school proms. You got to take your paycheck where you get it. You go ahead. Collect your money and do your story. Just don't be offended if I never read it."

I kissed the top of her head. "Don't worry. I wouldn't want you to anyway."

"What's it about?"

"A country singer named Billy Ray Rose."

"*That* prick? Why him?"

I had to think about that before responding. The truth was, I didn't know. "Dee, it's hard to understand. As near as I can figure, famous and infamous are practically the same word. He's a celebrity, even if most of America wants him lynched. He made it big, and people saw that side of him until they got tired of it. Then he showed the shadows of his psyche, and he fell. For a while, folks wanted to read about that until they got tired of it and him. Now he's in recovery, or so he says. He's reassessing himself and trying to reform. It's a sob story, and folks love a good sob story, even when the main character doesn't merit tears."

"So it's a fluff piece?" she said, cutting through the bullshit.

"Well…I never thought of it like that."

"Amazing," she said. Returning to an upright position, she looked away, staring distractedly out the window. "They give us two biting lines and *that* hick five thousand words of redemption. Wasn't he the one who said women should be swapped like bubblegum cards?"

I broke into an uncontrollable laugh, roaring until I couldn't breathe. My outburst ended with a flushed face and a few last gasps. "I hadn't heard that one. Wouldn't doubt it a bit. It's not out of character. I did hear him say he only slapped girls he didn't love."

"Oh, fuck me," she exclaimed.

"He would if you'd let him."

"I don't think so. I do have standards, believe it or not."

I took that playful jab in stride and responded, "Yeah, but I doubt *he* does."

She flashed a wry smile and said, "That's it. I'm out of here." She motioned forward with mock sincerity, implying she'd get up and leave in retaliation.

I grabbed her and pulled her naked body toward me. "You're not going anywhere," I said. "Now give me a kiss and I'll make you famous."

"How about infamous?" she joked, keeping her lips a few inches from mine. "Then you could do a fluff piece on me, too."

"You want fluff? I'll give you fluff. I'll give you all the fluff you can handle."

"Grrrr," she said in her best tigress voice. "Was that a come-on?"

I ran a hand through her tangled hair. "We passed the come-on stage a couple days ago. Now it's more like come back and do it all again."

An hour later, I was back at work while December showered. My thoughts weren't flowing so freely now. I couldn't seem to concentrate. After every sentence or two, I
drifted off into a trance, waking from a daydream moments later to find myself staring blankly at the ceiling or out
the window or at nothing in particular. The words just
didn't want to come. I tried to slip into my Pulitzer Prize
Winner routine, but it didn't help. Neither did my Careful
Observer or Eloquent Poet routines. Even my Tired Old
Hack routine failed to set my mind to work or my fingers
tapping out the words. The muse had forsaken me for the
moment. Most likely, she'd gone out for a burger and fries
or chocolate malt. Even muses deserve an hour off for
lunch.

I'd written less than a paragraph when Dee came
back. She was wearing my old Grateful Dead tie-dye and
some black sweats. "Well, well," I said with a grin. "Looks
like you've been raiding my drawers."

"What'd you expect, lover? My clothes smell like two-
day-old cigarette smoke and fermented sweat. It was steal
your clothes or keep cold."

"And naked," I said. "I liked that."

She laughed. "Not all the time. Right now, I've got
other needs."

"What kind?"

In a parallel motion, she ran both hands through her
soggy hair. It was more a gesture of frustration than sen-
suality. "I've been sober for more than a day and it sucks. I
feel like I'm being punished, only I didn't do anything
wrong. It hurts. Where do you keep your stash?"

"My stash?"

"The drugs, man. Your refrigerator's tapped out. No
booze, no beers, not even a bottle of wine. But you've got
to have something."

"Damn," I said, feeling like an imbecile. "I didn't
even think about it."

Her eyes widened. "You mean you *don't* have anything?"

"I'm not a buyer. It's rare that I go out looking, and rarer that I bring any home. The cats I know pass me what they've got. It's that communal spirit: share and share alike."

"You really don't?" Her voice was getting shaky.

"No," I said. "When I want to get high, I go out, find a friend, sponge a few hits, and then move on to the next friend. I do buy booze, but even there I get free drinks half the time. Still, I should've stocked up. I'm sorry. I forgot I was out."

"Fuck," she sighed. "Twenty-four hours is too much for me, Collin. I haven't been this straight this long since before I started the dancing gig. You've got to have something. Think."

"I don't," I said, but realized my error. "Wait. I might have half a joint. Just a butt, really."

"Where is it?"

"Check my closet. Look for a blue blazer. Right pocket. That's where I keep it if I've got any. There might be a butt in there. I don't remember smoking it, but it's hard to tell."

She was gone before I finished my last sentence. An instant later, I heard the scraping of metal coat hangers over an iron rod, squealing like cantankerous phantasms caught in an exorcism. When the shrill sound ceased, I called out, "Did you find anything?"

She came back holding a plastic baggy. Inside, I could see the inch-long remnants of a marijuana cigarette burned black on one end. "It's a start. You want to share?"

"I can't. I have to finish this."

"You're sure?"

I wavered a bit, then gave in. "Maybe one hit," I said. "Just one."

"Cool," she said, knowing I wouldn't say no to the second toke. She fumbled with the baggy until that small fragment fell out into her hand. Parts of it flaked off in her palm like dandruff, and I imagined the whole joint crumbling into dust like an old newspaper or a long-buried scroll discovered and brought out into the open air. "It looks like an antique."

"It's an heirloom," I rebutted. "Been passed down for generations. My great-great-great-grandpappy grew it on his plantation in the antebellum South. It's tradition for the eldest son to take a toke on his eighteenth birthday and then pass it on to his eldest son in turn. I want you to know, by smoking that joint you're breaking the chain, destroying a family custom."

"You sure you don't mind?" she cooed.

"Fuck it," I said. "I hate tradition."

"That's the spirit."

I saved my article, placed my computer on the floor, then went into the kitchen to find a lighter or a book of matches. The next thing I knew, December and I were floating on clouds, rolling around half-naked on the carpet, enjoying each other with our clothes on. We got lazy and lay on the floor with our heads resting on cushions from the sofa.

"You're better than any drug," I told her, holding her close at my side. "I mean it. You intoxicate me so much I don't want to stop breathing in your essence."

"You sound addicted," she said.

"Maybe I am."

We didn't say much after that. There was no need. We rested on the floor until our equilibrium returned. Then she left me and went off to do whatever.

Moving back to the sofa with my laptop, I went back to work. Well, I tried to work. The words still didn't come, though I couldn't blame the muse. Dope jaded my head with rainbows and fog. That's how it is with weed. You find your pot of gold and lose your way.

Dee returned, wearing her coat and a pair of my tennis shoes—about two sizes too big but still looking only half as absurd as if she'd put the platforms back on. "Come on," she said.

"Where to?"

"We need more drugs."

"I think I've had enough," I said, but she was having none of that.

"We need to get some stuff," she demanded.

"What kind of stuff?"

"I don't care. Whatever. This is your city. Who do you know?"

I laughed softly at the question. "It's not who I know," I said. "That's a junky's line. It's who knows me. And make no mistake, Dee, everybody knows me."

"Cocky, aren't you?"

"Not cocky. Just well-known."

Reaching down, she grabbed my arm to pull me to my feet. She tugged, sending a jolt through my shoulder. I stood up, careful to avoid further injury, using my other arm to slide my computer onto the sofa. "Prove it," she said. "Find a star maker to send us into orbit."

I nodded. "Why not? The story's coming slow just now. Maybe a break'll do me some good. Give me a minute to change clothes and we'll be on our way."

"Okay," she said. "Hurry." Despite the temporary placebo effect the wacky weed gave her, she was still fidgety with hunger. Her hands shook, her teeth chewed tenderly on her lower lip, and her eyes refused to focus on one spot for more than seconds. I don't think she was addicted to any particular substance. She needed *some*thing. She was hooked on being hooked.

I wanted to comfort her, perhaps to slip into my Good Doctor routine and reassure her while prying carefully about her cacoethes, but I didn't. That wouldn't solve anything. It might even offend her, push her away when I longed to have her close. The only comfort she needed came in a little plastic baggy filled with whatever precious plant matter she could find. She didn't want the Good Doctor. She wanted the Medicine Man. So, what else could I do? I accepted my responsibility and put on my Medicine Man routine. "I'll be quick. Don't worry."

Peabody Lucas was the only out-and-out "dealer" I'd ever bought from. Like I told Dee, I got most of my drugs for free from people like Mugwump. The few times I went looking, however, all roads led to *Sweetpea*. A dark-skinned man of mixed racial descent, he was in his late twenties, though his long, lanky form resembled that of an eighty-year-old. His skin clung to bones like a spandex dress to a girl's anorexic body. If you took the time, you probably could count every rib, muscle, tendon, vein, or artery. His eyes were bloodshot and surrounded by purple rings. His arms and legs wore many reddish-brown markings from a war with the needle. His fingers were stained yellow and orange, his lips scarred from burns.

Sweetpea dealt drugs just to satisfy his habit. He obviously didn't get rich from it. He lived in a modestly furnished one-room apartment on top of a Romeo's Pizza. The room had only a twin bed, bean bags, some cushions, and a short refrigerator, aside from several piles of clothes and assorted paraphernalia scattered about the floor. The bathroom could've been a closet.

I met Sweetpea a couple years back under different circumstances. He'd been healthier and more sociable, playing guitar for the reggae band Skaggadag. His group had a good sound. The band was going places. Skaggadag played to packed clubs, and the other members were talking about self-producing a compact disc. That was before Sweetpea's addictions got out of control, before he pawned his guitar for enough money to get himself a fix. By the time I took December to visit Sweetpea, Skaggadag was a year in the ground, and the band's former guitarist looked like he might be there soon himself.

"How you doing, Sweetpea?" I said, giving him a slow high-five.

"Tolerable," he replied. "That's the best I can hope for. How about you?"

"Going strong." Pointing to my companion, I added, "Sweetpea, this is December."

"*¿Que pasa?*" he said, in a lame attempt at Spanish.

"I'm alive. What's up with you?"

"About the same. That's the way I feel, too." He motioned for us to come in and take a seat on the bean bags.

We went inside but didn't sit. "Only got a minute," I said. "It's business."

"I figured," he whispered to me. "It's in her eyes."

I nodded. "So, what have you got for us?"

Sweetpea groaned a terrible gut-churning bellow. "It's a bad time," he said, which meant he had enough for his own needs. "Lousy month. I haven't seen my connections."

Laying down my Skilled Negotiator routine, I said, "No games, Sweetpea. We don't want your private stash. Just tell us what's for sale."

He rubbed briskly at his chin with thumb and forefinger, seeing a golden opportunity. A woman in need plus a man willing to do anything to fill that need equals good business. He knew it. I knew it. Dee knew it, though I doubt she cared. "I've got some C," he said.

"How much?" December said a little too eagerly.

He turned to search under dirty clothes. "Enough, but I got to warn you, it ain't very good."

"What's it cut with?" I asked.

"Sugar. Fact is, it's mostly sugar." Finding what he was looking for, he straightened up and turned back toward me holding a sandwich bag loaded with white powder.

"I'm allergic to sugar," he lied. I knew what he meant. His little cache was too diluted to do him any good.

December didn't give a shit. "What's your price?"

Sweetpea could hear the desire in her voice. Turning to her, he said, "Don't worry. I'll give you a fair number. I've had this batch and can't get rid of it at market value."

Maybe because it's not marketably valuable, I thought. "Is it that bad?"

"It's bad."

I shook my head. "I don't know, Sweetpea. How much do you want?"

"How about a hundred?" It had to be almost pure sugar. Looked like about three eight-balls in there. For Sweetpea to sell it for a hundred meant there was probably a little more than fifty dollars' worth of cocaine mixed with two or three grams of powdered sugar.

Still, coke wasn't my drug of choice. I'd sampled it once or twice. I didn't know if it would be any good at all that diluted. Leaning toward Dee, I whispered, "What do you think?"

She nodded vigorously as if screaming, *Take it, you son of a bitch!*

I knew where she stood, but I wasn't sure about Sweetpea. "I don't know," I said again. "If it's as bad as you say, it may not be worth ten."

December gave me a nudge in the back with her elbow. "Sounds like a good price to me."

"I don't know. I'll give you fifty, Sweetpea."

"You're breaking my heart," he said, and I'll wager Dee was thinking the same thing. Her slight nudge became a painful jab.

"Fifty?"

"Eighty," he said. "Just to get it out of here."

I was prepared to dicker a little more, but December wouldn't allow it. "We'll take it," she said, before I could open my mouth.

I glanced at her, Sweetpea, the drugs. "What the hell," I said, and reached for my wallet.

The rest of the day was a bust creatively. Instead of typing lines on my computer, I learned how to shape lines on a compact disc case and suck them into my nasal passages through a fragment of a drinking straw. Despite the low-grade product, Sweetpea's coke was more than enough for me. My inexperience with the drug made it more potent than it was for December.

Dee took two lines right away, and within ten minutes, she went back for another pair, followed by a group of three or four. It didn't matter. We had plenty. I wondered if Sweetpea might have underestimated his merchandise. Maybe the stuff sat around so long that he forgot how good it was or how much of it he had. Or perhaps he just needed the money to fill his own intense hunger. Whatever the case, Dee and I had plenty to satisfy ourselves.

We indulged our excess, not pausing for a second as we watched the day go by in a blur of numb faces and racing hearts. We did our drugs and made out on the couch before making love on the floor. When our energy levels lowered, we rested and then began again.

Somewhere along the way, we took a trip to Burger King for dinner, shoveling down burgers and fries like they were the last ones on the planet, pausing every now and then to talk about religion, politics, love, philosophy, and this and that nonspecific ritual topic, though I can't recall any of the comments we made. When we were through eating, it was home for more cocaine and more dancing naked throughout my apartment. Finally, too tired and spent to care anymore, we rested together on the bed or maybe the carpet, stroking each other's skin.

B.J. called before midnight. I didn't answer the phone, but I listened as he left a message on my machine telling Dee to be ready at six o'clock sharp on Tuesday. She cursed and groaned, and her mood took a downturn as she accepted the sad fact that she had to leave.

Unfortunately, I couldn't give her the night. I had to finish my story. December fell asleep at about a quarter past two, and that's when I staggered from bed and went into the living room to work. This time, I wouldn't be denied by muses or drugs. I sat with my laptop on my lap and the last trace of the day's excesses swirling in my head like a memory. My notes were beside me on the sofa, and I looked to them often, searching for good quotes and trying to fill in the story with Rose's words rather than mine. When that didn't work, I spoke my mind, trying not to be too harsh. To liven up the article I tossed in similes and metaphors wherever they fit, filling space with them. I kept finding words, whether Billy Ray's or mine.

Shortly after sunrise, I closed the piece with a quote from Rose, the same one I'd used to close the original story: "Don't know if I'll ever not be a bigot anymore. The best I can do is try not to offend folks, not to make 'em sad, and hope to somehow get past my roots." I punctuated the end, typed "—*30*—" at the bottom in the universal journalistic symbol that a story's over.

Looking at my watch, I saw it was almost eight o'clock. I was numb, tired, and in dire need of rest. So I slipped into my Weary Traveler routine and journeyed to the bedroom for some Zs.

CANTO SIXTEEN

She Edits the Story's Direction

I woke up after four in the evening. I was alone. Groaning, I threw myself out of bed like a weary soldier afraid to miss the final train from the front. If I wanted to catch Rowen before her flight, I had to be quick. Opening the closet door, I got down on my knees and rifled through my laundry basket, checking shirts and pants for Rowen's card. It was still in a pocket somewhere, but it wouldn't get away. Crumpled shirt, wrinkled pants, trench coat draped across the back of a chair—*Bingo!* There it was, wadded up with a chewing gum wrapper. I reached for the phone on my nightstand and dialed Rowen's extra number. After a few rings, a woman answered, though I couldn't tell if it was her. "May I speak with Rowen Rousseau, please?"

"*Collin,*" came the reply, "so good to hear from you." While I hadn't recognized her voice, she'd obviously recognized mine. "Have you finished the story?"

"It's done," I said. "When are you leaving?"

"My flight's at eight. You want to bring the story over?"

"Sure," I said. "Where are you?"

She gave me the address of a house in the North Hills, not far from the Rainbow Cafe.

"I'll be there," I said.

"The sooner the better."

I hung up and headed for the living room to get my laptop and print out the story. December was there, stretched out on the sofa and watching reruns of Battle of the Planets on TV. The cocaine baggy was on the coffee table beside her, open wide and more depleted than when I last saw it.

"Morning, Dee," I said.

"It's almost evening. Even I don't sleep this late."

I shrugged. "I was up all night working."

"You finished?"

"Yeah. Now I got to run it over to this chick before she splits town."

"Right now?"

"You want to come?"

"Can't. Got to wait on the band." She sounded depressed.

"Sorry, I forgot. What time?"

"Around six."

I looked at my watch. Quarter past four. "Shit," I said. "Sorry about that."

"It's no big deal," she said, but I could tell by her attitude that it was a big deal, and one not easily forgotten or forgiven. "It's been a blast." The inflection in her voice didn't share the sentiments of her words.

"Listen, I'll be quick."

"It's all right."

"No, really. I'll hurry. I just got to run this over and drop it off. I should be back before you leave, at least in time to say goodbye."

With an apathetic swipe of her arm, she waved me away. "If you make it, you make it. It's been a blast either way." With a smile, she added, "Just remember, next time have better drugs."

The promise of that mythical next time made me happy. "I'll keep that in mind." I wanted to go to her, to take her in my arms and kiss her until Armageddon, but I didn't. I was afraid. I knew there was a chance, however small, that she might reject me, retaliating for my rejection of her, my leaving her there before she could leave me. Instead, I let the conversation die.

Russell Rousseau, Rowen's brother, lived in a thoroughly modern embrace of failed eclecticism. His house looked like a sculpture. It was vaguely hexagonal, with large arrays of picture windows intermixed with clusters of bricks in different colors: reds, browns, grays. The roof looked like a castle's, with different segments, both square and conical, ascending to peaks in a random pattern. Someone had gone to a great deal of effort to design this house. It was exquisitely tasteless. I didn't get a chance to explain this to him, however. He wasn't home.

Rowen met me at the door, opening it and inviting me in before I had a chance to knock or push the buzzer. She was dressed in black, though more casually: Tragically Hip tee and loose cotton miniskirt covering bare legs. She smiled. "Glad you made it. Got the story?"

I held up the yellow envelope. "Right here."

"Excellent. Come in and have a seat while I take a look."

The front door led straight into the living room, with no hallway for a buffer zone. It was a semi-round chamber with pastel yellow shag carpeting covered up from wall to wall with expensive antique furniture—mind you, not the kind of antique furniture one might look at and say, "Where did you find this remarkable chair?" or "My God, what a beautiful totem pole you have there," but more the kind about which one might say, "Where did you get all this junk?"

There were statues and paintings, coffee tables covered with plastic sheets, and a dainty little sofa guaranteed to make Granny complain about her bad back. Off to the right was a spiral staircase that ascended into an opening in the ceiling. Having a picture of this house from without and within, I understood Russell like a book with a simple plot. He was one of those people who struggled so hard to be hip that he fell for every hipster's con, surrounding himself with absurdity. That, in turn, was what made him so uncool.

"Nice place," I lied.

Russell's sister was just the opposite: so calm and casual she'd be hip no matter how hard she tried to be dull. "Bullshit," she said, proving me right. "Even I don't like it, and I have a relatively open mind about these things."

"It is awkward looking."

"Russ got screwed. He just won't admit it."

"Where is your brother?" I pried.

"At the hospital. He's a surgeon."

"That explains it," I said.

"Maybe. But forget about him. We're short on time." She reached down and snagged the envelope out of my hand. "Sit down."

I did, dropping into the first chair I saw that didn't look like it would crumble under my weight. Rowen sat across from me in a fragile oak rocking chair. Opening the envelope, she removed my story and began to read it, scanning the pages and nodding after every few sentences or mumbling "Uh huh" or "Yeah" or "Hmm," and so on. I sat there watching like an eager lover waiting for a kind word. After a few minutes of this, she came to the end. "Very good. The editors should have no trouble running this. You seem to cover all the angles."

I sighed, relieved. "There aren't any problems?"

"Minor glitches here and there: word choices and split infinitives and such. But all that can be fixed easily enough by the staff. You've also got a lot of typos. Were you up all night?"

I nodded.

"Not a problem," she said. "It's good enough. The next issue's due out in about a week and a half. Look for it in there. You'll get your check in the mail shortly after."

"That's wonderful. Thanks for the opportunity. If you need anything else, don't hesitate to give me a call." I stood up, thinking our meeting adjourned.

Rowen had other plans. "What's your hurry?" she said.

I felt my face burning with embarrassment as I dropped back onto my seat. I was afraid I'd offended her. I didn't want to be rude. "Sorry," I said. "I thought we were finished."

"We are if you want to be," she said, and there was no mistaking her intent. "Stay for a while. Tell me about yourself. Can I get you a drink?"

My throat was dry as a desert wind, but I declined.

"So, tell me," she said, "what's *your* story?"

I wasn't sure what she wanted to know, so I told her about college, the newspaper, my love for music, and everything that led up to meeting Billy Ray Rose. She smiled at the points I found interesting and laughed at the lines I thought were funny, but she didn't interrupt. She just let me ramble on about this and that until I ran out of wind. When I wrapped up the synopsis, she touched her hands together in mock applause. She was playing me, toying with me.

I should've gotten up and left. It was my fault for staying, allowing her to trap me. But, I couldn't move. As a lover of all great cons, her scam intrigued me like a mystery novel. I couldn't forgive myself if I left too soon without waiting for the plot to unravel.

"That's a little more than I asked for," she said. "How about something more general?"

"Like what?"

"Do you have a girlfriend?"

I thought of December and the past few days. The memories sang Hosannas in my head. I heard her asking a similar question: Are you involved? I'd told her no. I wasn't involved. I didn't have a girlfriend. That was definitely the answer. This time, I wanted to say yes. Oh, how I wanted to. Then, when I opened my mouth to speak, I heard myself whispering, "No, I don't."

"A boyfriend, then?"

"No!"

Her eyes lit up, spitting fire at my feet. "Good," she said. "Let me show you the bedroom."

After twenty minutes of hurried intimacy, we were straightening ourselves up like two kids coming home from the playground, not wanting Mommy and Daddy to see the messes we made of ourselves. Though between us only a pair of black lace panties were removed, all our clothes were askew. My hair had developed a sort of multiple personality disorder, sticking up or out in different directions. Hers, however, retained a recognizable form. She was sweating and, were she wearing makeup, it would've run. The only additional color highlighting her face was the warm afterglow. She looked tired, weary, consumed. I could tell she'd rather rest for a while, perhaps with the two of us lying in her brother's king-sized bed as if we were longtime lovers instead of passing pleasure seekers. Even so, she didn't imply, didn't offer, didn't ask. "You're a mess," she said, running fingers through my hair to help me regain a facade of order.

"Don't I know it." I liked the feel of her hands in my hair. They moved with both the tenderness of a lover and the authority of a mother caring for her child.

Finishing up, she said, "Where's the rubber?"

"Trash can in the bathroom."

Without saying anything more, she turned and strolled off to find the dirty condom. She was only gone a moment. She returned holding a big wad of toilet paper with the loaded latex inside. "My brother's a bit of a prude," she explained, reaffirming my opinion that her bother stood no chance of ever being hip. Then she disappeared through a door on the opposite wall.

After a few seconds, I heard grinding gears downstairs, sounding like a can opener. I left the bedroom and walked down the staircase into the living room. Following the sound, I headed for the kitchen. Rowen was there, overseeing the operation of her brother's trash compactor. Seeing me, she said, "I buried it in the bottom. He'll never know."

"You and your brother are exact opposites," I said.

Rowen shrugged. "Our parents divorced when we were kids. I was five and Russ was ten. He went with Mom and I stayed with Dad."

"I see," I said, but not convincingly.

"Our parents were a couple of flower children. They were old hippies when we were born. And I'll bet you know the answer to this. What do old hippies become?"

"Yuppies," I said.

"Right. So, Mom became a yuppie and Dad, well, he just became an old hippie."

"I see," I said with more conviction.

When the machine had run its course, Rowen said, "There," as she switched it off. "That's that." She walked past me and I followed her like an obedient dog into the living room.

"Listen," I said. "I've got to be going."

She turned to me with that same clinical gaze she'd used to read my story and to study my face during sex. "Good," she said. "Can you give me a ride to the airport?"

It was almost eight before I made it home. Dee was long gone like a pleasant dream. I searched the apartment, looking for a note, but found none. She left neither metaphor nor message, not even a phone number where I could reach her. The only evidence she'd been there at all was a pile of my clothes on the bedroom floor and an empty plastic bag on the coffee table.

The moment had passed. She was out there and I was in here, and I knew nothing good would come from our separation.

Strange emotions assaulted my senses. I won't describe them because I refuse to believe in their existence. I wasn't prepared for guilt. I refused to accept remorse. Instead, I stretched out on the sofa with a forceful yawn. Slipping into my Coolest Cat on the Planet routine, I folded my arms behind my head, propped my feet on the arm of the couch, and stared up at the ceiling. Bleeding away my negative energy, I conjured up a smile.

Eventually, I drifted off to sleep.

CANTO SEVENTEEN

The next few months went by in a blur. I spent hours working or enjoying the shadowy parts of my job. I lived the life, but I wasn't living. A lot of familiar acts came through Pittsburgh in the late spring months: Metallica, Jimmy Page and Robert Plant, Nine Inch Nails, Cracker, Garbage, Ice Cube, Alice Cooper. I wrote their stories to keep busy, to defer thoughts of December until another day. Whatever I did, I felt this hollowness. It made my hands shake and my nerves twitch when I was alone. I felt the way I imagined I would at a friend's funeral, or after when the anxiety creeps in as the cemetery's bright green grass starts to fade in the rearview mirror. It wasn't so much that I mourned December. Her memory haunted me.

Everyone saw the change. On the street, if I ran into someone I knew, I nodded rather than saying, "Hello." In bars, I sat and stared at nothing. When I went from one club to the next to see another band, I felt apathetic. It wasn't Cancer Moon on stage, and it wasn't December teaching my ears to hear. Then, when bartenders that knew me offered their concoctions, I shook my head, saying, "Bring me an Absolut Screw." I even passed on a couple fiery flings. My friends at the newspaper noticed, too. Several asked about it, though only Hunter got me to open up. "What the hell's the matter with you?" he said, a playful inflection contradicting the forcefulness of his words. "You look like somebody sat on your favorite hat."

I didn't smile or laugh. I couldn't.

"Seriously, kid, you look like the poster boy for grim. What's wrong?" He paused before answering his own question. "It's a woman, isn't it? It's always a woman."

"You got it," I mumbled.

"Spit it out, kid. Give Uncle Hunter the gory details."

"Not much to tell. It's just a love that's lost, or maybe never was." I tried like hell to avoid the Chronically Self-pitying Loser routine, but it oozed from my pores, marking me with its stench.

"I understand. I've been there. It took me a score of trips before I fell down the right hole, and even in that one I hit bottom. Just got to climb back up and start again."

"Interesting theory, Hunter, but I'm not interested in theories."

Voice turning gentle, fatherly, he said, "Come on. Tell me about it."

I did. I gave it to him in exquisite detail: December, Bev, Rowen. He didn't seem to believe me at first, but when I finished I don't think he kept his doubts.

This story merited a cigar. I could see it in his eyes even before he reached for the pocket. Gnawing nervously on the end of a fat stogie, he said, "Forget what I told you, kid. You don't need to start again. You're falling in too many holes as it is. You just need to get old, like me. When you're my age, you won't be able to handle so much chaos in your life. For now, don't let it bother you. You'll figure out what to do. If it wasn't love, you'll forget her soon enough."

"What if it was?"

"If it was, then it is. You can't know that yet. It's too soon, and you're too emotional."

"Makes sense."

"Of course it does. Do you think I'd give you bad advice? Am I a professional or am I just a purveyor of useless tripe?"

"Well," I said, "according to the letters to the editor…"

Hunter took the cigar out of his mouth and raised it like a club to bash my head in. "See? You're making bad jokes. You're on your way to recovery."

Hunter might have been right. Still, I chose to ignore him. His advice seemed off the mark, though this is my fault. Looking back, I think I probably gave him inaccurate facts. I should've subtracted the word 'love,' perhaps replacing it with a word more appropriate like 'symbiosis.' She and I were symbiotic, sharing our bodies, emotions, thoughts, and hungers, feeding on them and growing stronger in each other's arms. We lived off each other's madness. Of course, I use the word 'we' because she shared the same sensations. When you remove a parasite, the parasite dies, but when you separate two organisms so intrinsically connected, both systems falter and fail. That's why I couldn't take Hunter's advice. I'd begun to falter.

In early June, tired of wallowing in my misery, I decided to catch up with December long enough for a quick fix. Day after day, I scanned the *Life* sections of every major newspaper the *Domestic-Chronicle* subscribed to: the *New York Times*, the *Washington Post*, the *Baltimore Sun* and twenty others. I searched for some hint that Cancer Moon might be passing through New York, Washington, Baltimore, even places as far away as Los Angeles, though I didn't know if I'd actually travel so far. I studied the pages, memorized them, hoping beyond hope that the band might play at some major arena or even a fly-by-night club.

I found nothing. Cancer Moon didn't have gigs in Philadelphia, Roanoke, Boston, Buffalo, Hartford, Annapolis, Indianapolis, or as far as I could tell, anywhere in between. Certainly the band didn't come back through Pittsburgh. I would've known about that immediately.

Aside from the papers, I read all the music mags and listened to college radio stations. I asked the four sisters at Shangri-La as if they were the wise old witches of myth. I kept my ears to the grapevine while hanging out in dives and joints and classier nightclubs. I tried to slip the band's name into every conversation, being as subtle as possible. "That reminds me of this band," I'd say, or "Have you ever heard of Cancer Moon?" Sometimes I'd say, "You guys sound like Cancer Moon," when interviewing an act passing through town. I recommended the band to everyone who liked music, whether rock, rap, or country. Each time, I studied the eyes and listened to the timbre of the voice, searching for reactions that might provide a clue.

Nothing.

It was as if the entire world had conspired to hide all traces of Cancer Moon. I found no leads. Not a word, not a thought, not a sign. Cancer Moon had vanished.

I felt like a performer in the theater of the absurd, with no point, no purpose, no meaning, and no structure. My existence staggered toward nihilism. My thoughts were futile. My hopes were futile. My search was futile. Most of all, I was futile—a ridiculous fragment of a ludicrous whole. But I didn't give up. I devoted every free minute to the quest.

Eventually, I figured out the problem. I'd been searching for answers somewhere in the future when I needed to return to the past. I had to go back to the start, where it all began. Mugwump knew the truth. Of all people, I should've asked him first.

It was an off night at Club Zero. Most of the college students, having finished their semester, were long gone on the summer party caravan to the beach or back home to visit family and find work. Only the locals remained to spend their cash at the Zero.

I was dressed in a faded orange tee and a pair of blue jeans, looking somewhat timeworn and weary, not my usual self. Even if I'd come dressed in my standard shirt and tie, however, I wouldn't have been recognized straight off. There was a new guy manning the door, a lanky older fellow with short platinum hair and a matching beard. I wasn't in the mood to lay my trip on this guy, so I paid the one-dollar cover and went inside.

Without the crowd and the blasting music, Club Zero looked almost like a museum—its black lights shining on twisted art and the shiny faux-marble floor. But the atmosphere had the feel of a funeral home when there's no funeral scheduled. The hustle and bustle of the respect-paying crowd isn't there, but the owners, undertakers, and employees still show their deeply sullen fronts, perhaps out of habit, but more likely out of a general sense of uneasiness that comes from being in a place of the dead when there are no dead in the place. Club Zero was like that. The staff and patrons were consumed by some macabre tranquility, a silence that wasn't supposed to be there.

Mugwump had that look about him, too. He sat at the bar with his feet locked tightly around one leg of a bar stool, his right hand stirring his drink with a straw, his left hand supporting his sagging head. Even his bright red Hawaiian shirt and Bermuda shorts didn't make him look the least bit cheerful. He seemed as depressed as I was.

I went to the bar and sat down on a stool beside him. "What's news?" I said.

He turned to me without a hint of a smile. "Hey, my friend." It came out as a tired sigh. "Not a thing. The whole world's going straight to hell in its average, every-day, boring old way."

"What's the matter?"

"It's the sunlight," he said.

"What do you mean?"

"A nightclub's dead in the sunlight," he said, "like a vampire. It melts into nothing. What's summer but several months of pure, undistorted sunlight?"

"Business is bad, I guess?"

He spat out a brief sarcastic laugh. "No business left to be bad. Now that school's out and all the kids have headed home, I'm sitting here watching my profits dry up."

I started to offer sympathy, but Cliff interrupted. "Hey, Collin, what'll it be tonight?"

"Absolut Screw." I reached into my jeans pocket and pulled out a five-dollar bill which I laid on the bar as my way of saying, *I understand your problem. Let me pay for my own tonight.*

Mugwump got the message, as did the bartender. Neither said a word.

"Keep it," I told Cliff. With no business, he had to be hurting, too.

"Thanks, man," he said, taking the money and walking away.

Getting back to Mugwump, I tried to cheer him up. "Don't worry," I told him. "Summer classes start in a couple weeks. The crowds are bound to pick up."

"Hope so. Goes like this too long, Club Zero could turn into Club Negative Balance."

"That sounds like a pretty cool name for an alternative bar."

"You may be right," he replied, "but what about Club Bankruptcy?"

I shook my head. "Sounds like a club for lousy lawyers and accountants."

"They tip well," Cliff interjected as he returned with my drink, and the three of us laughed long and hard, putting the solemn atmosphere to rest.

Raising my Styrofoam cup, I said, "Here's to lawyers and accountants." I slammed three quarters of the drink in one gulp before taking a deep breath and finishing it off.

In the same motion, without a moment's pause, I lifted my empty vessel toward the bartender as if to say, *Hey, Mister, why'd you go and give me this empty cup?*

Grinning, he said, "Thirsty?"

"Friend, there's a thirst in me that may never be quenched, a hole that may never be filled, a dry spot in my throat that no liquid has ever managed to reach." The statement was meant to be funny, but it came out dark and brooding. The ominous undertones tried to drag us down again.

Mugwump stopped staring at his drink and downed it. "Give me another, too," he said.

Cliff picked up both cups after a mock curtsy. "Damned bunch of alcoholics," he said, with a half laugh. "God love you."

By the time I emptied my fourth cup, the severe illness afflicting Mugwump's smile had eased. Tapping me on the arm with the back of his hand, he pointed to a pair of twenty-somethings who'd just walked in. "Hey, bottom fish," he said, "check out those two."

I glanced toward them and confirmed his description with a nod. Each looked beautiful in her own way. One was a bit heavy, but she masked it with dark clothes that blurred her form and forced the eyes to linger on her face, which was a study in symmetry. The other girl was a sculptured statue of an Amazon with an average face to match.

The ladies, apparently staring back, must have misinterpreted the nod. Both responded—one with a nod of her own, the other with a dainty wave. The Amazon pursed her lips in a mock kiss. I wondered what they thought of us—two goofs in colorful clothes.

"What do you say we go and check them out?" said Mugwump.

"I don't think I'm up for it tonight."

He sighed and slumped back into his previous pose, resigned and defeated.

"Really, I just want to sit here and lose all touch with consciousness."

Mugwump's emotional pendulum swung back to the good. "Hey, want to get fucked up?"

"Yeah, that's what I'm thinking."

"Why didn't you say so? Collin, my man, upstairs in my apartment I've got some of the best skunk you ever inhaled. Interested?"

"Sure. Why not?"

"Good. Help me collect those butterflies, and we'll go upstairs and share."

We sat lotus-like on Mugwump's floor, passing around a ceramic bong shaped like a giant penis. I think he chose that one for our guests, perhaps to see how they'd react. The husky one with the pretty face blushed the first couple times she put her mouth on the head. Her companion wasn't so bashful. The Amazon didn't hesitate to wrap her lips around the beast and pretend to suck it with a tease. To me, it was just another bong, one of many in Mugwump's collection. He had more paraphernalia scattered around his apartment than even a hardcore user like Sweetpea. There was a dinosaur and a space shuttle, a replica of the Statue of Liberty, several cartoon characters, three different interpretations of the Buddha—one of which looked like Elvis Presley—and a gigantic green space creature with four rubber tubes sticking out of its head. It's possible Mugwump may have liked the art of doing drugs more than the drugs themselves. That's not to say he didn't enjoy the high, but he collected pipes, hookahs, and bongs as if they were baseball cards or comic books and, as any collector will admit, nothing in the world matches the high of adding that special new piece.

Mugwump kept himself steady most of the night. It was almost impossible to tell when he crossed the line from low to high. He showed the same demeanor no matter how much he inhaled. The ladies weren't so lucky. They were high and happy, having a good time, drifting off noticeably, rocking back and forth while holding their ankles, giggling at the simplest comments, tossing phrases intended to be innuendoes but that came across more bluntly.

Before long, we were all under the spell of the weed, and we started playing around. Hermina, the Amazon, pinned Mugwump to the ground. Only half undressed, the two of them were thrusting back and forth in a mating dance of sorts. It was all make-believe, but I knew they wouldn't pretend much longer. I was with the other girl, Jan. She and I were pressed tightly together, kissing and playing Name That Tune with our hands.

It was all good fun, all very relaxing. But Jan really wasn't much interested in sex, and I felt indifferent to the possibility. After about twenty minutes of a hand under her bra and both of hers moving around on my lap, she stopped me. "I don't want to," she told me in a coy yet seductive tone. "I'm engaged." She said it in such a way that her message couldn't be misunderstood. It wasn't that she wouldn't do it, just that she'd rather not. She'd lie back, enjoy, and worry about her mistake when she sobered up. Still, she hoped I'd do the honorable thing so she could stay faithful to her true love, poor blind fool that he must have been.

I slipped into a weak Chivalrous Knight routine. "Don't worry. I understand."

She smiled and kissed me again.

"It looks like our friends won't be making the same pact," I said.

Jan giggled knowingly. "She's a slut," I heard her whisper.

"He is, too. They're perfect for each other."

"For a few minutes, anyway."

Caressing the back of her head with my hands, I pulled her close to me and said, "Maybe we should leave them alone. Would you like me to drive you home?"

She gave me a queer glance, perhaps deciding whether she could trust me. She must have concluded either that she could or that it didn't matter if she couldn't because she gave a nod in affirmation. She kissed me once more, long and slow. When she pulled away, she said, "You're a good guy, you know that? If I weren't engaged, I might keep you."

I smiled, accepting the awkward compliment. Kissing her on the forehead, I said, "Let's go," and forced myself to stand. I offered a hand and she grabbed it, pulling herself to her feet.

Our movements distracted the lovers. They paused from their frantic foreplay long enough to look our way. Each, in turn, spoke the same words: "What's up?"

"Don't worry about us," I said. "We're giving you privacy."

"We don't need privacy," the Amazon said, though I think she regretted it the moment she heard the words. Even so, she was right. She and Mugwump already were locked together. Only the most minimal garments prevented actual penetration. They would've gotten where they were going even if they were in the middle of a crowded mall at noon.

"He's just taking me home," Jan explained.

The Amazon feigned shock. "What about…?" she said.

"He'll never know." She must have realized how that sounded. "We're not going to screw. He's just taking me home." As an afterthought, she added, "It's not like we did anything wrong."

"It's cool," I said. "I'll drop her off a block away and watch until she gets inside."

Once our friends were certain we were leaving, they did their best to hurry us along, offering their rapid-fire goodbyes. But just as we were ready to walk out the door, Mugwump called to me. "Come by this weekend, Collin. Probably no crowd, but should be some good shows. I've got Aborted Starfish Jelly coming in from L.A. on Friday and the Creeping Neechees out of Baltimore playing Saturday night. Stop by. You'll love it."

"Sure," I agreed. And then it hit me. In all my weeks searching for December, I'd forgotten to ask the man who'd introduced me to her. "By the way," I said, "when are you planning to bring Cancer Moon back?" I tried to make it sound as casual as possible.

"You haven't heard?" he said, surprised.

"Heard what?"

"Cancer Moon split up."

"You're kidding, right?"

"Not at all. You really didn't know?"

"It's news to me."

"Yeah, they're done."

"They broke up," I said, shaking my head with regret.

"Yep. They couldn't work it out. Apparently there were some personality conflicts."

CANTO EIGHTTEEN

Forgetting the Past with Pills

Milan Kundera wrote that a single metaphor can give birth to love. If that's true, I was hopeless. What was I if not a walking metaphor for myself, an ever-changing outer image for the man inside. All my routines were symbols, confused representations of me. When I played the Eccentric Artist or Valiant Hero routines, I was neither an eccentric artist nor a valiant hero. I used those masks as metaphors for what I hoped was hidden. If that's accurate, and if Kundera was right, then my routines were leading me to love. I'm still not sure if I found it. I'll leave that for someone else to decide, someone sitting on a park bench reading a book or slipping into his own Casual Observer routine.

For weeks, my life swerved drunkenly. I skipped from routine to routine, not focusing on any one long enough to enjoy it or apprehend its significance. Aghast Archaeologist of Undiscovered Dreams, Remorseful Fan, Faithless Believer, Tired City Crumbling Back to Earth, Tired Philosopher Ceasing to Be, Maddening Monster, Wilting Orchid, and finally, Oblivious Abuser—I played them all,

"

one after the other, until I found the one that matched my mood.

I purchased all the reckless abandon I could afford. I skipped from drug to drug as often as I switched routines. The season was strong, and I could get whatever I wanted. I'd become a buyer to ease my pain, or maybe so I could know what Dee was feeling—wherever the hell she was, having completely vanished from my life.

Early in July I spotted Sweetpea while doing a story on a rap act called Da Zonez. I wasn't too interested in being a reporter just then, so I wasn't very focused on the sound. I grooved to the tunes, but rather that listen to Da Zonez, I stood there wishing I were zoned on drugs. I explained this to Sweetpea on my way out the door.

He had the answer. "How about pharmies?"

"What've you got?"

He grinned sardonically and coughed a sickly laugh. "Whatever you want, I got it. Uppers, downers, inbet-weeners. I got things that make you laugh, things that make you smile, things that make you come in your pants or fall off the edge of the world. I even got these little pink pills that'll help you out when you're trying to take a crap."

"What'd you do, knock over a drug store?"

He shook his head, still afflicted with that death mask of a grin. "Not me."

We left it at that.

I said, "I'm all about that falling off the edge of the world deal."

"How about Dannies?"

"You got Percs?" My mouth watered, and my spine tingled in anticipation. "I might stick my hand in that cookie jar. How many cookies?"

"More than enough. How many you want?"

"Dose and dollar?"

"Five on the pill," he said. "Five milligrams. The usual."

I nodded, not in a bargaining mood. "I'll take fifty."

"You know where I live. Drop by tomorrow. I'll be around. I'm always around."

That was that. The next day, I dropped two hundred and fifty bucks in the collection plate at the church of divine euphoria. Then I spent the week in a haze, eating pills like candy and trying not to let on to my colleagues. "What's the matter?" they'd say. "Back problems," I'd reply, so they wouldn't press it when they saw me pop another little yellow pill into my mouth and down it with a swig of bitter newsroom coffee.

The Dream Job

I was lying around my apartment in codeine calm when Rowen telephoned with another offer. Her voice came across as melodic, sending pleasure rippling through my skin. "Hello, Collin?"

"This is he. Is this…?" I had no trouble recognizing her now.

"Rowen Rousseau from *Musicade Magazine*." At first her statement sounded odd to me. It's not exactly normal to address yourself in formal terms to someone you've been to bed with. It seemed as if she thought I'd forgotten her. But it was just a standard introduction, the kind that becomes a habit, the same as my saying, "This is Collin Hearst with the *Domestic-Chronicle*," when talking to someone over the phone, and even when ordering a pizza or giving Mom a call on her birthday. We trained ourselves that way.

"Good to hear from you, Rowen. How are you?"

"Lively," she replied. "I've got my karma leveled off, and my aura keeps emitting new colors in comfortable hues. How about you?"

"I think my karma shot itself in the ass," I quipped.

She laughed. "And your aura?"

"Obsidian, with mind-numbing pink spots. Or maybe they're pink elephants. Hard to tell."

Turning serious, she said, "You're having a bad time of it?"

"I guess you could say that."

"Well listen up, Collin, because I've got news that'll change your life."

"Say again."

"It'll change your life," she repeated. "Might even cheer you up."

Not sure what she was aiming for, I joked, "Let me guess. You're selling subscriptions at sixty percent off the regular newsstand price, and if I order now, I get a free telephone shaped like a flying-V guitar and a chance to win a million bucks in your new sweepstakes."

"No," she replied, calmly serious, "but I might have to mention that to our sales staff. They aren't very creative, you know."

"I imagine. But if it's not that, then what?"

"Got a job open. One of our reporters quit. Thought you might be interested."

"You're offering me a job?"

"No," she corrected. "I don't have the authority to do that. But I recommended you, and my recommendation carries a lot of weight. Plus, the editors have seen your work. They loved the Rose story. You still have to go through the formalities, but my guess is the job's yours if you want it."

"What do I need to do?"

"Okay," she said. "Here's the trick. The editors haven't posted the job, but they want to get it sorted out ASAP, so you need to come up and meet with them. How's this weekend for you?"

"This weekend? Can't. I work weekends."

"No problem. So you tell me, what's the soonest you can be here?"

"How about tomorrow?"

This time, Rowen sounded surprised. "Tomorrow? Really? You *do* move fast. You can just drop everything and hit the road like that?"

"Nothing to drop. My only commitment's to my job, and mostly I work Friday through Sunday. I'm clear until Friday evening. If it works for you and your editors, I can drive up tomorrow, meet with them on Wednesday, then drive back on Thursday. Sound okay?"

"Collin, that's perfect. They'll be impressed, let me assure you."

"Great," I said, "so what do I need to bring?"

"Your résumé," she said, "not that they'll take any stock in it?"

"And?"

"Maybe five to ten of your favorite clips—all music related, of course."

"Of course."

"That's it. Oh, and you don't need to wear a shirt and tie or anything like that. They hate that. We're pretty informal up here. Just wear whatever you normally wear to work."

"I normally wear a shirt and tie," I said.

She found that amusing.

"What's funny?"

"Don't worry, Collin. After a couple months with us, you'll learn to relax."

CANTO NINETEEN

The Job Interview

I packed a shirt, tie, and a pair of black slacks, tossing them in an old duffel bag. For the trip, I went Rowen-style: black tee and jeans, dark and brooding but casual.

As I drove east toward New Jersey, all I could think of was *Musicade*. I could see myself interviewing all the big stars, or sitting at a cozy desk, staring out the window on a glorious autumn afternoon, holding the phone to my ear, and grinning wildly as the manager or agent for some new act sucked up while trying not to let on that he knew my words could mean Trendsville or Endsville for his group. Or, if that agent didn't call me, I'd get him on the line anyway, and in that calm, habitual manner—just like Rowen's—I'd say, "Collin Hearst with *Musicade Magazine*. That's right, the one and only *Musicade Magazine*. I'd like to do a story on your band. I heard the new tune on a college station and—let me be candid—this band is going places." Then that agent would go bust some heads to get the band sobered up for my call at whatever hour was most convenient for me. Yeah, let me be candid, I was going places.

When I arrived at Rowen's house in a small suburb just outside Newark, it was early evening. Her directions had been true, so I made it there without getting lost. She lived in a small, beige, ranch-style house in what appeared to be a peaceful community, not a place that seemed to fit Rowen's personality. I expected something with more chaos, perhaps a gray, glaring Gothic structure perched on a hill. Instead, she lived in the kind of home where one might raise a family.

Rowen sat on the front porch in a varnished wooden swing, sipping a Red Sangria wine cooler. She was dressed the same way I remembered her, though her clothes were brighter, with shades of rusty orange and light gray rather than blue and black. She didn't stand to greet me, staying still as she had at the Rainbow Cafe. She just tilted her bottle in my direction.

"Evening," I said.

"Hiya, lover. Glad you made it. Any trouble?"

"Smooth sailing all the way from Pittsburgh."

When I got to the top of the steps, she finally stood up, offering a friendly kiss on the cheek and escorting me into her home. Inside, I saw how different Rowen's style was from her brother's. Stepping through the front door was like stepping through a portal into another world. The traditional house in a traditional neighborhood transformed into a shrine of the damned or a home for the utterly deranged. The walls were speckled randomly with blotches of paint in uncertain splatterings of oranges, blues, greens, blacks. The carpet—the house's most normal feature—was ash gray, but covered with a large, round rug tie-dyed into a massive inward spiral of colors. Fat stone sculptures, or perhaps gargoyles, sat lotus-like on every side of the couch, two chairs, and a television set. These demons served as tables, coffee tables, lamp stands. Her brother had a few totems of his own, but his were forced and generally uncool. Rowen's, on the other hand, were somehow hip despite their gruesome features. Surveying the scene was like walking into Club Zero for the first time, only without the crowd. And that was just the living room. The rest of Rowen's house was equally intimidating, with mutant light fixtures, twisted tapestries, and curtains straight from the devil's bazaar. On every wall in almost every room hung paintings and photographs of nudes, both men and women, ranging from the artistic to the offensive. I couldn't tell if she had them because of a love for the human body or to fulfill some deviant sexual craving.

I'd never seen a house decorated like that before. When Rowen asked my opinion, my first impulse was to describe the place as 'intense.' I held back, choosing a different word, one I knew her type liked. "It's *eclectic*, like star clusters and sunlight in the same blue sky."

"So you like it?" she said.

"It's unique."

"So you hate it?" Her smile went from concave to convex.

"I didn't say that. It's unique. It's eclectic. It's a passionate expression of your personal view of the world. Therefore, it's part of you. I couldn't hate anything that's part of you."

The corners of her mouth again drifted up like two lovebirds carrying a piece of pink yarn. "I think you're a manipulator, Collin. But you have a way with words."

I leaned back against a wall, slipped my hands into my pockets, and worked up a rough version of my Lazy Sage routine. "Just trying to be objective. It's the reporter in me. I try to say what I see and hear, rather than what I think." I looked away, hoping to avoid her eyes, but she refused to let me.

Placing a hand on my chin, she pivoted my head until my eyes were locked on hers. "What do you think? Tell me. I really want to know."

I took her hand in mine, lowering both and holding tightly. "You want to know what I think? I think you're a beautiful woman."

"I was right. You're a manipulator, aren't you?"

"I don't know what you mean."

She didn't press the issue. Instead, she tugged on my arm and guided me back to the living room. "Sit down," she said, pulling away.

I took a seat on the sofa amidst her mass of meditating gargoyles, feeling somewhat intimidated by a couple staring straight at me. *Unique*, I thought. *Definitely unique.*

Rowen disappeared for a few minutes, returning with a crystal decanter and two obsidian goblets. "It's cognac," she said, sitting the glasses on the flat head of a gargoyle.

"Charming."

She filled each glass a quarter of the way and then sat the bottle beside them. With a servant's grace, she lifted the two vessels, handing me one. She sat beside me on the couch. Raising a glass, she said, "What should we drink to?"

I couldn't help flashing back to one of December's lines. *What should we talk about?* I'd asked, to which she'd replied, *What do people ever talk about? There's either you or me.* I don't know how Dee would react to hearing me use one of her lines on another woman, but I did it. I paraphrased and adapted it. "What else is there?" I said. "At this moment, this hour, this day, there are only three choices. There's you, there's me, and there's you and me. Everything else is another subject for another time, and for another toast."

She seemed to enjoy this Suave Dilettante routine. To prove it, her cheeks expressed themselves as two purple orchids blooming in a warm field of embarrassment. "All right," she agreed. "If that's the case, then we'll drink to you and me."

I touched my goblet to hers with a cheerful ping, and we sipped the warm brandy. It was smooth and sweet, rich with spice and a little nutty. She could tell I enjoyed it. Maybe it was the look in my eyes or the smile on my face or the way I seemed to savor each long, slow sip as if pressing my lips to Rowen's—or December's. She stared at me with this giddy, girlish look like children get when they win praise from their elders. "Not bad?" she said.

"It's magical." I didn't tell her that paint thinner would've been good if it took the edge off. I hadn't taken pills today, so the tightness in my gut hurt so much I strained to keep smiling.

"I'm glad you like it. It was a gift. My brother bought it for my wedding."

"You're married?" When I'd gone to see her at her brother's house, she'd asked me about my entanglements, but I hadn't thought to ask her.

"No."

"Divorced?"

"No."

"You don't look sad enough to be a widow."

"Stood up at the altar." She winced as she said it, marking the pain with her eyes.

"That's terrible," I said.

"He was an asshole anyway. Didn't deserve me."

"I believe it."

"Anyway," she continued, "I got to keep the cognac."

I gave a hesitant laugh that grew into empathy. "The pluses and minuses of life."

"What about you? Ever been married?"

"Not a chance."

"Why not? You seem like a solid candidate."

This topic intimidated me, leading me to thoughts of December. Slipping into my favorite Lost Cause routine— as all lovers are lost causes—I explained, "I'm just a tired hack without much hope. I write stories, not love letters."

She shook her head. "You're too negative," she said.

"Can't deny it."

"Awfully lame attitude."

I sipped my cognac, pausing to consider a response. "I'm not totally indifferent. I have goals, no matter how much I wish I didn't. They pop up at unexpected times, weighing on me as the overbearing obligations they are. They fill my head with grief, anxiety, despair."

"Why?"

"Because I want something, but no matter how much effort I put into achieving my goal, I can't control whether I succeed or fail. There are too many outside forces that determine success. So it's all hope, worry, and frustration."

Rowen obviously didn't share my views, but she saw the logic in them. Tilting her glass, she consumed the last of her drink with a disgusted grimace, as if the cognac were cough syrup and I were a bad cold. She wanted to cure herself of my thoughts. Needing more medicine, she refilled our glasses. "Tell me," she said. "What *are* your goals? What do you hope for?"

I sipped my cognac, not wanting to respond, but she prodded me on with a nod of her head. I could think of at least one goal that had run the gauntlet of hope, worry, and frustration without making it out alive. I wouldn't discuss that with Rowen. After an uneasy silence, I shrugged.

"Nothing?"

"Nothing," I said. "But it's only nothing at this moment, in this place, talking to this person. I'm too busy accepting my world as it rotates. I'm sure as soon as I make it back to Pittsburgh I'll get smacked in the face. That's the way it always happens."

She almost seemed to brighten after hearing me say that, as if I'd rejected her by rejecting the many things that cause me grief. It was almost as if she took pride in learning I could only engage in my metaphysics for a short time. Beginning to glow, she said, "Join the crowd. The rest of us spend a major part of our lives forcing ourselves to suffer. Scratch that. *Allowing* ourselves."

"I know," I said, and I think it came across as condescending.

She didn't call me on it. Tasting her cognac, she waited for me to go on.

I raised my glass and said, "To indifference."

"No, to dreams rather than dreads."

Our crystals clinked together and we drank—she to her toast, I to mine. From there, our conversation traveled many paths, twisting and turning, getting lost and starting over. We talked until after midnight before I got around to asking about the interview. "What's the plan for tomorrow?"

"What do you mean?"

"What am I expected to do?"

She'd moved closer to me throughout the evening, closing the gap almost in unison with the lowering of the cognac in her decanter. Our eyes were no more than a foot apart and her arm was draped along the back of the couch so her fingertips touched my hair. Occasionally she stroked the back of my neck in enticement. "Let's see," she said. "You'll be meeting with Carol tomorrow at four. Carol's the managing editor. She's a real nice person. You'll love her. I better warn you though, she's openly gay. Don't ask me how you'll know, but you will as soon as you meet her. She wears it like Cyrano's nose, and I hope you remember the rule about Cyrano's nose."

"Don't mention it or I'll get my ass kicked."

"Keep that in mind and you'll have no problems. Basically, she's a pussycat. Plus, she's easy to impress. If you impress her, you get the job."

"That's it? A four o'clock interview?"

"There's a couple other small details."

That worried me. It sounded as if she were about to break some bad news, almost the way a physician would talk about problems that popped up in a close relative's condition. *Well, son, we've got that blood clot pretty well fixed. We didn't have to amputate. It all went rather smoothly, and you'll be able to see your mother as soon as she wakes up. There's just a couple other small details.* To hear that is to anticipate the ominous. "What?" I said.

"Paperwork. All *kinds* of paperwork. You know how it goes. You have to give your name, social security number, references, how many times you've been laid in the past year."

"That's a tough one. I've only got ten fingers and toes to count on."

"Just take a guess. They won't check on it." We laughed together, drawing nearer toward a kiss. "Seriously, that's just a formality. As far as I know, nobody reads that stuff."

"So, what else?"

"Well, there's a long questionnaire you have to fill out. The editors *do* go through that. It's all music related. They want to see how much you know about music, how hip you are."

"That's cool. My hips are big enough."

She grinned. "Anyway, that just leaves the drug test."

I flinched. "Drug test? You didn't mention anything about a drug test."

"Don't fret about it," she explained. "Nobody cares if you smoke a joint or two here and there. It's not a problem. If the editors cracked down on weed whackers, they'd put the whole staff out of business. Themselves included. We couldn't print a magazine." She paused to gauge my response.

I gave her none, staring intently.

"No, it's no big deal. They just want to make sure their staffers aren't into the hard drugs, any potent narcotics. That'd be bad for business. Junkies aren't good workers. They don't meet deadlines, don't always show up for work. They're more likely to bring the cops around, too. We can't have that. It'd ruin the magazine's image. But a little pot? Don't worry." Again, she waited for a reaction. Then, with no reply forthcoming, she said, "You'll fit right in."

We were in the master bedroom racing through unskillful sex. My heart wasn't in it, but hers was, so I went along. I played the Happy Whore routine, smiling when I should smile, sighing when I should sigh, saying all the right words in time. She didn't notice my indifference that had flared up since I toasted it. The only thing I saw in her expression was happiness, and I was glad to give her that, even if I didn't feel it too. I played along, giving her what she wanted. Finally, I forced myself to suffer through one brief moment of bliss, and it was over.

Nothing further came of our affair. If Rowen wanted love, she didn't show it. At the conclusion of our escapades, we showered, each of us in different bathrooms. After that, we sat up and talked until about three in the morning. Then we went to bed separately. She showed me to a guest room, said, "Sleep well," and went her own way without so much as a kiss good night.

It didn't bother me that she slept elsewhere. Even if I lay beside her, she still would wake up alone. Within a few sleepless hours after she saw me to my room, I flew south for the winter of my soul—or rather, west back to Pittsburgh. I left behind a brief, impersonal note written on her own stationary in which I declined to pursue the job and gave neither reasons nor apologies. I went my own way without so much as a kiss goodbye.

Outside, the stars were beautiful, arrayed in their patterns and constellations. With their winks and sparkles, they beckoned me to make a wish. But I was having none of that. I was on the road back to Pittsburgh, forsaken and forlorn, to resume my routine lifestyle, hoping beyond hope to be reborn. But even that was a goal, and I wanted no part of goals, ambitions, desires, and wishes on stars. The moon was out, but I paid it no mind, refusing to see how cancerous it might be.

CANTO TWENTY

A Song Without a Melody

I made it back to my apartment shortly after noon, ready for a meal of Percodan and milk, the former to ease the pain of life, the latter to ease the pain of the former on a stomach rubbed raw from nerves. What else did I have to look forward to but leveling off my highs and lows?

Oh, but plans change…

Someone taped a scrap of pink paper to my door. It was too small to be a summons and too informal for an eviction notice, so I figured it for a note from a neighbor. What the hell, it could've been the black spot for all I knew, attached to my door as a harbinger of imminent doom. If that were true, I didn't care. I was in no mood for silly superstitions or foreboding.

I peeled the scrap of paper from my door and un-folded it gingerly as if it were a treasure map. Looking back, it seems that wasn't far from the truth. While it didn't lead to gold doubloons or pieces of eight, it led me to December. It read: *Sorry I missed you. Things always seem to work out that way. Well, I'll try one more time. Meet me at the Blank Verse on Webster Avenue at eight o'clock tonight. Don't be late.* The note wasn't signed, but I knew whose fingerprints could be found on the corners and whose handwriting formed the words.

I looked at my watch. It was early. I had plenty of time to prepare myself for the encounter. For months, I'd been waiting for December, wondering where she was and what she was doing, whom she was with and whose face she saw when her eyes were closed, someone else's skin pressed against her. At last, the time had come for answers.

Before the door closed behind me, I'd already tossed my duffel onto the bed and begun to undress—shirt first, then shoes, pants, socks, and underwear, imagining December's hands helping me along. Then it was a shower, shave, and a quick look at my fresh smile in the mirror. I felt that old ambition coming back despite my best intentions.

No tee and jeans tonight. That wouldn't do. I was going to meet December, so I wanted to look my best. But not overdressed, just the same. Jet black slacks, black socks, black shoes. Vivid purple and black short-sleeve dress shirt with the top three buttons undone. No tie, no hat, no jacket. Everything perfect. That classic first-date look, sharp and casual blended into one. It had to be that way. I refused to settle for less. Clean-shaven, splashed with cologne, hair brushed until not a single strand was out of place. The whole bit. Nothing lacking or held back. I checked and rechecked my appearance in the mirror, making sure there were no wrinkles, no loose hairs, no unexpected downturn in my smile. It was almost an obsession. Finally, when it came time to go, I studied my appearance one last time before slipping into my favorite Lovable Loser routine and heading for the door.

The Blank Verse was a bar about half the size of Club Zero, but the atmosphere felt easier in tone. The patrons weren't slaves to fashion or trends. They seemed more relaxed—most of the women in long, loose skirts and the men in corduroys and tees or flannels with the sleeves cut off. The regulars didn't want to stand out. To the contrary, The Blank Verse was a place for the hip and the hapless to dress down, come together, and fit in. There were unspectacular tables, casual lighting, and a subtle stage off in a corner bordered with stacks of cheap speakers.

"Collin," the redhead at the door beamed, "it's been months."

I doubted it had been so long. "Sorry, Connie. Been busy. You know how it goes."

She offered up a half smile, half frown. "Yeah, been busy here, too." Connie was the twenty-year-old daughter of Julie Morgan, owner of the Blank Verse. Being the owner's daughter meant little or no pay, but Connie didn't mind. She liked the people and enjoyed her job, working the door and occasionally waiting tables.

"How's your mother doing?"

"Still complaining about bad business and a bad back, but she's okay."

"She in tonight?"

"No, afraid not. You know *her*. Tries to take the day off whenever we book loud music." I nodded, remembering Julie's phobia about having fun. She left the enjoyment to her daughter and future partner as a sort of pre-funereal bequeath.

"Who's playing tonight, anyway? You got a big-name act?" I was digging for information, trying to find out about December.

"Just our monthly open-mic night. You want to play?"

I grinned. "You know, I could take that a couple different ways."

She grinned back, twice as devilish. "I guess you could. But my boyfriend's due in here any minute now. He gets paranoid about people getting my intentions wrong."

"Yeah, yeah, yeah."

"So, you want to get up on stage, maybe play a song or two?"

"Next time," I said. "I'm not prepared tonight. Got a lot on my mind."

"I know how that goes, too," she said. "Anyway, I'll be expecting you next month. You better be ready to perform for me."

"If I were of a mind to, I could take *that* a couple different ways."

She replied, "I guess you could," this time with no mention of her boyfriend.

I stared at her calmly for a moment before looking away. Changing the subject, I said, "What have you got tonight? Anybody good?"

"Just the regulars. Country band, alternative band, a couple soloists, a handful of poets—you know the routine. There might be a couple new acts, but I don't know. You'll have to ask Lisa. She handles that end. I just collect the covers."

I took that as a hint and reached into my pocket.

"Not you," she said, with a flirtatious grin. "You practically work here."

Making my way to a table by the stage, I took a seat with my back to the wall so I had a clear view of the entire room. Scanning the scene, I searched for signs of December. Not seeing her amidst the people scattered about the club, I sighed and made a mental note of my surroundings.

I saw Lisa across the room, fiddling with knobs on her sound board. She had that same serious look she always wore on open-mic nights, a look that said, *Don't mess with me or I'll fill your head with white noise.* That look summed up her personality. She was a control freak. She demanded everyone's respect and courtesy, as well as their patience and deference to her abilities. All the regulars knew that, and they understood what it meant: To have a good show, they'd best not fuck with Lisa. She owned the dials. She could turn the volume up or down. She could jump back and forth between effects so a bad musician sounded good or vice versa, depending on her mood. If she didn't like someone, she could make him not want to come back by humiliating him on stage with a barrage of pitch shifts and tone adjustments that the musically un-knowledgeable would presume to be the performer's lack of talent. Were anyone stupid enough to piss her off, she might never call his name at all, leaving him sitting there, growing more nervous, and wondering, *Am I next? Maybe next? How about now?* But that was a treatment she reserved for only the most egregious offenders: folks who found her sensitive spot, wherever that might be. Basically Lisa was defined by a single word scrawled in black magic marker across the front of her silver cap: *Soundchick!* Every-body knows you don't fuck with the Soundchick if you hope to get anywhere in the music business.

I was contemplating this when Bub, the long-haired heavy-metal waiter dropped by with a pair of drinks. The first was a tall glass of thick fluids layered in a variety of colors that seemed to shift in the light. The second looked more familiar. "How's it going, Collin?"

"Good, Bub. What's up?"

"Couple drinks for you."

I started to explain that I hadn't ordered any drinks, but that would've been redundant. Everyone knew me well enough to anticipate my desires.

"The first one's from Paula," Bub continued, refer-ring to the tall black woman behind the bar. "She said she calls it an Uzi because it's got a lot of shots and not much control when firing."

I laughed and waved to Paula, who accepted the gesture as thanks.

Bub sat the drink on my table and reached for the other. It was a smaller glass with a familiar orange glow inside.

"Absolut Screwdriver," I said.

"Yeah," he replied. "This one's on that young lady over there." He pointed to a shining star over by the bar who waved at me when she saw I was looking.

I didn't recognize her at first. She could've been a stranger for all I knew. But I saw the eyes, and they were December's eyes, looking through holes in someone else's head. If she'd blinked or turned away, I might not have figured it out. She had gone through a transformation, emerging from her chrysalis as an angel rather than a butterfly. Her skin, once pale as the full moon on a cloudy night, now flashed a passionate tan. Her short black hair had been cut shorter, squared off and looking almost professional—not to mention, it was now a bright, natural blond. Even her clothes were different, with a long-sleeve, pen-striped men's dress shirt—mine, I realized—hanging untucked over a flowing brown skirt. Other than the eyes, nothing about her was how I remembered, and even those eyes had changed. I could see they were happy eyes, magical eyes, *sober* eyes. As if to prove this, December lifted her glass in toast, and I could tell right away it was filled to the rim with water.

"Enjoy," said Bub.

I turned to him just long enough to thank him. When I turned back, December was gone, having vanished like a vapor in the sunlight. I remained in my seat, knowing that she didn't want me to search for her. She had something planned, and she wanted me right where I was.

The night drifted by like dead leaves in a pond, slow and morose, without much hope of reaching one side or the other. I had no interest in the show beyond the inevitable glimpse of December. In spite of this, I stayed in my seat through song after song, set after set, paying little mind to the young performers or the ebb and flow of the crowd.

I listened inattentively as Charlie Pearl chirped and twanged about all the loves he'd lost or never found to begin with, and every time he sang of drowning his troubles in the bottom of a glass, I took his advice and tried to drown my own. As Charlie and his band left the stage, I applauded politely and drank a little more.

The next act was a folk duet I'd never heard of—Christian and Kelly something or other, a married couple apparently. They had some talent, but their slow, soft, steady arpeggios and harmonies nearly put me to sleep. I signaled to Bub, ordering another drink.

The duet was followed by a comedian who wasn't very funny and a handful of poets. One by one, they took the stage, each offering two and sometimes three poems. A few were inspiring, a few despairing. Some amused, while many more spoke of love. The most passionate of the poets was a young brunette in her late teens—named Aurora, I think—who sang her poems rather than reciting them. Each *a capella* verse could've filled ten books about emotion, even without the words. She touched me, and for the first time that night, I snapped out of my trance and thought like a professional. I made a mental note to do a story on her.

She was followed by the last of the group: a lanky fellow wearing only black swim trunks and a pair of sandals. He was the only one I would describe as pretentious. He grabbed his cock as if it were something special and babbled an absurd piece about cutting off his testicles and crushing them like soldiers underneath a tank. The sad part isn't that he recited such drivel, but that by the look on his face it was obvious he genuinely didn't understand why people were laughing at him. To this madcap orator, he must have thought his words profound, though to the rest of us, he was a poser. Three times he offered an awkward verse, and three times he received the same response. When the last line dripped from his lips with a spray of spittle, he bowed his head and carried himself off the stage. Aside from his friends, nobody applauded—not even Soundchick, who clapped for almost everyone, even those she despised and embarrassed.

At the failed poet's passing, I drank a toast to dejection.

I had to sit through one more act before December took the stage. Kenny Durante, a former classmate of mine, got up with his beautiful ash-gray sunburst guitar and strummed goofy renditions of classic rock songs. With the grace and precision of a circus clown, he played the Beatles, the Stones, Elvis, and some comedic originals. Unlike the poets and bands before him, Kenny owned the crowd. When people laughed, they were laughing with him rather than at him. When he grabbed his cock, folks understood the scorn he conveyed. And when Kenny left the stage, it was with head held high while everyone cheered.

Kenny didn't take his guitar with him, however. He left it plugged in. The next thing I knew, there was December, sticking her head and right arm underneath the strap. She didn't say a word in introduction. She just stepped to the microphone and sang three of the most amazing songs I've ever heard. Often, she glanced my way, making sure I was paying attention.

I was. I knew from the first chord her songs were all for me.

The first built a slow, steady blues groove. Its hook drew me in, controlled me, sustained my curiosity, and forced me to tap a foot to the rhythm. Closing my eyes, I focused on the words:

Face flushed with booze and contentment, I did just as she said, smiling and reflecting on that special scene, that day in Mugwump's sound room. She opened me up with the music and drew the memories out as she told the story in vivid detail, reminding me of the unexpected moment shared between us. I lived it and relived it a hundred times, feeling her lips against mine, her hands on my head, her smoke ripping into my lungs. I thought I heard my heart beating faster, but it might have been the music. Yes, that's it. It had to be the music.

When the first song was finished, Dee didn't pause before plunging into the next piece. This one was a tranquil ballad filled with a well-practiced voice and fragile mix of arpeggios much like the ones that almost put me to sleep earlier. With December's hands fingering each note, I felt no drowsiness. I listened, under the spell of the song. It was a melodic chronicle about misunderstanding, about the night I went home with Bev instead of Dee. I was saddened, but at the same time, invigorated. She put so much emotion into the performance that at times I thought she might start to cry while at other times she seemed to sin the biggest sin of all by confessing some-thing akin to love. But she didn't dwell on these, and I understood it was part of the show. She'd written the story of our relationship, and she'd turned it into a musical—not a gentle musical like *Grease* or *Annie*, but a deranged rock opera like *Tommy*, *Operation Mindcrime*, or *The Wall*. I watched, nearly crying.

The third song was a straight-out rocker about addic-tions, whether hers or mine. It started out with four simple lines, the same four metaphysical, metaphorical lines that repeated throughout the piece like echoes of the final plea from a lost soul stumbling to his death on a canyon floor.

The words reverberated through the bar, picked up in mad synchronicity by patrons who sang along:

> *Give me some sugar, baby.*
> *Give me some love.*
> *It's just the three of us together like*
> *a mean little dream about us.*

It was so catchy that, despite the melancholy undertones I recognized and understood, I too began to sing along. By the end, everyone had joined in, even Lisa. Though Kenny Durante had owned the room, December brought it to life. It was hers to command, a crowd of puppets dancing as she pulled their strings—the copper strings of a guitar.

After, all sat silently waiting for a fourth enchanting soliloquy, but it wasn't to be. As I said, she gave us three perfect, passionate outpourings, and no more. That's not to say, however, that her performance was over. She had one last piece to play for me. I'm not sure it can be called a song, although I can't think of another word to describe it, except perhaps 'insanity.' Staring straight at me, she introduced the piece, speaking for the first time. "This next song was written for a very dear friend of mine. It's different from anything I've ever done, so please bear with me. Try to understand how difficult it is to capture the essence of a person, especially a person as confused as my friend." She smiled, frowned, then tried to smile again but couldn't make it stick. "Anyway, here goes."

She rocked back on her heals and then lunged forward, strumming harsh chords and errant notes, alternately picking and pounding the strings with disdain or sorrow or venom. The notes came at random, a mix of harsh chromatics and dire riffs leading into dreadful runs. She would play a fragment of the song and then move on, never repeating the same chord pattern or note progression twice, playing each once and then leaving it behind. The music—if it can be called music—ripped apart the air in a cacophonous rage like a train wreck, a metal shop, or the collective wails of a thousand banshees predicting their own ends.

The patrons looked at each other in disbelief. Some held their ears or winced whenever a shrill sound split the air like atoms in a bomb. A few even looked as if they were mourning, with eyes glistening from tears, cheeks flushed, hands covering mouths to muffle gasps and terrified shrieks. The song tortured everyone's ears—everyone's but mine. I listened, fascinated, as she began to sing a series of random words and phrases, having no rhyme or rhythm:

> *The moonlight matinee is closed.*
> *An imaginary car stalls*
> *in the parking lot of dreams.*

I tried to make sense of her lyrical implications, but they were as incomprehensible to me as December herself—or perhaps, as I was to her. She paved a path through my life, building a road leading nowhere. I couldn't follow. I couldn't keep up.

> *Time transcends the rainbow*
> *into darkness grim as father's love.*
> *The sublime sufferer awaits*
> *tired and alone in a chicken coop*
> *to be eaten by the wolves.*

Despite the discord, no one interrupted December's performance by heckling her or yelling for her to get off the stage. No one ran screaming from the bar. No one cried out, "What the fuck?" No one dared. Not even Soundchick.

The song lasted somewhere between ten minutes and a lifetime. When it was over, Dee said, "Thank you," and made her exit. Lifting the guitar over her head, she freed herself from its grip.

No one applauded, but not because of any disrespect. The crowd, which only minutes before had been jumping with the music, sometimes singing along, now was filled with apprehension, an uneasy sense of having experienced something unique. All of us knew that song would never be played again. Finally, after a long silence in the bar, I alone lifted my hands and forced myself to clap—a stinging crescendo to the song, almost as discordant because of its solitary nature.

Kenny met December at the edge of the stage to get his guitar and say a few words. I'm not sure what he told her, but she nodded in reply and I could read her lips as she said, "Thanks."

Meanwhile, the crowd was coming out of its daze, forsaking mass hypnosis or group psychosis for a few mumbled sparks of communication spreading quickly into a conflagration of words. The bar returned to normal, everything loud and unfocused like December's song.

The next musician headed for the stage.

I took a last sip from my drink. When my gaze came back from the bottom of the glass, I was face to face with the woman I craved like a thousand Percodans. Grabbing a chair across from me, she sat down. "Hello, Collin," she said. "You look bleak."

"It's nice to see you, too," I said—half sarcastic, half sincere.

She smiled tenderly.

"Everything about you's so different."

She shrugged. "Times change. People change. I've changed. But you've stayed the same. You're exactly as I remember you."

"Why would I want to change?" I replied.

"You tell me, Collin."

"I don't know. I like the way I am."

"Do you?" She flashed me a halfhearted smile.

I shrugged.

"You don't like it. Not really. But you're used to it. It's comfortable."

"Comfort isn't everything," I said. As if to prove this, I got up and moved over to the chair on her left. I wanted to be close to her, to touch her, to breathe in the sweet scent of her skin hidden under clouds of smoke. I cupped my palms on top of her left hand. "Let me look at you. You're more beautiful than ever." It was redundant. She already knew she'd improved.

"I've shed my dark side like an old, dead skin," she said. "I had to clean up my act before my show got canceled. Things weren't going well. You heard about the band, I take it?"

I nodded. "What happened?"

"Disagreements," she replied.

"That's what I was told."

"I was out of control, but I tried to control the band. It didn't work. I just made everybody hate me. We had it out one night after a gig in Columbus of all places, back where it all began. I told'em it was my way or the highway, so they took a hike. Hit the road and never looked back."

"I'm sorry to hear that."

"Don't be. Things always work out for the best. Cancer Moon was a bright star flashing briefly to supernova before burning itself out. When I realized that, I took a look at myself and saw the same symptoms. I knew if I didn't straighten up, I might burn out, too. So I've changed my styles, changed my views, changed my looks, and changed my tune. You're looking at the new me, Collin, the new December Leigh."

"You're beautiful," I said again.

"Thank you," she said.

I started to tell her something else, something important, but I couldn't.

"Enough about me. What's your story? Like I said, you haven't changed a bit."

"I almost changed," I told her. "I had a chance." I spent the next fifteen minutes filling her in on my *Musicade* fiasco, beginning with my search for Cancer Moon, ending with December's note, and not skipping a word, a pill, or a thought in between. She listened close, smiling at the happy parts, but mostly shaking her head. When I was finished, I said, "That's it. That's the way it went. I just got back this morning. Now I'm here."

"It's too bad," she said, showing true empathy.

"It wasn't important to me."

Again, she shrugged. "That's your business. If it means that little, no problem. If you don't want to change, then don't. It's up to you. But take it from someone who knows, you're blighted with madness. If you don't change, it'll just get worse. Trust me, this time. You'll hear my song in your head, and it won't fade no matter how much you beg or plead or cry out in the middle of the night. The song's a part of you, and you're a part of the song. I pulled it from your heart after waking from a nightmare—one that you were in. I heard your heart beating rapidly, erratically, and I knew then as I know now that it wasn't just a dream."

"What does that song have to do with any of this?"

"Don't you see?" she said. "That's your life, Collin: a song without a melody, rapid and random, dark and disillusioned. All you can do's mouth the words and hope they have meaning, or listen to your heartbeat, as I did, searching for a better rhythm. That's it for you unless you give up all the songs and start to change your tune."

"Maybe so," I said, sinking deeper into myself.

"It's the truth, Collin. You know it and I know it, because believe me, it was my song, too. But I've already changed my tune. Now I'm going further. I've got a new band, a good band."

"Really?"

"We haven't got a name yet, but we've already found an agent who loves our sound, and she made us promises.

Big promises. She's got gigs lined up for us in New York and L.A., Dallas and Detroit. She says she's got big-time producers coming out to see us. She says they'll think of a name once we're signed."

"That's amazing, Dee. I'm happy for you." And I was, though I was also sad for me because I knew she had to leave me yet again.

"We're on our way, Collin. With Cancer Moon, I let my addictions lead. I couldn't think straight. We had all this talent, but I didn't know what to do about it. That band was going nowhere. Not this one, though. We'll make it. I'll make. Nothing can stop me but me."

"I hope you're right. I wish you the best." It was true, however cheerless I sounded. After a momentary pause, I gave her hand a squeeze and said, "I've missed you, Dee."

"I've missed you, too," she said, but it came out in a less than encouraging tone. "There's more I have to tell you, though. I'm getting married next month."

"What?" It was all I could say. The word escaped with a gasp, while the erratic heart she'd described skipped a few more beats, rumbling to the staggered tempo of disbelief.

"It's true," she said.

"Who?"

She said nothing at first.

"Who are you marrying?"

"His name's Collin, too. He's my lead guitarist."

"I can't believe it," I said, a lie. I believed it, and the truth hurt so much.

"It's true," she repeated. "I'm going to be Mrs. December Leigh Casey."

My passionate self dug its claws into my chest, demanding that I stand up and proclaim my affections, that I scream, *No! You just can't do it! You can't!* But my rational side fought back and won, and in its winning, I lost. With my throat nervous and dry, I grunted, gasped, and coughed out one simple word: "Congratulations."

The night went by in a blur, as had my whole life before it. Much was said between us, but none of it mattered. Maybe I was too drunk to remember more, if that's an excuse. But the real story came to an end with that one word, those five simple syllables mouthed but not really meant, expressing joy in a voice filled with sorrow. At closing time, Dee walked me to my car, where she said goodbye with one last glorious kiss. It was both an ending and a new beginning. After all, how can the phoenix rise from the ashes without the ashes to rise from? How can a sinner be reborn without having sinned? How can an addict overcome his addictions without his addictions to overcome? And how can a man, a sad, tired, fragile shell of a man, recover from lost love without having loved and lost?

"Dee," I said as she started to walk away, not sure what I wanted to tell her.

"Yes?"

The words just sort of came out. "Don't forget, you still owe me a cup of coffee."

"Another time," she said, smiling.

"Another time," I agreed, smiling too. Not as bold as hers, it was the most honest smile I ever gave her. Not watching her as she walked away, I looked down at my hand as it worked the lock and opened the door. Tired from toes to intestines and everything above, I collapsed into the driver's seat, starting the engine with a slow turn of the key. I slid the transaxle into gear. Then, for just a moment—one brief, hopeful moment, an instant toward the infinite—I eased into my Collin Hearst routine and went on with my life.

-30-

ABOUT THE AUTHOR

Ace Boggess is a freelance writer and editor living in Charleston, West Virginia. He is the author of two books of poetry: *The Prisoners* (Brick Road Poetry Press, 2014) and *The Beautiful Girl Whose Wish Was Not Fulfilled* (Highwire Press, 2003).

His writing has appeared in *Harvard Review, Notre Dame Review, Lumina, Mid-American Review, River Styx, North Dakota Quarterly,* and hundreds of other journals. He received a fellowship from the West Virginia Commission on the Arts and spent five years in a West Virginia prison. But that's another story.

ABOUT HYPERBOREA

Hyperborea is an independent book publisher based in Canada.

Visit us online at hyperboreapub.com, and follow us on Facebook and Twitter (@HyperboreaBooks).

Read more. Read better.

9 781988 292052